Former Things

Gail Lowe

Eloquent Books

Copyright © 2010

All rights reserved – Gail Lowe

No part of this book may be reproduced or transmitted in any form or by any means, graphic, electronic, or mechanical, including photocopying, recording, taping, or by any information storage retrieval system, without the permission, in writing, from the publisher.

Eloquent Books
An imprint of Strategic Book Group
P.O. Box 333
Durham CT 06422
www.StrategicBookGroup.com

ISBN: 978-1-60911-514-2

Printed in the United States of America

Book Design: Suzanne Kelly

Dedication

Former Things is a love letter to everyone who has experienced the heartbreaking consequences of family estrangement.

To Kathy,
Your hard
work made
Former Things
possible!
Gail

Acknowledgments

Thank you, Nancy Allshouse, for encouraging me to write *Former Things* one word, one sentence, and one chapter at a time. Thank you to my husband and best friend, Tony Giannetto, for your endless patience while I sat next to you night after night writing and seeking your guidance and wisdom. A final thanks to my readers—Barbara Donahue, Jane Hakanson, Kathy Mac-Neill, and my mother and other best friend Gladys White—for your gentle criticism. A final thanks to Michael Sullivan for your technical assistance.

Forget the former things
Do not dwell on the past
See, I am doing a new thing
Now it springs up; do you not perceive it?

Isaiah 43:18 (NIV)

Former Things is a work of fiction and any resemblance to actual people is purely coincidental.

Emily and Nicole

CHAPTER ONE

It was mid-morning on an unusually warm blue-sky Friday in December 1985, but the unseasonable weather visiting Rye, New Hampshire did nothing to lift Emily Preston's spirits. There was a brightly colored Georgia O'Keeffe sunflower print hanging on the pale yellow wall of Dr. Juliet Talbot's examination room, but even that failed to cheer her. Emily, at age fifty-one, had felt unwell for the past month so she'd made an appointment with Dr. Talbot to see what might be wrong. Her symptoms were vague—heart palpitations, fatigue, wakefulness in the night, and a few missed periods. She suspected that her doctor would tell her she had entered menopause, and the thought frightened her. Emily thought that to enter menopause was to have life fold in on her, and she was not prepared to become a woman past her prime.

Emily was dressed only in a paper gown and seated at the end of the examination table when finally, after a twenty-minute wait, the door opened and Dr. Talbot stood at the threshold. It was then that Emily felt the scream rise from somewhere deep inside of her, a visceral, wretched scream of desperation she had been holding back for months. It was the kind of scream a mother ape would release upon discovering that a predator had captured her young, guttural and enduring. But she continued to hold it inside by clenching her teeth and balling her fists.

Emily didn't know this—how could she?—but Dr. Talbot's day had started off with a series of missteps. First thing that morning a man complaining of chest pains had been brought to her office by his anxious wife, and Dr. Talbot had had to make arrangements for him to be admitted to the hospital for a suspected heart attack. No sooner had she taken care of that

Gail Lowe

emergency than one of her medical assistants called in sick. The final crack in her morning happened when her au pair left a message saying that Joy Lynn, her youngest child, refused to get on the school bus. When Emily started to cry, Dr. Talbot wished she hadn't come to work at all. Still, she put aside all thoughts of what had already marred her day and moved toward her patient. "What is it, Emily? What's wrong?" she said. Her voice was filled with genuine compassion in spite of the early morning trip-ups. For the past four years, Emily Preston had been her patient—ever since Dr. Phillips retired—and Dr. Talbot had never known her to be anything but stable and calm.

Emily wiped her tears with the corner of the paper gown and averted her eyes from Dr. Talbot's gaze. "It's my daughter," she explained, her voice cracking. "Nicole left six months ago and I have no idea where she is."

Dr. Talbot had never met Nicole Preston, but Emily had spoken about her in the past. She knew that Nicole was about twenty-seven and that she was Emily's only child but not much else.

"I don't understand," she said, placing her hand on top of Emily's. "What do you mean Nicole left six months ago? And why don't you know where she is?"

Emily took a few deep breaths to quiet her emotions, but when she glanced at Dr. Talbot the tears started again. The young doctor looked so much like Nicole—the dark hair cut in a chin-length bob, the acorn color of her eyes, the oval-shaped face. Emily took the tissue Dr. Talbot offered and wiped her eyes. Still crying softly, she told Dr. Talbot her story.

"My husband died of a heart attack in January, right after the new year," she explained. "It happened while he was shoveling snow. I suggested that he hire someone to do it, but he insisted . . . well, anyway, Nicole went with me to my attorney's office for the reading of my husband's will because she expected an inheritance. Without telling me, he apparently promised Nicole that he'd leave her a portion of his estate. She said he even told her he was going to set up a trust fund for her. My husband never mentioned anything about it to me, and now I'm paying the price."

Former Things

Dr. Talbot handed Emily another tissue, and she blew her nose before continuing. "When Nicole found out he didn't leave her anything, she went into a rage and accused me of getting him to change his will before he died. Nicole has always had a hair-trigger temper, and she let it get the best of her that day."

Dr. Talbot recalled reading John Preston's obituary in the *Portsmouth Herald*, and she meant to send Emily a sympathy card but, like so many other things, it had slipped her mind. She had met John Preston once at a Rotary Club meeting when she was invited to speak on behalf of the medical community and recalled now his striking silver hair, his mannerly ways, his engaging smile. He was well respected in town and had been a member of the board of directors at the local Chamber of Commerce. "I'm so sorry to hear about your husband," she said, consolingly. "It must have been a terrible shock for you. You're still very young to be a widow."

"I never expected him to die so young, so yes, it was a shock," Emily said before continuing her story. "I told Nicole I'd share what her father left me and that she would never go without, but she wouldn't listen. Nicole has always been headstrong and difficult, you see. She refused to listen to reason."

Dr. Talbot stood back and thought about what Emily had just told her. She knew what Emily needed more than anything was reassurance that Nicole was not gone forever but was only taking time to sort things out in her mind. In her own experience, she'd had arguments with her mother and they had not spoken for weeks. She was sure that this mother-daughter spat would blow over as most others did. "I'm sure she's just taking a little time to think things through," she said after pondering the situation. "Nicole will be back soon. You'll see."

"No, I don't think she will," Emily insisted. "I found out that she quit her job and left town. I've asked the police to help me find her, and I hired a private investigator, too, but no one can help me. I'm sorry I'm such a mess. It's the holiday season and . . . well, I just lost it today because my emotions have been building up for so long. And you remind me so much of Nicole. You look enough like her to be her sister."

Gail Lowe

When Dr. Talbot heard this, she wondered if it would be better for her associate to see Emily. "Would you rather see Dr. Raymond today? I mean . . . if I remind you of Nicole so much, it might be better for you. He's in this morning."

"No. I'm fine. Really. I'll be okay."

"Are you sure? Maybe I could write you a prescription for something to help you sleep. Or refer you to someone you can talk to. And I'd recommend that you take some time off from work at the hospital." Dr. Talbot knew the pace of the emergency room at Portsmouth Regional Hospital where Emily was on the nursing staff could be hectic and overwhelming at times.

"No, I can't take time off. And I don't want to rely on medication, either. Really, I'm fine. I'll be okay." But she was not fine, and she was not okay. After Dr. Talbot took Emily's blood pressure—she told her it was sky high—listened to her heart, checked her reflexes, ordered blood tests, and confirmed that she was probably in menopause Emily hurried out of the office and ran to her car. With the windows rolled up and her forehead pressed against the steering wheel, she squeezed her eyes shut and bit down on her finger to keep from screaming, but in the end what had been building inside of her for months was finally unleashed. It was a monstrous, hideous torrent of sound that spilled from the deepest part of her, and she wailed until her throat was raw and her chest hurt. Her daughter—her only child—had left her, and there was nothing she could do to bring her back. She blamed her dead husband for what had happened, but most of all she blamed herself. A wedge had formed between her and Nicole, one that she was powerless to remove.

CHAPTER TWO

In the beginning, the wide gulf between Emily and Nicole left Emily in a state of despair, and when she went to sleep nightmares were her constant companion. In the morning she felt groggy and dizzy, as if hung over from a night of too much champagne. In her dreams, she was running down a dark, narrow street in a frantic effort to get away from someone, or something. Who or what, she couldn't say. She only knew she was being hunted. The nightmares occurred over and over and the details were always the same. In her waking hours she puzzled over the meaning of the dreams and considered taking Dr. Talbot's offer to refer her to someone she could talk to, but what would be gained? She finally concluded that she would probably never know what the dreams were about. Maybe they were about nothing more than the past trying to catch up with her.

Still, the images had been as disturbing during her waking hours as they were while she slept. Dark shadows. Whispered accusations. And that presence, sinister and foreboding, was always with her. She tried everything she knew to keep the dreams from taking over her sleep, but the warm bubble baths before bedtime and journal writing proved futile. She had even tried prayer. Nothing worked. The dreams made her tired, worn out, and at times peevish. She wished she could turn back the clock and relive the day that changed the course of her life, the day Nicole walked out of her life. Then maybe her sleep would be peaceful, but she knew this was only wishful thinking. Nothing could ever change the past. What happened could not be undone.

Eventually, the nightmares diminished, then left entirely, and Emily came to realize that they were tied to her broken relation-

Gail Lowe

ship with Nicole. Now, twenty years later, all she had left of her daughter were memories dimmed by time. The nightmares had ended long ago but her grief was still very much with her, though it had grown old, just as she had.

In the early years after Nicole left, the lonely spells nearly did Emily in. Out of the blue, depression would gather momentum the way thunderclouds do on a hot, humid summer day, and whenever that happened she gained comfort by going to the wooden chest where she stored photograph albums and scrapbooks from Nicole's childhood. Sometimes, she would go to Nicole's old bedroom and open the closet door where taffeta, organza, and lacy prom gowns in shades of pink, aqua, and purple still hung on satin hangers and breathe in the faint fragrance of perfume that still clung to the fabrics.

Nicole had been twenty-seven when she made her exit, Emily, fifty-one. Now at age seventy-one, Emily was reconciled to the unpleasant truth that she might have to face the end of her life alone. She'd come to terms with this probability, though she still continued to hold out hope for Nicole's return.

On the day Emily and Nicole visited Attorney Gerald Bramhall's office to hear details of John's will, years of bottled-up rage inside Nicole had boiled to the surface. John's sudden death had left Emily confused and shocked, and in all the tumult of arranging for his wake and funeral she had put off settling his estate until Attorney Bramhall called to remind her that she needed to tie up loose ends. She had invited Nicole to join her for the reading of his will, and Nicole was only too eager to accompany her mother. She fully expected to leave the attorney's office a far richer woman, but her expectations took a detour when she learned that she would inherit nothing. On the way home, Nicole stewed after learning that her father had left everything to Emily—the waterfront house in Rye, a retirement fund, a large portfolio of stocks and bonds, savings accounts, and a summer cottage on Prince Edward Island. When Emily pulled up beside Nicole's car in her driveway, she asked Nicole what was wrong and she told Emily what her father had said long before his death. Money, Emily knew, had always been one

Former Things

of the great dividers among people, and it was something that would probably never change. A few minutes later, they were standing in the middle of Emily's kitchen when Nicole lost her temper.

"Daddy told me he would leave me a big chunk of his estate and said he was going to set up a trust fund. He would never have left me out deliberately," Nicole had grumbled, her face set in a dark scowl. "You got him to change his will before he died. You must have."

Emily looked at Nicole, horror written on her face. "I did no such thing, Nicole! I would never do anything like that. You will inherit what is left after I'm gone. As for a trust fund, your father never mentioned anything about that to me," Emily had answered firmly. "Please, Nicole, you must understand. You are my sole heir, but your inheritance just won't come to you at this time. Right now, I need to think about how I'll manage in my old age. Do you have any idea how much nursing homes cost? I might have to live in one eventually, for all I know. Come to think of it, what I am doing is giving you the freedom from having to worry about how I'll manage financially at the end of my days so you won't have to." Emily hoped this would put an end to the matter and that Nicole would not let her temper take over.

But Nicole glared at her mother and felt the heat of anger rise from the bottom of her feet to the top of her head. Emily noticed the muscle working in Nicole's jaw, always a danger sign that her daughter was about to become unhinged. Emily clutched her slim gold necklace and twisted it until it became a knot that later she would find almost impossible to undo.

"You've never loved me! If you loved me, you would share what Daddy left in his will!" Nicole shouted. "I hope you die a lonely old woman! And I hope it *is* in a nursing home!"

Nicole fumed as she moved toward her mother. Emily knew she had to choose her words carefully or risk her heightened wrath. "Nicole, please, let's not quarrel. I do love you. I always have and always will. And I *am* willing to share what your father left. Don't you see? I said you would never want for anything. What more can you ask for?"

Gail Lowe

"I want half of what Daddy left, and I want it settled today!" Nicole demanded. She was only inches from her mother's face now, and she jabbed Emily in the chest with her finger.

"I'm sorry, Nicole. I cannot give you what you want. You'll get your inheritance in due time. Just not now," Emily said, backing away.

"Then you can keep your fucking money! I don't give a rat's ass what happens to you!"

"Nicole, your language!"

Before Emily could stop her, Nicole turned toward the kitchen counter and picked up a delicate crystal fruit bowl her own mother had given to her before she died and smashed it onto the floor. Emily stared in horror at Nicole, then at the bowl, heartsick that the beloved heirloom was now lying at her feet shattered into a thousand pieces.

"Now look what you've done!"

"See? You care more about that fucking bowl than you do about me! I'm glad it's broken! It was nothing but pretentious anyway—just like you!" Nicole turned away from Emily and grabbed her purse and keys off the kitchen counter. Before she stormed out of the house, she went to her mother and stared her in the eye. "You know . . . as much as I hate you, I feel sorry for you," she said through her teeth. "Someday maybe you'll face up to the truth that I was a mistake. You never wanted me!" And then she was out the door.

Stunned, Emily ran to the front window of the living room and watched while Nicole got into her car and slammed the door. Emily raised the window and called out to Nicole, but she sped away, leaving skid marks on the driveway. After Nicole's car was out of view, Emily returned to the kitchen, careful not to step on any of the broken glass. With shaking hands, she got a broom and dustpan out of the utility closet and swept up what was left of her mother's bowl while tears leaked out of her eyes and flooded her cheeks. She tried to tell herself that it was only a bowl, but it had belonged to her mother and she would have been crushed to know that her granddaughter had destroyed it in a fit of rage.

Former Things

Emily knew how difficult Nicole could be, but in the days following her tantrum she grew more and more concerned that Nicole would not be coming to her senses anytime soon. She couldn't forget what Nicole had said and worried that she had meant every word. Emily eventually learned that Nicole's perception was also her reality when she refused to return Emily's phone calls. She sent cards and letters, too, but they all came back marked "return to sender." At first, Emily thought Nicole would call to apologize and make amends but after a month of silence there was still no word from her.

Three weeks later, Emily drove to Nicole's apartment and waited for her to come home from work. When Emily spied one of her neighbors walking along the street, she got out of her car and approached the woman to ask if she had seen Nicole. Emily was shocked when the neighbor told her that Nicole had moved the previous weekend. When she asked the woman if she knew where Nicole had gone, she shook her head. "She seemed to be in a hurry. The landlord told me she left quite a few things behind," the woman said. "I'm sorry I can't tell you anything more."

Emily stared at the woman, for the first time noticing her dyed platinum blond hair and gaudy pink jacket with big rhinestone buttons. At first, she was angry with the woman for telling her such distressing news but quickly corrected her thinking. She was merely a messenger, not an enemy. Emily thanked her and then hurried home.

Emily called Nicole's landlord as soon as she got through the door, but all he could tell her was that Nicole had left without paying her rent. Not only that, but he was furious that she had left without cleaning out the apartment. "What do you expect me to do with all her stuff?" he asked gruffly.

"Keep it. Or sell it. What else can you do?" she had replied. "I certainly have no use for it."

"You're her mother. Do the right thing and put it in storage," he said, attempting to induce guilt, but his attitude upset Emily even more and she hung up, disgusted. If Nicole didn't care about her things, then neither did she.

Emily drove to the police station after speaking with the landlord, but Lt. Harmon told her that because her daughter was a grown woman she could come and go as she pleased and there wasn't a single thing he could do to help her find Nicole. The next day she called a private investigator, hoping that he might be able to track down Nicole, but after a few weeks of searching and a bill for more than two thousand dollars he reported back to Emily that Nicole was not leaving a paper trail. Soon the days turned into weeks and the weeks turned into months, forcing Emily to face the fact that Nicole had meant business the day she stormed out of the house and wasn't coming back.

As Emily began to feel the extent of her loss, she fell into a deep depression she couldn't snap out of. The loss of John and the disappearance of her only child was more than she could manage. Now she knew what an old house felt like when a raging storm blew through and tore off its shingles and shutters and a tree came crashing through its roof. When she was at home, she cried morning, noon, and night and there was nothing that brought her any comfort. She called Nicole's office every few days, hoping that her co-workers had heard from her, but they all said the same thing. Nicole had left her job without giving notice or even saying goodbye, and no one had talked to her since.

The photographs Emily kept in her old wooden chest helped some and so did looking at the scrapbook she had made for Nicole. There was a photo of Nicole building a sand castle on Prince Edward Island that Emily loved. Nicole had been six years old that summer, and she'd grinned into the lens of the camera, her two front teeth missing. Another photo was taken on the day of Nicole's school play when she was in the third grade. She had played the lead role in *Alice in Wonderland* and looked so adorable in her little white dress with the red pinafore. Emily found another one John had taken on her high school graduation day. It had been a breezy June day, and Nicole had had to hold on to her mortarboard to keep it from flying off her head. In the

Former Things

scrapbook, she found old report cards, blue ribbons Nicole had won for her drawings, and letters she had written to Emily and John while she was at summer camp in Maine.

As much as the photographs stored in the albums offered comfort to Emily, occasionally a photograph would trigger an especially touching memory and grief would come crashing over her again like a rogue wave.

As the months passed, Emily settled into an uncomfortable, lonely existence, one that most people would have found intolerable. It was as if she'd been diagnosed with a chronic, incurable illness and was forced to live with painful symptoms day in and day out. She felt as if she had been stripped of her identity as a mother and left for dead. Her work at the hospital became her salvation, and she was grateful she could help in a meaningful way by nursing people back to health. At night when she came home from work, she took out a journal she'd bought in a boutique in downtown Portsmouth and wrote down her feelings. One night she wrote:

> *At night when I close my eyes and think of you,*
> *You come to me in images only my soul can interpret*
> *Giving me hope that you are nearer than I know.*
> *The tender threads that bind us may have stretched,*
> *But they can never be broken.*
> *Knowing this is my comfort. It is my peace.*

And every year on Nicole's birthday, Emily wrote a letter to her and placed it inside a card before sealing it.

> *Dear Nicole, this year you are celebrating your twenty-eighth birthday, and I miss you so much. I hope you are well . . . Happy birthday, darling . . .*
>
> *Dear Nicole, you are celebrating your thirtieth birthday today. What a milestone! I hope you find a special way to welcome your third decade . . .*
>
> *Dear Nicole, I can hardly believe I am writing this but today you are thirty-eight years old. Are you happy and at peace? I can only pray that you are . . .*

Gail Lowe

Dear Nicole, forty years ago today I gave birth to you. Not a day goes by—make that a minute—when I'm not thinking of you and wishing you well. I miss you more now than ever before . . . Please come home. I want to make things right between us.

Always, she signed the cards *Love, Mom.*

Every Christmas she bought one special gift for Nicole, wrapped it in holiday paper, and stuck a bow and name tag on it. The message was always the same. *To Nicole with love, Mom.* One year she bought Nicole a pair of cultured pearl earrings. Another year she found a 14 karat gold bracelet with a Siamese cat charm. Nicole had grown up with Soo-Lin, her Siamese cat, and Emily thought Nicole would love it. One Christmas she bought Nicole a music box that played *Clare de Lune.* Nicole had learned to play the Debussy composition on the piano when she was twelve, and the piece had become one of her favorites. In her safe deposit box at the bank, Emily had tucked away a letter in an envelope with Nicole's name written on it telling her that though they were apart, Emily continued to think about her every day. She also set up a bank account with Nicole named as beneficiary and made deposits on every holiday. Emily kept hoping for a phone call, but as the years slipped by, one after another, her hope for a reunion began to diminish.

Even now, thoughts of Nicole occupied Emily's thoughts from the moment she opened her eyes in the morning until she closed them at night. Nicole would be forty-seven now. Emily wondered if she had married and had children. Was she living close by or on the other side of the country? What did she think about the state of the world? What had she done with her life? Who were her friends? There were so many questions Emily wished she had answers to but didn't. Before she went to her grave, she wanted nothing more than one final chance to see her daughter and to repair their broken relationship.

She wondered what would happen if she ran into Nicole on the street or in a shopping mall. Would there be instant recognition? An awkward hello? A turning away? A meeting of the eyes and a reaching out in love and forgiveness? When Emily was out

Former Things

and about—in downtown Portsmouth or Boston or some other place—she found herself scanning the crowds for a glimpse of Nicole, but though many young women looked like her from a distance, none of them were ever her. She fantasized about their conversation if they came face to face. *Why hello, Mom . . . it's so good to see you after all these years . . . how have you been . . . I'm so sorry for what happened.* And Emily would respond, *Me, too. It's all in the past. Why don't we leave the past in the past and be friends.* She also realized that such an encounter could go the other way. Maybe Nicole would ignore Emily and pretend she didn't know her.

The emotional pain caused by the loss of her only child over what Emily thought of as a misunderstanding and unmet expectations on Nicole's part had lessened over time but when she allowed thoughts about her daughter to linger longer than a minute or two, that old gnawing pain of grief had a way of slipping back in and taking hold. For mothers whose children had died there was at least closure, but for her there was none. Hers was an open-ended grief that even time could not dispel.

CHAPTER THREE

When her seventieth birthday approached, Emily thought it might be time to retire. The pace of the emergency room left her exhausted, and her old Victorian home was getting to be too much for her to handle alone. After a particularly difficult week at work when three patients came to the hospital dead on arrival, she handed in her resignation letter. A few days later when her second floor toilet overflowed, she decided it was time to sell the house.

One afternoon on her way out of the Senior Center she picked up the monthly newsletter and saw on the back page an advertisement for Emerald House, an elegant residential community for senior citizens at Moody Point on Great Bay in Newmarket. When she got home, she picked up the phone and made an appointment for a tour, and a few days later she met with the property manager. When Donald Magnuson showed her around, she was impressed with the spacious great room where blue and gold striped upholstered sofas and chairs were grouped in front of a fireplace. There was also a formal dining room and landscaped grounds where rhododendrons, azaleas and lilac and peony bushes grew along winding pathways. Before leaving, she had signed a one-year lease for a four-room apartment that had a kitchen painted pale blue where she could bake her own bread and make spaghetti sauce if she wanted to. Even better, she could bring Callie, a Siamese cat Emily had adopted from the local animal shelter. A few days later, she drove to L. L. Bean in Maine to buy dishes with a blueberry pattern, and she found an oven mitt, kitchen towels and napkins to match her new dishes at a kitchen boutique in Portsmouth. She also bought a new oak kitchen table and ladderback chairs painted white and

Former Things

deep pink towels and floral soap dish for the bathroom. Before she moved to Emerald House her neighbor, Mary Ellen, helped Emily organize a tag sale for furniture and other things she no longer wanted, and what she didn't sell she donated to Goodwill and the Salvation Army. When it came time to say goodbye, Mary Ellen gave her a set of cobalt blue glasses to match her new dishes.

In August, she settled in at Emerald House and a few months later she was feeling right at home. One Sunday afternoon in late October Emily stood at the threshold of the community dining room and peeked in, noticing that only a few people were seated at the tables. Some sat alone while others were grouped in twos and threes. A fresh wave of loneliness moved over her when she realized that maybe today, like countless other Sundays, family members had come by to take their elderly relatives out for dinner. It was also possible that the dining room was nearly empty because the residents had gone on a field trip that Marie, the activity director, had arranged for coastal Maine with stops in Portland, Kennebunkport, and Ogunquit. Emily had been to those places many times before and had had no desire to join the others.

She got up early that morning and after showering she put on a pair of cream-colored woolen pants and a black angora sweater. Her short silver blonde hair, brushed away from her face, was a striking contrast against the black sweater, and no one would have guessed she had reached the seventy-year mark. She moved toward the table she shared with Alice, Rita, and Tess and sat down in a pale gray upholstered chair.

While waiting for her friends, she looked around the room and wondered where Evan was. The young man worked as a waiter at Emerald House, and he and Emily had become good friends soon after she moved in. It was Evan who was usually bustling about the dining room, filling the water glasses, and cleaning the salt and pepper shakers, not Mikayla. Yet there she was at the back of the room, stainless steel pitcher in hand, icy water droplets clinging to the shiny cold metal, moving from table to table like a butterfly drifting from one flower to the next.

Gail Lowe

She hoped Evan wasn't ill but had only taken the night off and hadn't remembered to tell her. Or maybe he'd switched jobs with Mikayla and was in the kitchen right now washing lettuce, peeling cucumbers, and cutting tomatoes into wedges for the residents' salads. Emily studied the menu while she waited for the other women to join her. Roast beef au jus, baked stuffed chicken, and salmon with dill sauce were tonight's choices. All decent selections, she thought. While she was deciding what to order, her three friends came into the dining room.

Tess, a retired chef, arrived at the table first and leaned over Emily's shoulder to see what was on the menu. "Anything good tonight?" she asked. Her face darkened when she read the selections. "Same old thing. I'd love a good Italian stew sometime. That was one of my specialties," she said, settling into her chair with a look of disgust on her face.

Emily had grown accustomed to Tess's constant longings for something other than what was offered on the menu at Emerald House and had learned to tune her out, the way one eventually learns to tune out a dog's relentless barking. Alice and Rita breathed a collective sigh of relief whenever Tess's daughter took her out for dinner or to her home for the weekend, and Emily couldn't help but feel a sense of relief, too. She wondered why Tess didn't cook her meals in her own kitchen, feeling the way she did.

Alice had her share of complaints, though she rarely mentioned them and they were never about what was on the menu. For one thing, she was in constant pain because of arthritis in her right hip and knee caused by a number of falls she'd suffered when she was younger. For another, Alice was also a widow with one son who lived in Arizona. He rarely came to New Hampshire, which meant that she was alone except for when his business brought him east once or twice a year.

Rita, a tall, heavy-set retired librarian, fussed about the sloppy housekeeping habits of Miranda, the woman who cleaned the residents' apartments. Tess and Alice had considered moving to another table in the dining room so they wouldn't have to listen to Rita, but Emily talked them into staying put, reminding them

Former Things

that Rita, a single woman with no children, was a good person at heart and that her white glove approach to cleaning might have more to do with having nothing to keep her mind occupied than it did with Miranda doing a poor housekeeping job.

Emily had refused to join in any criticism and tonight, instead of listening to Tess complain about the food, she changed the subject and pointed to the thickly padded clouds outside the floor-to-ceiling dining room window and proposed that after dinner they all go to the atrium at the back of Emerald House where they could watch the sun go down over the bay. Since Evan didn't seem to be around, Emily knew they would probably not be playing their regular Sunday night chess game, and the last thing she wanted to do was sit in her apartment with only Morley Safer and Andy Rooney to keep her company.

When Emily first moved to Emerald House she had not known what to expect, only that Marie kept the residents busy by hiring local entertainers. Piano players led sing-a-longs, tap dancers hoofed to old Broadway tunes, and comedians came to tell their mother-in-law jokes. Marie also took the residents on day trips, taught exercise classes, and called the numbers at bingo games. Anything to keep their aging bodies and minds in shape, Emily supposed. Upstairs on the second floor were a library, board games, a fitness center with bikes and treadmills, and a lounge where a flat screen TV hung on a wall. Emily had taken her time getting used to her new home and soon found that she enjoyed sitting in the library reading magazines and taking best sellers from the bookshelves back to her apartment. She had even formed a reading club, and in the last month she and five other men and women had taken up reading *To Kill A Mockingbird*. She'd read the book in high school but found the story much more interesting now. In the fitness center, Marie had shown her how to use an exercise bike hooked up to a computer monitor that took her over virtual coastal, mountain, and woodland terrains, and she was thankful that her legs were still strong enough to take five-mile rides on her favorite route through a redwood forest.

On Wednesday afternoons, she played bridge with three other residents, and once a month she spent the entire day

Gail Lowe

shopping in Portsmouth and having lunch with Mary Ellen at The Old Ferry Landing. Sometimes they topped off the day by going to a movie at the Screening Room over in Newburyport, and they wouldn't dream of missing one if Tom Hanks was the leading man. In hindsight, Emily had to admit that she had been nervous after the sale of her house and feared losing her independence, but now that she was settled in she felt at home. Though Nicole had cast her aside, she was determined to be cheerful by focusing on everything good in her life.

"So will you all come with me?" she asked, looking around the table. "The weatherman promised a magnificent sky tonight. He used colors like violet, pink, and salmon to describe it. In fact, he said it would be a salmon sky, whatever that is."

"Probably something he made up," shrugged Tess, shaking out her blue linen napkin and spreading it across her lap. "I guess you can count me in." And Alice and Rita agreed to go, too. A moment later, Mikayla came to their table.

"Where's Evan tonight?" Emily asked. "I don't see him around."

Mikayla wiped the bottom of the water pitcher with a crisp white towel before setting it down on her metal cart. The dark-haired woman's hands were so chapped and reddened one might think they were submerged in water all day. Emily knew she supported three young children by herself and lived in a small one-bedroom apartment. Mikayla had told Emily once that she slept on the living room couch, but she never complained. "Just something I have to do so my kids can have their own bedroom," she said. After her shift ended at Emerald House, Mikayla went to Emily's old stomping ground where she worked in the emergency room, just as Emily had, except that her job was to answer phone calls from people with all kinds of medical problems. Emily knew how busy and chaotic the emergency room could be and wondered how Mikayla kept up the pace of working two jobs. The woman did not have an easy life, Emily knew, and on occasion she would press ten dollars into Mikayla's hand to help her out.

After setting the pitcher down, she turned to Emily. "No, Evan's not sick. He called yesterday and left a message saying

Former Things

he had an important exam to study for. He'll be back to work tomorrow night."

Emily wondered why Evan hadn't let her know that he wouldn't be at work but was relieved to learn that his absence wasn't due to anything serious. He had joined the kitchen staff around the same time that Emily first moved in, and they'd taken an instant liking to each other the first time they met. Now she thought of Evan as one of her lifelines. Conversation came easy for them, and they laughed and talked about everything from politics to art.

Before moving to Emerald House, Emily had looked at condominiums and townhouses near Portsmouth and had found many of them beautiful with extras like swimming pools, tennis courts, and exercise rooms, but they all seemed to be occupied by people much younger than herself. She wanted to live with her peers, people she would feel comfortable with, somewhere she would fit in. Over 55-communities were an option, too, but the closest one was more than fifty miles inland and they would not accept pets. She wanted to stay close to the seacoast so she could take drives in her gray '98 Volvo along the curving coastal roadway where waves crashed over the rocky shore on windy days. She also wanted to continue riding her old three-speed Raleigh from Rye to New Castle where she always stopped to have lunch at Wentworth-by-the-Sea.

While at dinner on her first night at Emerald House, Emily had watched Evan with amusement while he moved from table to table with the finesse of a Parisian waiter. When he finally got around to hers, she asked his name. "Evan Pierce," he told her. "You remind me of someone. I know—the mother in *The Brady Bunch.*" His voice was teasing and friendly.

"You must mean Shirley Jones. You're not the first person to say that. I'm Emily Preston."

"Nice to meet you, Emily. That's a beautiful string of pearls."

Emily took stock of the young man standing before her in his white shirt and black pants. He had dark wavy hair, green eyes, and a dimple in his left cheek. She imagined that he had quite a few girlfriends.

21

Gail Lowe

She brought her hand to the pearls John had given to her on their twenty-fifth wedding anniversary. Someone had once told her that pearls brought tears, and they certainly had, but when she first saw them in a display case in the jewelers building in downtown Boston she wanted to own them, to feel their cool luster against her skin. She had dropped a hint at dinner that night, and on their anniversary John presented them to her while they were having an intimate dinner at home. He had cooked filet mignon and lobster and when she sat down at the table, he stood behind her and had instructed her to close her eyes while he placed them around her neck and closed the clasp. The dinner and pearls had been lovely, but she eventually realized they had not been a gesture of love but a way for him to make up for what was lacking in their marriage.

"They were a gift from my husband. He passed away twenty years ago," she explained.

"Well, they're very pretty. You know, my mother's name was Emily. I've always liked it."

"Really? Now isn't that a coincidence."

He smiled and filled her water glass. "I suppose it is."

In the coming weeks she got to know Evan better, and at every meal she found something new to ask him. Where did he grow up? Exeter. What football team did he root for? New England Patriots. Where did he go to school? University of New Hampshire. What was he studying? Journalism.

"Do you know how to play chess?" she asked one day.

"No. My parents played, though. Their games lasted for hours sometimes."

"It's a great game for the mind. Keeps it in good working order. How would you like to learn?" She'd asked the question with measured caution. She didn't want to put Evan on the spot, but she did want to get to know him better. She'd not yet asked him about any girlfriends, and if he did have a special friend he might want to spend his free time with her, not some old woman he barely knew.

"I don't know when I'd find the time. My schedule is so busy. There's school work and my job and . . ."

"Well," she said, "if you ever do find the time, I'd love to teach you. It wouldn't take long for a smart young man like yourself."

Evan studied Emily and suddenly felt sorry he'd cut her off so abruptly. He thought a moment before answering. "I could probably make some time tonight since my classes tomorrow don't start till noon . . . if you're free, I mean . . . but I could only stay for about an hour."

"Wonderful! My apartment number is 129A. Seven o'clock?"

"I'll be there."

As soon as he finished work, Evan went back to his dorm to shower and change before returning to Emerald House. Since Emily knew he was coming, she'd arranged for delivery of two dishes of vanilla ice cream and a container of hot fudge from the kitchen.

At six-thirty, she changed into a pair of black slacks and white cotton sweater. Standing before the mirror, she scrutinized her reflection with a critical eye. She was still youthful with her stylish short haircut and clear blue eyes, and thanks to her mother's good genes her skin had remained unlined except for a few spidery lines radiating from the corners of her eyes. Satisfied, she fluffed her hair, put lotion on her hands, and went back to her living room to wait for Evan.

He arrived a few minutes before seven and after she hung his jacket in the hall closet, he noticed a row of beautifully framed photographs of exotic landscapes, eighteenth century buildings, and desert scenes lining the wall that led to Emily's living room. "I see you like photography as an art form," he said.

"Very much. These are pictures my husband and I took on our many trips. This one was taken from the Left Bank of Paris, or Rive Gauche, as the French call it," she said, pointing to a photograph of the Seine. "And here's one of the sunset over the Grand Canyon. My husband and I enjoyed being on the go. We traveled far and wide."

Stepping further into her apartment, Evan's feet sank into Emily's plush maroon and cream-colored carpet, and his eyes

Gail Lowe

came to rest on a magnificent arrangement of long-stemmed pink flowers in the middle of a glass coffee table. He also recognized one of Chopin's nocturnes playing in the background.

He leaned over to sniff the heady scent of the flowers. "Where'd the bouquet come from? They're so unusual. Do you have a secret admirer?" he said, reaching out to touch one. A secret admirer? She smiled to herself. Looking back, she supposed she could have had several romances, but after John's death she had decided to go it alone and pushed all thoughts of love out of her mind.

"They're African lilies" she explained. "Before he died, my husband was in the habit of arranging flowers for me when they were in bloom. I might as well spend my money on something I enjoy." John had been an avid gardener, and he had carefully planted the flowers that came up every spring at their home in Rye. Blooms of every size and color from the garden had once graced her tables. Now she ordered flowers from a local flower shop. They were an indulgence but one she believed she had earned.

Evan wandered over to the Steinway and glanced at a row of framed photographs on display across the top of the piano. "Family members," she said, picking up one of the photos and running her finger along the top of the frame. "They're dusty, I'm afraid. This one is of my husband and me when we went to Italy the summer before he died."

"Isn't that Venice? St. Mark's Square?" he said.

"Actually, it is. You recognized it. Have you been there?"

"The pigeons were the dead giveaway. I was there once when my parents took me to Italy on my father's spring break. He's a professor at my school. I think I was twelve or thirteen. And who is this?" he asked, pointing to a picture of Nicole.

"That's my daughter," she said, resting her hand on the silver frame.

"She's pretty. I don't think I've ever seen her at Emerald House."

"No, you haven't."

"Does she live close by?"

Former Things

"No . . . as a matter of fact . . . I don't know." A cloud covered her face, and Evan gave her a puzzled look. She answered quickly to cover the awkwardness of the moment. "It's a long story, and I'll tell you sometime. But now it's time for your first chess lesson. Are you ready?" she asked cheerfully, changing the subject.

"Sure. Let's get going, teacher."

Emily laughed and left Evan in the living room while she went to the hall closet where she kept her chess set. She returned a moment later and invited him to sit across from her at the dining room table. Once the chessboard was set up and the ivory pawns, knights, bishops, rooks, and king and queen were all in place, she set about teaching Evan the basics of the game. Much to her surprise, he caught on quickly and came close to beating her in the first game.

"I'll bet you had no idea how easy it is to learn," she said.

"I didn't. Who taught you?"

"A doctor I once worked with at Portsmouth Regional. Early in my nursing career. We played on nights when the floor we worked on was quiet." She hadn't thought of Martin Jackson in a long time and now wondered what had become of him. "In fact, this very chess set was a gift from him. You had mentioned that your mother died. What happened to her, if you don't mind my asking?"

"A blood clot. It went straight to her lung. She died instantly," he said. "It happened two years ago. Ever since then my dad and I . . . well, we've never been close. I doubt he'd be all that impressed if I told him I'd learned to play chess."

"No? And why is that, do you think?"

"He tells me in so many words that he's disappointed I'm not planning to follow his career path, but I have no interest in his field—chemistry and physics. That's what he teaches. I want to be a journalist."

"I know that sometimes parents are disappointed when their children don't follow them in their careers, but we all have to follow our own path. He probably realizes that. I always told Nicole to go with her bent, that it would take her where she

25

Gail Lowe

needed to be in life. That's what I did when I decided to become a nurse. I'd suggest that you do the same."

"Exactly. That's what I'm doing. And what about your daughter? What did she study?"

"When Nicole went to college, she had no idea what she wanted to do so she ended up with a liberal arts degree."

"What kind of work does she do?" He sensed a sadness come over Emily, one that he didn't understand.

"I think she would have made a great teacher, actually, but that's not the path she took. She still didn't know what she wanted to do after she graduated, so she took a job at an insurance company," she said wistfully, then paused. "Well, enough about that. It's almost eight o'clock, and I promised to keep you for only an hour. How about some ice cream before you go?"

He looked at his watch. "I guess I can squeeze in a little dessert, but then I have to get back to my dorm. I've got an exam tomorrow."

"It's a deal."

While they ate, Evan told her about the classes he was taking, and Emily thought his father lucky to have such a fine young man for a son. While they talked, she learned that Evan helped out at the local food pantry and had gone to a prestigious high school in Massachusetts on scholarship.

"I must say, Evan, I am impressed with your resume. You are quite the young man. Tell me, do you have grandparents?"

"I do but my mother's family lives in Tennessee and both of my father's parents died when I was only four. They were killed in a car accident. I only have vague memories of them. And I haven't seen my other grandparents since my mother's funeral."

"I'm sorry," she said. "That must have been a traumatic time for your family. I mean when the accident happened."

"I suppose it was. My father rarely mentions it. He kind of lives in his own little world. I'm an only child, so when it comes to family . . . well, it gets kind of lonely, you know?"

"Yes, I do. More than you think."

When Evan finished his last spoonful of ice cream, he rose from his chair. "Thanks, Emily. I had fun."

"Me, too. Do you think we could do it again? Maybe next Sunday?"

"I can't make any promises, but I'll let you know."

"Fair enough."

She walked him to the door and waited while he zipped up his jacket. Then she watched him saunter down the hallway toward the elevator. When the door opened, he slipped inside and was gone. Next time she'd ask him what kind of writing job he hoped to have one day. There were a million other things she wanted to ask, but her questions would have to wait. She was looking forward to getting to know Evan Pierce. She liked him. In fact, she liked him very much.

In the parking lot, Evan headed back to his car. He thought that maybe he'd give his father a call this week. Tell him about his chess game with Emily. Maybe he'd even suggest that they set aside some time to play. Spending the evening with Emily had stirred up his grief over the death of his mother, and he realized that with every passing day he missed her more and more. Pulling his cell phone from his pocket, he punched in Nina's number. He had been dating the co-ed for a few months and had got in the habit of checking in with her every night. She picked up on the first ring.

"I thought you'd be back in your dorm by now," she snapped. "Where are you?"

"Just leaving Emerald House."

"How come so late?"

"Had some things to do. That's all." A flash of annoyance caught him by surprise and then he softened. "You want to come to my room, watch a movie with me? I'll pick one up at Quick Flick."

"I guess so. Sure."

"Shouldn't take me long."

"Okay. See you later."

Gail Lowe

On Wednesday, Evan called his father to tell him about his chess game with Emily. "There's a woman at Emerald House who taught me to play, Dad. How about if I challenge you? I'm pretty good at it," he'd said.

"Not right now," his father had replied. "I'm up to my ears grading term papers. Call me again in a few weeks. I might have some time then."

Evan had thought that learning how to play chess would please his father and that maybe it would even surprise him, but his father's response had been flat and unenthusiastic. He'd call again, as his father had suggested. If he still wasn't interested, then Evan decided he wouldn't bother him again.

The following Sunday night, he and Emily met for chess and the week after that, and soon their Sunday night games became a ritual. In fact, Evan looked forward to seeing Emily almost as much as he had once looked forward to his dates with Nina.

CHAPTER FOUR

Christmas and New Year's Day came and went, and the cold, snowy New England weather kept Emily confined to her apartment. After one of her chess games with Evan in mid-January, Emily washed and dried their dessert dishes after saying goodnight and went to the living room and sat at the piano. Listening to classical music had always relaxed her, and she found even more serenity while playing her favorite pieces. She loved how composers like Mozart and Rachmaninoff had written arpeggios and glissandos into their great masterpieces, and she'd mastered a few of them herself. She struck the first few notes of Rachmaninoff's Concerto No. 2, the leitmotif from her favorite love story, *Brief Encounter*. While she played, she envisioned in her mind Celia Johnson's and Trevor Howard's final scene in the refreshment room at the railway station.

John had taken her to see it at a film festival on Valentine's Day when they were married only three years. On the drive home to their apartment in Portsmouth she'd given him a Valentine of her own—the announcement that she was pregnant. She'd been suspicious that she might be expecting a child when she missed a period, then two. Early morning nausea only heightened Emily's suspicion, and when Dr. Connor confirmed that she'd probably give birth in late summer, she was elated.

Emily remembered John's reaction was one of both happiness and fear. John owned his own medical supply company and traveled frequently, which meant that he was out of town for days at a time. "What if you have the baby while I'm on the road talking to doctors about the latest in hypodermic needles?" he said, fearing that he wouldn't be home when the time came for Emily to go to the hospital.

Gail Lowe

"Don't worry. Even if I go into labor while you're away, I'll let you know. First babies usually take a long time to be born."

"I was thinking just the other day how beautiful you look lately, Em. Now I know why." He'd reached for her hand across the car seat and squeezed it. "Imagine that. We're going to have a baby. A son, maybe. Or a daughter. And you, the mother of my child."

Rebecca, or Becky as they called her, made her entrance into the world on September 1, 1956, and John had been at Emily's side until it was time for her to be wheeled off to the delivery room. Her labor had been long and difficult, but when the doctor placed Becky by her side all wrapped up in a pink receiving blanket and she saw her baby daughter for the first time, she cried tears of joy. Emily marveled at the infant's full head of hair, golden as tints of sunrise, heart-shaped mouth, rose pink cheeks, and tiny fingernails. She fell instantly in love.

Emily stepped into the role of motherhood easily and confidently. She and John had decided before Becky was born that she would stay at home while he continued to build his business. The arrangement suited them both, and mother and baby fell into a pleasant daily rhythm of feedings, naps, and play time. The months passed quickly and soon Becky was ten months old. She had grown into a chubby, healthy baby, one who smiled brightly, even at strangers. People often stopped Emily on the street or in a store to remark about how adorable Becky was, and the comments always filled Emily's heart with joy. Becky was already saying a few words, creeping, and waving bye-bye. Soon, the doctor told her, she'd be feeding herself and pulling herself up to walk.

John was at work when Emily's cozy world suddenly stopped spinning. July 17, 1957 had been a warm sunny day, and everything in the world felt right to her when she put Becky in her crib for an afternoon nap. While the child was sleeping Emily went to the kitchen to make a cake for dessert. She got out her red Pyrex mixing bowl and went to the refrigerator for eggs, milk, and butter and to the pantry for flour and sugar. Then she took her Betty Crocker cookbook from a shelf next to the sink and hummed while putting the ingredients together.

Former Things

As soon as the cake was in the oven, she went to the living room and picked up the latest issue of *Good Housekeeping* off the coffee table. She enjoyed cooking and liked trying new recipes to serve to John when he came home at night. He always lavished her with praise for her efforts, even when the recipes didn't turn out to be quite as good as they looked on the pages of the magazine. That morning she'd awakened early, even before Becky started to stir, and by three o'clock that afternoon she was exhausted. After taking the cake out of the oven and placing it on a wire rack to cool on top of the counter, she went back to the living room and fell asleep while reading a recipe for chicken Kiev. She woke up an hour later and found that the magazine had fallen from her lap onto the floor.

She yawned and stretched and looked at the small brass clock on the table next to the couch. Four-fifteen. Becky normally didn't take long naps and that caused Emily some concern. The house was unusually quiet with only the hum of the refrigerator and the barking of a dog somewhere in the neighborhood. Leaning forward on the couch, Emily listened hard for the baby sounds she had grown accustomed to—chattering, fussing, and crying—but the house was as silent as the bottom of a well. Her concern continued to mount as she moved toward the door of Becky's room. When she turned the doorknob, all she could hear was the pounding of her own heart.

She opened the door a crack and peeked in. Emily thought the sound of the door's creaking hinges would wake the baby, but Becky still didn't stir. She crept toward the crib, careful not to make any noise. A moment later, she looked down at the child, at first not understanding why Becky was still sound asleep. She seemed so peaceful dressed in her little yellow overalls, the ones with the yellow duck appliqués Emily had sewn on herself and Becky's favorite stuffed teddy bear lying near her feet. Emily reached into the crib, touched Becky's cheek, and froze when she felt the chill of her skin. Then she saw the tightly clenched fist of Becky's right hand, pale as a pearl, and the white froth tinged with blood covering her lips. Her fuzzy pink blanket was bunched up under her face, and

Gail Lowe

Emily knew in an instant what had happened. Two years of nursing school had taught her all she needed to know. In an act of desperation, Emily moved the baby onto her back, then shook her from side to side, willing her to breathe, hoping against hope that she would wake up and start to cry, but she just laid there, her eyes closed, her jaw slack.

"Oh, God . . . oh, no . . . Becky, wake up!" she whimpered. Shaking uncontrollably, she lifted the baby from the crib and shook her but she was as limp as a rag doll. Emily raced through the house and outside to the street. "Someone, please help me!" she screamed. "My baby! My baby!"

Althea Marcotte, Emily's best friend and next door neighbor, heard Emily's pitiful cries for help while she was getting supper ready and rushed outside to see what was causing the commotion. When she saw Emily running up and down the street with the baby clutched to her chest, she ran to her side and wrenched the child away. After placing Becky on a mound of grass, she checked for a pulse and listened for a heartbeat but was unable to detect either.

"Make her breathe! For God's sake, Althea, make her breathe!" Emily screamed.

"Emily, you've had nurse's training! You must know how to revive her!"

"I can't remember what to do! My God, somebody do something!"

Emily's hysterical sobbing brought people to their doorsteps, and one neighbor who lived across the street called an ambulance. Seconds later the wailing of a siren could be heard in the distance, and in a matter of minutes a medical technician was leaning over Becky, the silver disc of his stethoscope firmly planted against her tiny chest.

Too late, he covered the child with a blanket and a police officer cleared the sidewalk of spectators. He stood up and looked around for the mother but didn't have far to search. Moving slowly toward the sobbing Emily, he placed his arm around her shoulders.

Former Things

"Here, let me help you," he said, leading her to the front stairs of Althea's home. "I'm so sorry, ma'am. So sorry." She heard his words, saw the brown of his eyes, felt the rough fabric of his shirt, but nothing made sense to her. She put her hands over her ears to drown out what he was saying and shook her head, but somewhere deep inside she knew what he was trying to tell her. "No, no, no . . ." she murmured, crying and sinking to the sidewalk, almost taking him with her.

The baby was whisked away in an ambulance with Emily at her side while Althea followed behind in her car. At the hospital, Althea found a pay phone to call John's office and his secretary pulled him out of a meeting when she heard that there had been an emergency. "John, it's Becky," his secretary said.

"What about Becky?"

"I'm not sure. I think you better get to the hospital. Portsmouth Regional."

He didn't ask questions. The look in his secretary's eyes told him that whatever the problem was, it was serious. He left the office without bothering to take his jacket and briefcase and wove in and out of rush hour traffic to get to the hospital where he found Emily and Althea sitting on a bench outside the emergency room. When Althea saw him approach, she moved toward him, touched his arm, and went to the rest room to give them some privacy.

"What happened to Becky? What happened to our baby? Where is she?" His face was ashen, his face tense, his eyes blazing.

When Emily failed to answer him, he pulled her to her feet and shook her. "For God's sake, answer me! What happened to Becky?" But Emily only stood there, unable to do anything but shake her head and cry.

A doctor approached then and moved the couple into a private area. "Are you Mr. Preston," he asked softly.

When John nodded, Emily moved away and turned her back to them. "I'm so sorry," the doctor said. "Your baby came here by way of ambulance. She was . . . we did our best to save her.

Gail Lowe

We're almost positive it was crib death, I'm afraid. It's a mystery that medicine has yet to solve. No one is at fault. Please accept the hospital's deepest condolences and my own, as well."

John looked at the doctor in shock, then at Emily. Time seemed to pass in slow motion when he heard the doctor speak about a possible autopsy, death certificate, and insurance papers that needed to be signed, but his words all seemed jumbled together and he couldn't make sense of what was being said. Finally, the truth struck him that their beloved baby daughter would not be going home, and he hit the wall with his fist. Then he turned to Emily. "What happened this afternoon? What happened to Becky?"

Emily's words came out haltingly. She told him about putting the baby in for a nap and how she had fallen asleep on the couch. "I never heard a thing . . ."

The doctor left to answer a page, and when Emily and John finally came out of the room John went to the doctor and told him he'd arrange to sign papers later. And when they arrived home and went inside their dark and empty house, John began ranting at Emily. "Why didn't you check on her while she was sleeping? For God's sake, why? And when you found her, why didn't you try to bring her back?"

Emily looked at John and hated him in that moment. "It's not my fault. Do you hear? It was not my fault!" she shouted, emphasizing each word. "I was a good mother. And don't you ever forget it!"

John went to Becky's room and stood in the doorway, hoping there had been some kind of awful mistake and that it was all a bad dream and he would wake up at any moment and find Becky lying in her crib, jabbering away like she always did. He stood there sobbing, his head hung low, hands shielding his eyes. Emily pushed past him and when she went into the room, he grabbed her by the shoulder but she tore away from his grasp and went to the chair where she had rocked Becky to sleep. "I want to be with her," she sobbed. "If I can't have my baby, I don't want to live."

Former Things

The following day funeral arrangements had to be made, and that took up Emily's and John's time as they went through the motions of telling family and friends their tragic news and picking out a burial dress for their baby, casket, and cemetery plot at Wedgewood Cemetery.

Reverend Henry Lord from the Church of the Good Shepherd had officiated at the small private service and, though lost in a thick fog, Emily could still recall bits and pieces of his homily.

We are gathered here today with many questions deep within our hearts. How did this happen to an innocent child like Becky? Why did God allow her to leave us so soon? I am certain these two questions have been asked again and again by Emily and John and their family members and friends.

I cannot answer these questions, nor will I even try other than to say that God works in mysterious ways. He gives and He takes away, and it is not ours to question why. Instead, we are gathered here today to mourn the loss of this infant whose name was Becky and to ask for nothing more than that God accept her into His almighty kingdom. We are here also to ask God to help Emily and John and their families cope with their grief and help them to gain understanding that their beloved child is in the best of all possible places—with the Almighty Lord.

When I think about Becky—or any child who has met an untimely death—I think about what occasionally happens in a garden full of beautiful roses. Now and then, a rosebud fails to bloom. Becky is like that rosebud. She came for a short time but, like the rosebud, her life ended before it had a chance to truly begin. One day this mystery will be explained, and we are called by God to exercise patience until that day comes.

Just as Jesus Himself wept over the death of his friend Lazarus, we weep today for the loss of this precious child.

Gail Lowe

Even if we could venture a guess as to why God chose to take her, we might not come close to the truth. Please reach out to Emily and John in the coming days, weeks, and months. They will need your support, for what they have experienced is a pain that no parent should ever have to endure. And now, please join me in prayer.

When Reverend Lord finished praying, Emily went to Becky's small white casket and ran her fingers along the baby's lace-trimmed pink and white dress. The fragrance of the gardenias, gladiola, and chrysanthemums surrounding the casket had a dizzying effect on her, and the room suddenly felt unbearably hot. Her head felt light and she thought she might faint. Gripping the side of the casket, Emily stared at Becky for a long time before, much to John's horror and everyone else's, she reached into the casket and lifted the infant from the satin pillow beneath her little body. She held the baby close to her and rocked back and forth while crying. John went to her side, but she refused to acknowledge his presence.

"Emily . . ." he said, his voice brittle and broken. "What do you think you're doing? You have to put Becky back!" But she only clung to the child more tightly, unwilling to give in and refusing to let go.

While she played the final strains of the concerto, Emily allowed her gaze to fall on the photograph of Nicole. Behind the photo, inside the frame, was a picture John had taken of Emily holding Becky outside their home a month before their baby's death. She had hidden the photograph there in secret, but now and then she would take the frame apart and look at the photograph of the baby she had loved and lost. Almost fifty years had passed since Becky's death, but she still continued to think about her every day.

She recalled now the difficult hours, days, and weeks after Becky's death and funeral. Her mother and father had traveled from their retirement home in Florida, and John's parents had come from Pennsylvania. Her brother, Ben, had flown in from Michigan, and John's two brothers arrived from California.

They had all tried their best to share in John's and Emily's grief, but not one of them had any idea what it was like to lose a child. Only she and John knew. At times she felt as if she were floating outside of her body, so disconnected was she from her physical self. Her breasts, still swollen with milk, begged for her baby, and every night she cried herself to sleep and again in the morning upon waking.

She'd been inconsolable for months on end, and at one point John thought she might need medication for depression, but she refused to see a doctor and instead wrote about Becky in poems and essays in her journals long into the night.

A year after Becky's death, Emily decided that life had to go on and she needed to do something to keep her from going insane and thought that going back to school might help. After talking over her ideas with John, they agreed that going back to nursing school might be good for both of them. It would give Emily something to focus on besides Becky's death and relieve John of having to come home to a wife who had lost her reason for living. After enrolling in nursing school, she threw herself into her studies, finally having found a new purpose.

While training to be a nurse Emily had little time for John or her friendship with Althea. Visiting her best friend had become painful since they'd both given birth around the same time. Althea's baby, Wendy, was now well past two years old, and it tore Emily's heart out to think that Becky would have been the same age had she lived. Even on weekends when John was home she spent most of her time at the dining room table, textbooks spread out before her. Emily didn't notice the dishes piling up in the sink, the dust on the end tables, the crumbs on the kitchen floor. She was also unaware of what was happening to her marriage, so consumed was she with her studies. At night when she got into bed she was too tired to respond to John's touch. When Althea called one morning to tell her that her husband had left her for another woman, Emily was startled. "It can happen to

Gail Lowe

anyone, Emily. I had no idea Peter was so unhappy. I had no idea at all," Althea had said through her tears.

After she hung up, Emily thought about her own marriage, then shrugged off any concerns that John might one day do what Althea's husband had done. He'd never leave her for another woman. No, she was sure of it. John would never do such a thing.

Six months later, Althea called Emily, excited about a dress she'd found on sale at Jordan Marsh in Boston. Over the phone, Althea described the dress to Emily in detail. She did her best to sound enthusiastic about Althea's shopping treasure but in truth wondered what the fuss was all about. She had more important things to occupy her mind than a bargain dress, like the anatomy exam she was scheduled to take the following day. She told Althea she only had a few minutes to talk.

"I want you come over to see it, Emily," she said. "It's a white silk cocktail dress and has a matching cape trimmed with red feathers. I couldn't resist it. I can't wait for the perfect occasion to wear it. You never know. Maybe I'll have a new boyfriend one of these days and he'll take me to someplace fancy. I wanted something new in my closet, just in case."

Emily wanted Althea to be happy and told her friend that one day love would come her way again. She hoped that would be the case. Emily had no time to spare now that she was so close to graduation. If Althea had a boyfriend, she wouldn't feel so guilty about not spending time with her. As it was, it was all she could do to study, take care of a house, and keep meals on the table.

In early May, Emily set off for Boston where she was enrolled in a weeklong training program at the Boston Shriner's Hospital. She cooked and froze a few meals ahead of time so John wouldn't have to think about what he would eat when he came home from work. After packing her suitcase and gassing up the car, she left on Sunday afternoon and checked into the women's dormitory where she was going to spend the week with other nursing students while learning how to handle severe burn cases.

Emily was overwhelmed and fascinated by what she saw at the hospital—a three-year-old boy who'd suffered burns at the

Former Things

hands of his mother, a fireman recovering from burns while putting out a fire in an apartment building in East Boston, a woman whose apron had caught fire while she was making beef stew on top of the stove. She saw for the first time in her young life how strong the will to survive could be when she witnessed up close the burn victims' fight for their lives.

The following Sunday she came home exhausted but exhilarated over what she'd learned. When she unlocked the door and came into the living room, she found John lounging on the couch watching a football game. He hardly looked up at her when she set her suitcase down in the middle of the room, and when a commercial for shaving cream interrupted the game, he got up from the couch and gave her a token kiss on the cheek before going off to the kitchen to get himself something to drink.

"So, you managed without me around?" she had asked when he came back.

"I guess so," he'd muttered. "Sorry . . . it's been a long week. I'm not in the mood for a chat. I want to watch the game."

And that was it? He wasn't going to ask about her training? She considered forcing the issue by telling him that she'd been gone a full week and would like him to at least take a little interest in her even if he had to fake it, but she decided to let things be.

He turned his attention back to the game and she picked up her suitcase and carried it to the bedroom to unpack and wash up. After putting her dirty laundry in the hamper, she went to the bathroom and turned on the faucet in the sink. While bending over the basin, something in her peripheral vision caught her eye. She turned and saw a small red feather lying on the floor. She turned off the faucet, dried her hands, and picked it up. Cupped in the palm of her right hand, Emily examined the feather closely and recognized it as the kind that circled the hem of a woman's elegant ball gown, the kind found in a stripper's boa, the kind that might have fallen loose from a sex toy stored in a bedside drawer. It took on the proportions of a five-pound weight when she pondered where it might have come from.

She raised the feather to her eyes and studied it. The sweet scent of gardenia—or maybe it was jasmine—clung faintly to

Gail Lowe

the bit of red fluff, and she brought it to her nose to breathe in its essence. She recalled Althea's description of her new dress a few months before. *". . . a matching cape trimmed with red feathers,"* Althea had said.

What had happened while she was in Boston? Was it possible that Althea and John had betrayed her? Had Althea found John as irresistible as her bargain dress? Had her perfect occasion come about while Emily was at the training?

The discovery of the feather and its implications gnawed at her for the rest of the night, and when she went to bed, sleep would not come. When John turned to her in the night and gruffly told her to stop tossing and turning, she got up and took her pillow and extra blanket to the couch and struggled to get back to asleep. Troubling thoughts ran through her mind, and a few times in the night she thought about waking John to ask him about the feather, but she knew he had an important meeting first thing in the morning and there was no sense in both of them losing sleep. To rouse him and confront him with her suspicions seemed ludicrous. Just before sunrise she finally fell into a troubled sleep that was filled with disturbing images of a crying baby and wilted flowers.

Just before sunrise Emily smelled the aroma of coffee brewing in the kitchen. She heard the water in the shower running and knew that soon John would be leaving for work. She sat up, looked down at her hand, and studied her wedding ring. At the beginning of their marriage, it had held promise of a life they would share together, for better or worse. The worst had come too soon with the death of Becky and though John had blamed her for their baby's death, time had begun to heal that deep and painful wound. At least she thought it had. Her inner self raged against the idea that he had been unfaithful to her with Althea, but in the final analysis, she knew that people were fallible. Maybe she'd been too trusting, too complacent, too idealistic, and too focused on her studies. The thought also occurred to her that John might have left the feather on the bathroom floor on purpose. For what reason, she could not imagine.

Former Things

She picked up the feather off the coffee table, noting for the first time that it was the color of blood. Her lower lip began to tremble, and the start of tears blurred her vision. She shook her head to clear the accusing, intrusive thoughts, for she did not want her imagination to run riot. She would not become an accuser, nor would she confront John about what she'd found. She realized now that she was still too fragile emotionally from Becky's death to want to know the truth. She'd simply let the matter drop and not mention the feather at all.

Emily went to the kitchen and held the feather over the wastebasket. Behind her, she felt a presence and turned to see John standing in the doorway with a white towel wrapped around his waist. His eyes fell from Emily's face to the feather then rose again to her face, holding her gaze. Neither of them blinked. She bit her lower lip and waited for him to speak, but he continued to stand there in silence. Finally, he raised a hand to his face and tugged on his chin. "Um . . . I . . ." he said, his words trailing off.

Emily knew that the future of their marriage rested solely with her. In an instant, she'd become a tightrope walker, teetering back and forth on a high wire, uncertain of her footing, fearful that she'd lose her balance and come crashing to the ground at any moment.

The blue of John's eyes darkened with dread over the exposure of his indiscretion. She wanted to impale his heart with a kitchen knife, for he had impaled hers, but instead she let the feather drift its way into the wastebasket. The flicker of relief that fell across her husband's face was unmistakable.

"Well?" she said.

"Well what?"

"Finish what you were going to say."

"It wasn't anything important."

He was right. It wasn't important. Her own perfect occasion no longer hung in the balance. Her own perfect occasion, she knew, was not what had happened while she was in Boston or what would happen this week or next. Her own perfect occasion occurred the moment she decided to forget about the red feather and move on.

A river of relief flowed through John when he saw the feather disappear into the wastebasket. He chastised himself for being careless. Emily's posture told him everything he needed to know—that she had intuited his infidelity. Hadn't she told him about visiting Althea a few months back to see a dress she'd bought—a dress with a cape trimmed in red feathers? His wife, he knew, was a smart and clever woman, one who caught on quickly. He'd thought long and hard about asking her for a divorce, but to do so would mean financial devastation. He had no intention of sharing what he had worked so hard for with an ex-wife. No, it was better that he stayed married and have some action on the side. Next time, though, he'd be more careful and it wouldn't be with anyone Emily knew.

The following Thursday, Althea called to ask if Emily wanted to make a date for lunch at The Wellington Room in Portsmouth. She touched lightly on the subject of Emily's training in Boston, but Emily knew Althea well enough to know that she was only feigning interest. Emily declined the invitation, afraid she might accuse Althea of cheating with her husband after a second glass of wine and even more afraid of what Althea might have to say. Emily knew that what might start out as a casual lunch between two friends could take a sudden turn for the worse, and wouldn't that be an ugly thing to happen inside such a nice restaurant. No, she'd made the right decision. She would not have lunch with Althea Marcotte. In fact, she didn't care if she ever saw the woman again.

CHAPTER FIVE

In June, Emily graduated with high honors from nursing school, and John's sales volume had increased so dramatically that they could afford to buy the beautiful Victorian home in Rye they'd had their eye on for months. As soon as they were settled, she went to work at Portsmouth Regional in the neurosurgery unit. Though her marriage to John was still intact, she no longer looked to him to meet her needs. Instead, she called on her own inner reserves and threw herself into her work.

On the job, Emily was a good nurse if not a bit aloof. She would not allow herself to get close to any of her patients but instead held them at arm's length. She knew that many of the people she cared for were terminally ill, and she was not about to subject herself to another broken heart if one of them died. She worked alongside a team of doctors and nurses who specialized in brain diseases and head injuries. One doctor in particular captured Emily's attention. Dr. Martin Jackson.

In the operating room, she watched with fascination while he opened a patient's skull to work on the brain. His movements were precise and swift, and she admired his confidence and the intensity and agility of his hands. While he worked, the room was silent except for the occasional scuff of a nurse's shoes, the clatter of metal instruments, and classical music coming from a transistor radio on a shelf.

There was a mystique about Martin Jackson that drew Emily to him. He was tall, like John, but more broad shouldered and thicker at the waistline. His sand-colored hair was closely cropped, his blue eyes as pale as beach glass, and his jaw strong. In spite of his insistence on silence in the surgical suite, he was a kind and patient man once an operation was completed, and he

Gail Lowe

demonstrated extraordinary compassion while his patients were recovering. She went on morning rounds with him and watched as he held his patients' hands, some fighting for their lives. She had come to know his encouraging words by heart, *"You are doing just fine. You are going to get better, and I want you to believe that,"* he told one sick patient after another.

Slowly, her broken heart began to heal and she was grateful to Martin Jackson for that. Occasionally, he had to remind Emily that patients were not made of just skin, muscle, and bone. "They have souls, too," he told her. He had seen how detached from her patients she could be and showed her through his own actions how to treat people who were not only sick but, in some cases, facing the end of their lives.

Emily had heard rumors that Martin's home life was not a happy one. His wife, a fellow nurse had told her, suffered from some kind of mental illness and at times had to be admitted to a psychiatric hospital to adjust her medications. Emily had met Melinda Jackson once at a Christmas party for the neurosurgery staff and had studied her from across the dining room at Wentworth-by-the-Sea.

Where Martin was tall and broad at the shoulders, Melinda was small and bird-like. Her legs were wire-thin and her body straight, like a boy's. The night of the Christmas party she had on a short black dress, and the tight skirt accentuated her skeletal body. Her lips were painted red, and Emily thought she looked like a hooker. Emily wondered if the woman might have some kind of medical problem, and her suspicions deepened when they were in line at the buffet table. Melinda had been next to her as they progressed from one chafing dish to the next, and Emily couldn't help but notice the two-karat diamond on her ring finger as she pointed at the food and commented about how everything looked delicious but there was so little of it she could eat.

"I have a sensitive stomach," Melinda had said, explaining the few ounces of food she put on her plate, but in the next hour Emily watched her drink three martinis, one right after the other.

When the evening ended and they met again in the ladies room, Emily noticed that Melinda's eyes were bloodshot and

Former Things

glassy and that she was unsteady on her feet. She wondered then if maybe Melinda Jackson's problems were related more to alcohol than anything else.

Minutes later, when they were in the lobby, Martin told Melinda he would start the car and warm it up and that she should meet him in front of the hotel. Emily was startled at his wife's cold response. "You do that," Melinda had muttered. "You owe me that much." Martin heard his wife's comment and gave Emily a pathetic look before going through the front door.

Melinda turned to Emily. "You nurses all think my husband is some kind of god," she said, her speech slurred. "Well, let me tell you something. He's not. He's a self-centered beast and if he didn't make so much money, I would have left him long ago. I rue the day I married him."

Shocked, Emily murmured goodnight and left Melinda Jackson standing there, struggling to find the sleeve of her coat.

Outside, Martin sat in the cold waiting for the car's engine to warm up. He stared out into the dark night, and the muscle in his jaw worked while he thought about his wife's rude remarks. He ran his hand over the black leather seat of his brand new Porsche and thought about the new tri-level home he and Melinda had just bought in Exeter. On the surface, he had it all: the car, the house, a thriving surgical practice, and the respect of his colleagues. But underneath the veneer of what looked like success, his life was as hollow as a rotted out log. He'd had reservations about marrying her even as they stood at the altar, but his father had pushed him into it. "Melinda will make a good wife," his father had said. "So she drinks a little. No one's perfect. And look, her father is one of my golfing buddies. The family is well off. Between your career and her family money, you'll be set for life. You're both in your thirties. How long are you going to wait to settle down and give your mother and me some grandchildren?" Martin had listened to his father, had followed his advice and now he was married to a woman he didn't love, and the grandchildren his father had hoped for were nowhere in sight.

He'd considered leaving Melinda in the first year of their marriage, but even more so now that he had met Emily. Only he knew that she would never leave her husband, and Melinda would end up with at least half of what he'd worked so hard for if he asked for a divorce. Being around Emily was becoming increasingly difficult. He found her exciting, intelligent, and wise in a way that Melinda was not. Maybe his best option would be to make a career move that would get him out of New Hampshire and away from temptation, but that would take time and he'd have to convince Melinda. He'd been invited a few years back to join the staff of a teaching hospital in Chicago. Maybe he'd make a few calls and see if there were any openings. He'd be willing to give anything a shot.

The following day, Martin cornered Emily in the hospital cafeteria and apologized for his wife's behavior. "Melinda is basically a good woman," he said wearily, "but a troubled one. She's had her problems. I try to be as compassionate with her as I am with my patients, but believe me it's not easy."

"You don't have to explain," she had replied. "I understand. Perhaps not in the way you think, but I've been through a lot, too. My baby girl died when she was ten months old. We all seem to be carrying some kind of anchor that keeps us stuck in the sand, don't you think?" He looked at her for a long moment before answering.

"I suppose you're right. I'm so sorry about your baby, Emily," he said, placing his hand on her shoulder. "I had no idea. Please accept my sincerest condolences. I truly care . . . about you."

She nodded and when she looked into his eyes, she saw that he was desperately searching, pleading almost, for something as simple as a human connection. From that point on a bond between them formed that went far beyond doctor and nurse, and they turned to each other for solace and comfort.

Martin taught Emily to how to play chess, and she brought him books from the library she knew he would enjoy reading. Over time, their conversations became more intimate. Martin told Emily about Melinda's drunken episodes, and Emily told

Former Things

Martin about her own marital difficulties. She shared with him her grief over Becky's death, and he shared with Emily his disappointment about having a childless marriage.

On the night a man arrived at the hospital brain dead after a motorcycle accident, they met in the doctor's lounge for a cup of coffee after the death certificate was signed. They were alone in the room, and Martin took the opportunity to hug Emily. Her desire for him intensified in that moment but she pushed him away. "I'm sorry, Emily," he said, "I just thought . . ."

"Martin, for better or worse, we're both married," she said, struggling for words that wouldn't cause him pain. "I will not allow us to become a cliché. We are both worth far more than that."

He kissed her hand then and said he understood, but truthfully he didn't understand at all. She deserved to be loved, and he was the one to love her.

At home, Martin gave in to pensive moods and became more withdrawn. It wasn't that he was cruel to Melinda, but rather detached. After dinner, he closed himself off in his office to read medical journals, but Melinda didn't mind. She kept herself busy by mixing martinis and after her third or fourth drink, she fell asleep on the couch and stayed there until morning.

CHAPTER SIX

Two years after starting her nursing career at Portsmouth Regional, Emily found herself pregnant again, this time with Nicole, though her excitement over the impending birth could hardly compare with the excitement she'd felt over the news that she was pregnant with Becky. The night she conceived had started badly when John called to tell her he had to take a client to dinner at the last minute.

"But we have dinner reservations," she had protested. "It's my birthday."

"Emily, there's nothing I can do about this. A deal is riding on this meeting. It's my job and our livelihood."

"And our marriage is riding on your following through on a promise to take me to dinner. Your job is more important than me," she had said, twisting the phone cord in her hand. Since the episode with Althea, she had been suspicious of John's whereabouts when he called at the last minute to tell her he had to meet with a client.

"I'm sorry. We'll have to celebrate another night. The guy has a ton of money, and I want his business."

"And I want you to keep your promises to me!"

She had hung the phone up in anger, not giving him a chance to respond. When he got home later that night, he'd leaned over to kiss her hello and she'd turned from him but not before she smelled liquor on his breath. His jovial mood only confirmed that he'd had too much to drink. Later, when he reached for her in bed, she tried to turn away but he held onto her tightly, determined to have his way. In spite of her protests, he climbed on top of her and she finally gave in, pretending, much to her surprise, that he was Martin Jackson. In

48

Former Things

the morning, they barely acknowledged each other, and when she missed a period, then two, she knew why. The thought that she might be pregnant again horrified her and filled her with resentment and rage.

She told Martin after Dr. Connor confirmed that she was, indeed, pregnant, and he merely looked at her without commenting. He could see by her downcast expression that she wasn't happy and that the baby had been unplanned. "When are you due?" he asked flatly.

"The middle of November."

"What will you do after the baby is born?"

"I don't know. I can't bear the thought of leaving my job."

"Come back to work then."

"I don't know how John would feel about my working with a new baby."

"Then work part-time. I need you here, Emily. There isn't a nurse within a hundred miles I can count on the way I count on you."

"Time will tell. At this point, I have to take things a day at a time."

When Emily was six months pregnant, she went through the motions of buying diapers and blankets and other things she knew the new baby would need and also a blue musical teddy bear that played Brahm's lullaby, hoping that the new baby would be a boy. In fact, she fervently wanted a boy. Another girl, she knew, would only cause her grief over Becky to come rising to the surface again. She bought new outfits, too, and packed all of Becky's old baby clothes in her wooden chest.

"Why don't you just donate Becky's things to a thrift shop?" Althea had asked during one of their now rare conversations. Emily had never confronted Althea about the red feather, and she probably never would. It hardly mattered anymore. She and John were still husband and wife, but in name only. At best, they were companions who happened to live together, and they were about to become parents again.

Gail Lowe

"A thrift shop!" Emily had replied, tightening her grip on the phone. "I can't bear the thought of giving Becky's clothes away."

"Emily, she's not coming back, and if you have a girl . . . well, would you use them for the new baby?"

"Of course not! I'm keeping Becky's clothes for my own reasons."

"Well, I'm sorry if I offended you."

"You did. You know nothing about losing a baby. And I hope you never do."

After that, Althea stopped calling and Emily was just as glad. She had a new baby on the way, and she didn't need to be reminded of John's infidelity. Maybe things would be different once the baby arrived. She hoped.

CHAPTER SEVEN

When Evan returned to work on Monday, Emily waved to him at the back of the dining room. He acknowledged her and continued to work as he moved from table to table. She wanted to ask him how he'd made out on his latest exam and if he'd done anything interesting over the weekend.

"I missed you yesterday," she said when he arrived at her table.

"One day off and you missed me?"

"I did, didn't I, Rita?" she said, glancing at her friend.

Rita didn't respond but fixed her eyes on Emily's face. "I really didn't notice," she said, and Emily suddenly wondered if Rita and the others were jealous of the attention Evan paid her.

"Well, I did. And that's the truth. Are you up for a chess game tonight?"

"Sure. Why not?"

"Good. I'll take care of refreshments."

Evan arrived at Emily's apartment promptly at seven o'clock, and when she opened the door to let him in, she noticed immediately the luxurious brown leather jacket he was wearing.

"It's gorgeous," she said. "Was it a gift?"

"A birthday present. My girlfriend gave it to me." Emily had remembered his birthday, too, by giving him a book on the history of chess she had found at the River Run Bookstore.

"Well, she has good taste. It looks great on you."

"My girlfriend thought so, too. She picked it out herself."

"What's her name and will I get to meet her someday?"

51

Gail Lowe

"Nina. She's a journalism student, too, in her junior year. And yes, I'd like you to meet her. Actually, she got a job here a few days ago."

"Really? Doing what?"

"Kitchen work. Same as me."

Emily's heart sank. If Nina worked with Evan, would she expect him to escort her home after work and would Evan have to give up his chess games with her?

As if to read her mind, he told Emily not to worry. "She's fairly independent. We mostly see each other on weekends. We both have a lot of studying to do. In fact . . . well, I probably shouldn't be taking time away from my studies to play chess. At least on Sunday nights."

"But chess is good for you. Think of it as part of your education. Chess helps you make good decisions. It forces you to focus and concentrate. I think your professors would agree." Emily knew she was practically begging Evan not to give up their chess games, but the thought of not seeing him outside of the dining room was deeply disturbing to her.

"Probably, but playing chess also means I have to rush to get my papers in on time."

Emily knew that Evan was sacrificing study time to be with her, and she wondered if she was expecting too much of him. He put her wondering to rest when he mentioned that in the summer he'd have more time. "A few months from now I'll have a break from school work. I can hardly wait."

Yes, a break from school would do Evan good, Emily thought. Over the five months she'd known him she'd seen how hard he worked in the dining room, and she knew he worked just as hard at school and his volunteer jobs. He'd shown her the papers his professors returned after grading his work. Most came back with high grades and complimentary comments in the margins. That made her proud.

"Well, here, let me take your jacket. You do trust me with it, don't you?" she said, teasing.

Now, I don't know about that . . ." he teased back.

Former Things

She gave him a lighthearted tap on the arm. "Come with me. Right this way."

They played one game, and Evan won. While they played, they chatted. "So what do you plan to do this summer?" she asked.

"Work at Emerald House and try to do some freelance writing," he said.

"What would you like to write about?"

"I haven't thought about it yet. Someday I'd like to do some traveling. Like you and your husband did. I'd like to go somewhere this summer. Somewhere like Prince Edward Island. Maybe I'll rent your cottage. Then I'd write about the experience and try to sell my work."

"I'd be glad to give you the keys to the cottage," she said. "You wouldn't have to pay me to use it. I was just wondering . . . what do you think about becoming a travel writer?"

"The field is too competitive, though I would love it. Very few people can make a living at travel writing. That's what my professors tell us. It's more of a sideline for most writers."

"It sounds like such a glamorous thing to do, though, don't you think?"

"I'll say. Did you keep journals of your travels, Emily?"

"Actually, I did. At least for the trips that most impressed me."

"Tell me about them"

She thought a moment, then said, "One time my husband and I went to Tenerife. It's one of the Canary Islands. And we took one day while we were there and flew to Morocco. Of all the places I've been, Tenerife and Morocco were the most exotic."

"How so?"

She sat back in her chair and in an instant she was back in Tenerife. In her mind's eye, she saw herself with John, walking along the boulevard in Puerto de la Cruz. They had been married for ten years and had left Nicole with John's mother while they were away. As she spoke to Evan, she could almost feel the Sahara breeze coming all the way from Africa brushing across her winter weary skin and smell the combined sweet and salty fragrances of frangipani and almond blossoms and brine from

Gail Lowe

the sea. She recalled their hotel room and how they could hear remnants of the mistral as it howled its way southwest down through Europe toward the Canaries.

The tour guide had told them that Tenerife was a microcosm of an entire continent with gold sand beaches in the south, mountains and banana plantations in the central region, and pine tree groves in the north. She had been amazed at the landscape and formations in a lava field that extended for miles all the way from a mountaintop down to a black sand beach. And the beautiful blue carpet they bought at one of the bazaars while on their excursion to Morocco still lay on the glistening wood floor of her bedroom at Emerald House. Life in Morocco had been unlike anything she had ever witnessed—dentists performing tooth extractions in open-air markets, beggars whose eyes had been gouged by thieves, and persistent vendors who refused to leave tourists alone until they bought their wares. As fascinating as the trip was, Emily's hope that maybe some alone time would help their marriage had not materialized. Their time away had had little effect on their relationship and her loneliness only intensified after they returned home.

Evan listened to her descriptions of Tenerife and Morocco, captivated. "It's your move," she said, bringing him back to the present.

"I guess I'll have to put Tenerife on my list of places to see," he said, moving a bishop. "Where else did you go?"

"Well, I'll give you the short list. The blue ribbon goes to Prince Edward Island. You see, my brother—his name was Ben—owned a pop-up camper when his children were young. You know, the kind you pull behind a car. One summer his wife, Susan, and I took our kids on a camping trip to the north coast of the island to a town called Cavendish. Nicole was about six years old. We took my mother along, too. That was the year after my father died. My mother was such a good sport because she was always so easy to please. She loved having fun."

Emily told Evan how they'd hitched the camper to the car and driven four hundred miles through New England and New Brunswick before finally arriving at the ferry that would take

Former Things

them to Prince Edward Island. When they arrived less then two hours later, they found a campground where they parked the camper for a week.

"We took the kids swimming and boating while we were there," she continued. "The Gulf Stream runs from Florida up the coast and that makes the water surrounding Prince Edward Island the warmest anywhere in the north." She told him about the pink-red sandy beaches and explained that the color came from the iron content in the soil.

She told him also about the lobster suppers held in the island's churches and that she and her family had sat around a campfire at night and slept under the stars and that they had cooked scrambled eggs and bacon for breakfast on a Coleman stove.

"I loved the island so much that I convinced John to take Nicole and me there the following summer," she said, continuing her story. "We ended up buying a cottage in Cavendish. I still own it. My brother and his wife took their children there every summer, too. They both passed away a few years ago, and their children are scattered all over the country now, but I'll bet they have fond memories of that trip."

"I'll bet they do, too," said Evan.

A thought suddenly popped into her head. "Do you like lobster?" she asked.

"It's my favorite seafood."

"How about having a lobster dinner with me next Sunday night? Nina, too. I'd love to meet her."

"No way—lobster! I'll ask her."

"Good. We'll have ourselves an old-fashioned Prince Edward Island lobster supper."

She finished her story, telling Evan that she had found an Anne of Green Gables doll in a storefront window in Charlottetown, and that she had bought the doll for Nicole. What she didn't mention was that Nicole had rejected it, calling the doll ugly in front of the store clerk and having a temper tantrum because Emily had refused to buy another doll that was twice as expensive. Nicole ended up sulking for the remainder of the trip.

For the rest of the night, thoughts of Nina occupied Evan's mind. He would ask her to dinner, but he hoped she wouldn't come. Nina, he had discovered over the past month, had a possessive streak he didn't like, leather jacket or not. What would she think if he knew he was playing chess on Sunday nights with a woman old enough to be his grandmother? On second thought, hanging out with a woman Emily's age was far better than hanging out at some bar in Durham with a bunch of co-eds. How could Nina argue with that?

After Evan left that night, Emily poured herself a glass of wine and went to the living room to sit in her recliner. The room felt chilly, and she pulled a pink woolen throw over her shoulders. Callie came out of the bedroom where she'd been napping in her favorite spot on Emily's bed and jumped up on her lap. She ran her hand over the purring cat's soft fur as she stood on her hind legs and rubbed her face against Emily's cheek. Such comfort—from a little cat, no less, thought Emily. Outside, a late March snow was falling and she could hear the cold wind whistling around the corners of the building. Even though the indoor temperature was a comfortable seventy degrees, she shivered from simply thinking of being outside. Emily had always preferred the warm summer weather when she could work in her garden and tend her plants and flowers. Winter had always been another story. Right after the New Year, she and John always packed their luggage, flew to West Palm Beach, and didn't come home until the end of March. She thought about turning on the television, but Evan had stirred up so many memories that she just sat in her chair quietly and allowed her thoughts to drift back to the time when Nicole was born.

The date had been November 18, 1958, just as the doctor had predicted, after Emily endured an especially grueling and difficult pregnancy.

During her pregnancy she had gained more than fifty pounds, developed edema and awoke every night with agonizing back pain. Every time she looked in the mirror, she turned away

Former Things

at the sight of her bloated face, round as a pie. To top it off, if giving birth to Becky had been a painful experience, the birth of her second child was far worse. Nicole had been born breech, in spite of all Dr. Connor's maneuverings to turn her around. The pain had been unbearable until the doctor mercifully gave her an anesthetic in her spine.

Unlike Becky, and despite her weight gain, Nicole turned out to be a much smaller baby and, unlike Becky, she was born with spiky black hair. From the start, Emily had trouble nursing her and she became so frustrated that she resorted to pumping her breast milk and giving it to Nicole in glass bottles. To make matters worse, the baby had colic and screamed every night from suppertime until nine o'clock, wearing Emily out. As she grew, Nicole rarely smiled and seemed tense and unhappy, even when Emily tried everything she knew to comfort her. She questioned her doctor about the difficulty she was having with Nicole, but he could offer no advice other than to say that the baby would grow out of it.

"She'll get over her colic one of these days and everything will be fine," he said. He'd been right about the colic, but everything was not fine.

Emily was often exhausted from taking care of Nicole and her fatigue made her irritable and overly sensitive. John would only have to look at her a certain way before she was reduced to tears. Secretly, she wished she'd refused John the night Nicole was conceived. If the entire truth were known, she wished that Nicole had never been born, realizing that her grief over Becky was still too fresh. But she was here and there was nothing for Emily to do but try her best to love her and take care of her the best she could.

When Nicole was six months old, Emily told John she wanted to return to the hospital to work part-time. Martin Jackson had called to tell her that the hospital was short of staff and that her help was desperately needed. He didn't say so, but she sensed he needed her, too, in a more personal way. John had protested, insisting that her first responsibility was to Nicole, but she ignored him and, after hiring Cora, she went back to work three days a week.

A kind and gentle black woman from Jamaica, Cora stood five feet tall and wore her hair in a thick braid that trailed down the length of her back. She had come highly recommended by one of the nurses Emily worked with at the hospital, and she thought Cora might welcome the extra income an additional job would bring.

Emily's co-worker had been right. She interviewed Cora a few days later and when Emily offered her the job, she accepted right away. Emily was relieved to know she could go to work and not have to worry about who was looking after Nicole. But on the days that she was home with the child alone, Emily found herself becoming more and more impatient and short-tempered.

"I know what it's like to be a mother," said Cora gently when she stayed late one day and saw that Emily was on the verge of tears after Nicole woke up from her nap in a cranky mood. "I raised four children myself," she said, placing her fleshy arm around Emily's shoulders. "But you need to let yourself relax and not be so uptight with Nicole, Miss Emily. Babies know when their mothers are tense, and the last thing you want is an anxious baby because they grow up to be anxious adults who have all sorts of problems. Try to relax. Nicole needs a calm mother." Emily concluded that though Cora lacked a formal education, two things she did not lack were common sense and wisdom.

Try as she might, though, Emily couldn't find it within herself to let go and relax. She watched every move Nicole made and found fault with her child from morning until night. She knew that she was over-reacting to what in most instances amounted to nothing more than a molehill, but she was unable to contain her thoughts and words. She never put a hand on Nicole, but her words often came out sharp and cutting and she had trouble trying to soften her approach.

When John came home at night, Emily could finally relax because he took over for Emily. He was far more easy-going than she was and she thanked her lucky stars that he was.

Former Things

By the time Nicole was a toddler, Emily had grown used to having another child around, though she rarely took time to play with her or do things with her that other mothers did with their children. They never visited the park where there were swings, and she encouraged Nicole to play by herself so she could read, knit, and cook. She blamed her lack of time with Nicole on the number of hours she worked at the hospital, but even Emily knew this was only an excuse. If she were to tell the truth, her job at the hospital was the most important thing in her life. Her friendship with Althea had ended long ago, and she and John had grown farther and farther apart. The only reason they stayed together, she finally acknowledged one day, was for the sake of Nicole.

When Emily was at the hospital, she was free to be herself and she laughed freely in spite of life and death situations swirling around her every day. She knew, also, that Martin Jackson was responsible for her lightheartedness. The more she got to know him, the more she realized that he was an amazing man with an equally amazing sense of humor and compassion. She looked forward to going to work as much as she dreaded coming home. One morning after rounds, Martin asked Emily how Nicole was doing.

Her face darkened and he sensed something was wrong. "You can tell me, Emily. Is there a problem?"

Emily lowered her head, ashamed that she was so transparent. "You know me better than I know myself," she said. "It's not Nicole so much as it is me. I can't help but think about the baby I lost. I know it's not fair to Nicole, but I can't help myself."

"Don't be so hard on yourself. It takes a long time to heal a loss as profound as the death of a child, especially one like Becky."

Emily nodded. "I know that."

Martin thought he might be overstepping his bounds but asked the question that had been on his mind for a long time. "Have you considered seeing someone about your grief? Someone you can confide in?"

Gail Lowe

"If you mean a psychiatrist, no. But maybe I should. Poor Nicole. It's not her fault that Becky died."

"I wasn't thinking about a psychiatrist. Just someone you can talk to. Your clergyman, for instance. Someone who can be impartial. Someone you can trust."

Emily felt so close to Martin that she was comfortable telling him anything, even the most personal truths. "I'm finding it hard to feel affection for Nicole, Martin. I'm afraid to love her. Afraid of what might happen if I do."

"You mean you're afraid that if you love her, you'll lose her like you lost Becky?"

"Yes, I think of what could happen. And then anger seems to bubble up inside of me for no reason at all. I find myself getting upset over the most trivial things, and Nicole always seems to get the brunt of it."

"Emily, you suffered a terrible loss, something no parent should ever have to face. Nicole is not responsible for Becky's death. If you let her in, she can help you heal your grief. You need to find out who it is you're really angry at."

She looked at her hands and twirled her wedding ring round and round her finger. Before she could say another word, Martin was paged. He stood up and looked down at Emily. "I need to go now, but give it some thought. A professional might be able to help you. You have nothing to lose."

CHAPTER EIGHT

When Emily arrived at Reverend Lord's office the following Thursday to talk to him about Nicole, she was nervous and relieved at the same time. She was relieved because she was finally going to share her deepest feelings about her child with someone other than Martin. Yet, she was nervous because she had no idea how her minister would react. She had not engaged in any kind of meaningful conversation with him since Becky's funeral service and felt a bit awkward approaching him now. Still, she knew Martin was right. She had to talk to someone who could be impartial and not judge her.

She had chosen a simple outfit to wear for the appointment—black wool trousers, a white shirt, and single strand of pearls. On her feet she wore a pair of black leather pumps and she carried a purple leather clutch purse to add a splash of color. She wanted Reverend Lord to think of her as organized and stable, not some kind of out of control neurotic housewife and mother.

Before leaving for her appointment, Emily had studied herself in the mirror. She was dismayed to see dark circles under her blue eyes and a too-pale complexion that begged attention from the sun. She smeared a nickel's worth of rouge on her cheeks to give her face some color and added a touch of red lipstick. When she ran a comb through her hair, she noticed a few new strands of gray and made a mental note to ask her hairdresser what to do about it. She didn't want to look any older than her thirty-two years.

After pulling into the lot behind the Church of the Good Shepherd, she parked her car and went inside where she found

Gail Lowe

Reverend Lord's secretary, Pauline, sitting at her desk sorting through a pile of checks and cash.

Pauline, a plump, matronly woman with gray hair, greeted Emily and asked her to have a seat. "Reverend Lord is just finishing up a phone call. He'll be right with you," she said. Emily sat in a chair opposite Pauline's desk and noticed a Bible on top of a small table next to her. Emily picked it up and flipped through the pages to the book of Isaiah. Scanning one of the pages, she read:

> *Forget the former things,*
> *Do not dwell on the past;*
> *See, I am doing a new thing!*
> *Now it springs up; do you not perceive it?*

Forget the former things? Impossible. How could she forget the sweet crown of Becky's golden hair, her baby scent, the soft skin of her back, the promise of a beautiful new life?

Emily was pondering these things when Reverend Lord, a tall slender man with thinning gray hair and a kind facial expression, poked his head out of his office and invited her inside.

Emily found his office as warm and comfortable as the man himself. The walls were painted a soft yellow and on the hardwood floor was a deep brown rug. The lighting came from a pair of lamps on end tables and sunlight filtered through a stained glass window over his desk that depicted Jesus holding a lamb. On his desk was a highly polished hourglass made of wood and framed photographs of people Emily recognized as his wife and children.

"Sit down wherever you think you'll be most comfortable," Reverend Lord said, his hand gesturing to a green sofa and matching wing chair. "Would you like some tea? Earl Grey?"

"No, thank you."

Emily waited patiently while he went to his desk to get his pen and notebook. For the first time, she considered her minister's name. Henry Lord. The Reverend Henry Lord. Why was it that people's names so often matched their professions, she wondered. She remembered reading about an attorney in Boston

Former Things

once whose last name was Law. Attorney Richard Law? Yes, that was it. And a doctor who specialized in hand surgery she'd met while in nursing school also had a name suited to his profession. His name had been Dr. Fingerhut.

The minister sat down in a chair opposite Emily and asked what had brought her to him. He had spoken briefly to her a few times after Becky's death, but with all the demands of his job he had little time to spend with a grieving mother and had assumed she was healing as time went on. Today, Emily looked tired and worn down, and he wondered if she might be suffering from post-partum depression. "When I spoke to you on the phone about coming in, you said you wanted to talk to me about your daughter. Is that still the case?"

"Yes, among other things," Emily nodded. "I know you have a large congregation to tend to, but I truly feel the need to talk to someone. Since you know my family and the circumstances of Becky's death, I thought I'd turn to you first. I'll get right to the point, Reverend Lord. My feelings about Nicole are at war within me. To be perfectly honest, I'm having a hard time feeling a connection with my own child."

While Emily talked, Reverend Lord listened patiently and jotted down some notes. Her story spilled out in a torrent, like water suddenly bursting through a stopped-up dam—about Becky's birth and death, about the night Nicole was conceived, about her distance from John and her unrelenting grief. And finally, about how she found no joy in playing with Nicole and finding fault with everything she did. When she finished, tears were raining down her cheeks, and Reverend Lord handed her a box of tissues, which Emily gratefully accepted.

"What you're feeling is not unusual," he said soothingly. "Your feelings about Becky's death—whether anger or grief— are being transferred to Nicole. You need to get through your grief before you can hope to have a meaningful relationship with your second child. Tell me, how did you and your husband meet?"

Emily told Reverend Lord that she and John had met in high school, that he had been a star player on the football team,

Gail Lowe

and that they had parted when John left for college. "He went to the University of Connecticut and I went to nursing school, but I only stayed two years," she explained. "We kept in touch and saw each other when John was home on semester break. I never looked at another man. I knew from the start that he was the one for me."

She continued, telling Reverend Lord that she had fallen in love with John the instant she first spotted him at a school dance. "He was tall and slender and had the most beautiful wavy hair. I loved his eyes, too. They're a beautiful shade of green. The sad thing is, my husband is a handsome man, but I'm not at all attracted to him."

"How have you been getting along?"

"Not well. When I'm at home, I'd rather be at work."

Reverend Lord leaned toward Emily. "Are you fighting . . . I mean, in front of Nicole?"

"No. It's more like there's a wall between us. Like we're living in two separate worlds."

"Have you tried to talk to him about how you feel?"

"Yes, many times. But it always comes back to the night Nicole was conceived. If he hadn't come home drunk . . . if he hadn't forced himself on me . . ."

"Nicole never would have been born, is that it?"

"Yes."

Emily could see where the discussion was going. In her heart she had not forgiven John for forcing himself on her when she had no interest, nor had she forgiven herself for giving in. Worst of all, she had not forgiven Nicole for being born.

"I need to get past what happened that night, don't I? And I need to let go of Becky."

"If you expect Nicole to grow up normally, yes on both counts."

He regarded Emily for a moment before continuing. Certainly she was a bright woman with insight and heart and he admired her honesty. Not many mothers would come right out and admit they were having this kind of trouble with their children.

Former Things

For the next hour Reverend Lord told her how resentment, blame, and a lack of forgiveness had a way of creeping into human relationships and destroying them and how it was both hers and John's responsibility to rebuild their family on a foundation of forgiveness. "The last thing you want to do is make Nicole feel unloved," he pointed out. "She will feel the sting of your rejection and you will pay a king's ransom in the end. What I suggest that you do—and you need to take this advice seriously—is to learn to accept and love Nicole for who she is and not compare her to Becky. She has a right to her own unique qualities."

Emily agreed and asked for his help. "I know what you're telling me is true. I want to accept Nicole," she said. "I just don't know how. My heart feels like it's filled with tears."

He hesitated a moment then had an idea. "Let me ask you something. What do you imagine Becky might be like if she were alive today?"

Emily looked down at the floor and for the first time noticed that Reverend Lord was wearing two different colored socks, one navy blue, the other dark brown. She wondered if he had discovered his mistake after arriving at the church and had too many appointments during the day to take the time to go home and change. She wondered if his wife did the laundry, if she sorted his socks, if she . . .

"Emily? Can you answer my question?" he asked, interrupting her thoughts.

"I'm sorry. My mind wandered. What did you say?"

"I asked what you think Becky might be like today if she had lived."

"She was such a sweet and pretty baby," she replied softly. "And good natured, easy going. She rarely cried. Becky was sleeping through the night soon after she came home from the hospital. I had no reason to think anything bad would happen to her."

"But now let's take her life forward a few years. What do you think she would have been like at two years old?"

"She would have been talking and walking and she would be funny and we'd go for walks in the park and I'd be taking her

Gail Lowe

to the library . . ." Her voice trailed off when she realized that her imagined life with Becky was far different from the one she had with Nicole.

"Go on."

"I would have bought her little dresses and patent leather shoes and books and dolls," she said, crying now. "She would have loved climbing onto my lap and having me read books to her. We would have had wonderful times together . . . "

"Do you think Becky would have been a perfect child?"

"Of course not. No child is perfect."

"In your mind Becky was. But you're right when you say no child is perfect. Do you think it's possible that you may have idealized Becky? That you have allowed your imagination to make her perfect when, in fact, she may not have been much different from Nicole in the long run?"

Emily nodded and twisted the crumpled tissue in her hands.

"Let's consider for a moment that in spite of Becky's good nature at ten months she might have developed a personality trait that you didn't like. A bad temper, perhaps. Or a stage where she preferred to play by herself rather than spend time with you."

Reverend Lord continued, suggesting that while it was true that Nicole had been a disappointment in some ways, Becky might also have brought disappointment to her in one way or another. "I'd like for you to think about this for a while. Turn it over in your mind. Would you like to meet with me again so we can talk more about this?"

"Yes, I would." She was hopeful now. Maybe Reverend Lord could help her through her ordeal. Maybe he could help heal her wounded heart. "Reverend Lord . . ."

"Yes, Emily?"

"While I was waiting for you, I turned to a page in the Bible that talked about forgetting the former things and not dwelling on the past. How can God ever expect me to forget Becky?"

"God doesn't expect you to forget Becky, Emily. He wants you to remember her. But what He's saying is that He wants us to concentrate on what is happening now so we can pour all our energies into what we have before us, which, in your case, is

Nicole. He wants us to live in peace and to have faith that He's taking care of Becky until you can be reunited again. Learn to trust God, Emily. Having faith in Him is what He wants most. Does that answer your question?"

"Yes."

He smiled and went to his desk to get his appointment book. "Can you come again next Tuesday? I have time at eleven o'clock that morning," he said, glancing at her.

"I'll make arrangements for Nicole."

"There's something I want you to think about, Emily."

"What's that?"

"That God loves all of us in spite of our flaws. We often disappoint him, but He loves us anyway. And He calls us to do the same with the people we meet in life, especially those closest and dearest to us. Most of all, He wants us to forgive others so we, too, will be forgiven."

"I'll think about that."

"Until next week, then. And, by the way, at some point I think it would be a good idea for you and John to come in together."

"I'll think about asking him to come with me,"

Reverend Lord got up, moved toward his desk, and stopped. "Emily . . ." he said, his back to her.

"Yes, Reverend Lord?"

"There's something else."

"What?"

"I want you to watch for the consolation in the desolation."

"Consolation in the desolation? I don't understand."

"The good things that come your way. Nicole is only one of many. I know she can never replace the baby you lost, but she is a gift from God. Enjoy her."

Emily considered his words before answering. "I'll remember that," she said.

"Now, before you leave, why don't we pray?"

Tired now, Emily rose from her chair and turned off the living room lights. She wondered what had happened to Martin

Gail Lowe

Jackson. She'd heard that he'd accepted a position at a teaching hospital in Chicago after leaving Portsmouth Regional some years ago. As for Reverend Lord, he was now retired and spent the winter months in St. Augustine. That's how life was. People came into your life, sometimes for a little while, and then went on their way, including children if they had a mind to leave. After changing into her nightgown, she pulled back the covers on her bed and slid in between the sheets. Sleep was a long time coming but when it finally did, she dreamed about Nicole. In her dream, she and Nicole were in a house that had many rooms. One room at the back of the house looked out from a large picture window onto a smooth flowing river with a stand of trees on either side. Emily called Nicole to the window and pointed to the river where it became turbulent over a bed of rocks.

"It's beautiful, isn't it, Nicole?"

"Yes. It's kind of like us, Mother."

"Like us? What do you mean?"

"The river. See how it flows? Where the water spills over the rocks it's interrupted and there's turbulence. In the case of the river, the fault lies with the rocks. In our case, it's Becky."

"Becky? I don't believe I know anyone by that name."

"Yes, you do. You know very well who Becky is, and so do I. I've always known about her. At least since I was old enough to read. I know I had a sister who died a few years before I was born."

"You're mistaken, Nicole."

"Am I? Mother, please don't lie to me. I found my sister's death certificate on top of your bureau when I was ten. You must have forgotten to put it back in your strong box. Why did you keep Becky a secret all those years?"

"Nicole . . . you are mistaken."

"I am not mistaken. I know the truth."

Emily's breath caught in her throat. The dream jerked her out of a sound sleep, and her heart thumped inside her chest. Could Nicole have somehow found out about Becky and not let

Former Things

on that she knew? Could she have kept the knowledge to herself all those years, even though she had known the truth all along? She recalled the day she found Nicole's diary when she was a teenager. She had read some of the entries and one cryptic message had been written on Becky's birthday. Had Nicole known the truth? For the rest of the night she tossed and turned and slept fitfully. In the morning, she felt as if she hadn't slept at all. She hoped the dream wasn't some kind of premonition of what was to come. She and John had decided it would be best to keep Becky's life and death a secret, both of them agreeing that the tragedy was best left in the past. There was nothing to be gained from sharing their grief with Nicole, they had both thought.

CHAPTER NINE

At breakfast, Tess commented on the dark circles under Emily's eyes.

"I didn't sleep well last night, that's all," she replied, reaching for a slice of toast.

"Well, you should ask your doctor for something to help you sleep. I hate to say it, Emily, but you've been looking piqued lately. To be perfectly honest, you look awful."

"Tess, when I need your advice, I'll ask for it," Emily answered sharply. "Furthermore, I would appreciate it if you would keep your opinions to yourself." She wanted to suggest that Tess take a good look in the mirror, but she held her tongue. Her own face was a jigsaw puzzle of lines and whorls, no doubt etched by her negative attitude about everything in life.

Just then, Alice and Rita came into the dining room and joined Emily and Tess at the table. "Don't you two think Emily looks tired today?" Tess asked.

Without waiting for an answer, Emily stood up. "I think I'll have breakfast in my room. Enjoy your day, ladies."

"Wait! Emily!" Tess pleaded. "I didn't mean to hurt you."

Emily didn't acknowledge Tess, nor did she want to hear what she had to say. Instead, she stiffened her back and returned to her apartment. Then she ordered breakfast to be sent to her apartment, and when it arrived, she ate her oatmeal and toast while watching the *Today Show.* After the program ended, she decided to go back to bed. The weather was rainy and gloomy outside and Tess's remarks had not helped matters. She only hoped that she wouldn't dream of Nicole again.

Former Things

Around eleven o'clock, Emily checked her grocery list to make sure she hadn't left anything out. She would do the bulk of her shopping today and buy three lobsters at the fish market downtown on Sunday morning. She was looking forward to meeting Nina Sunday night. Evan hadn't told her much about his girlfriend other than to say she was also studying journalism. She hoped she would like her as much as she liked Evan. After taking her long black wool coat from the front hall closet, she put it on and took her keys and purse from the closet shelf. Then she went outside to start her car.

The day was cold for early April, and a stiff bitter wind was blowing down from Canada. The weatherman had said the air temperature would feel like twenty degrees with the wind chill factor and he'd been right. He had also forecast a spring snowfall sometime in the next twenty-four hours, and she hoped the weather wouldn't interfere with her plans for dinner with Evan and Nina. She had no desire to eat a lobster dinner all by herself. Shivering, she sat in her car and waited for the engine to warm up.

A few minutes later, she shifted the car into reverse, pulled out of the parking lot, and headed for Farmland to buy rice pilaf, lemons, ingredients for a salad, and a few other odds and ends. Once inside the little market, Emily picked up a shopping basket and proceeded down the aisle to the produce section. The store was empty except for the clerk who was standing near the cash register at the front of the store. While she was looking at the tomatoes, Emily thought she heard someone crying. She stood still and listened. Sure enough, someone at the front of the store was crying. Emily hastily put a head of lettuce, two tomatoes, cucumber and a red onion in her shopping basket and went to the other aisles to finish her shopping. Halfway to the checkout counter, she could see the store clerk crying into a tissue. She stopped for a moment, not knowing what to do. She didn't want to embarrass the woman, but she had to pay for her groceries and get her other errands done. She finally cleared her throat, went to the front of the store, and placed her groceries near the cash register.

Gail Lowe

The woman glanced up at Emily. "I'm sorry," she said, wiping her eyes.

"No need to be sorry. Is there anything I can do?"

"No. I'll be okay. It's just . . ." The woman started crying again.

Emily waited. "Can I call someone for you?"

"No. I'm really sorry. It's nothing. I'm just having a problem with my sister. We had a disagreement and now she won't speak to me."

"I'm sorry to hear that. Family arguments . . . they're no fun, are they?"

"No," the woman said, "not at all."

Emily weighed her words carefully. It was not her business, but since the woman had shared an intimate detail of her life, she felt called to say something about the importance of not letting an argument go too far.

"I might be out of line saying this, but if I were you I'd call my sister to talk things over. Believe me when I tell you that being on the outs with someone you love can turn into a long and lonely road. Do what you can to turn this situation around now before it's too late."

"I've tried."

"Does your sister live in town?"

"Yes. A few blocks away from me."

"Then go knock on her door. After you finish work today, go see her and try to straighten out whatever the problem is."

"I'll think about it."

"When all is said and done, you'll be glad you made the first move. It's just not worth going through life with hard feelings."

"I didn't ask for this."

"No, you probably didn't. But one of you has to make the first move. Be the bigger person. You be the one to take the high road."

The conversation ended when an elderly man entered the store and asked for directions to a church. Emily passed the woman ten dollars to pay for her groceries and left without waiting for her change. She only hoped she would take her advice and get to the bottom of the problem, whatever it was. One thing the world didn't need was another family estrangement.

Emily arrived home an hour later and unpacked her groceries, happy that she was going to entertain Evan and Nina on Sunday night. Cooking was something that she rarely did anymore, even though she had her own kitchen. When John was alive, they enjoyed cooking for their friends and playing card games after the dishes were washed and dried. Being in the company of other people had been the glue that held their marriage together, and she had made a commitment that she would raise Nicole with two parents under one roof. One of these nights she would invite the Sterlings, the couple who bought her home in Rye. The last time she'd seen them was when they had invited her for dinner at her old homestead. Elizabeth Sterling had hired a professional decorator from Boston and the results were astounding. She owed them an invitation. Maybe she'd offer to cook lobster for them, too. Maybe they knew how to play whist. She knew that Rita played. She would ask her to be her partner for the night.

She planned to serve chowder before the lobster and decided to make it ahead. She took a stockpot from a hook above the sink and added a few inches of water. Then she set the pan on the back of her gas stove, turned on the burner, and went to work peeling and slicing an onion. Next, she cut the haddock she'd bought that afternoon into bite-size chunks and added it to the water along with the onions. Finally, she peeled three potatoes, diced them, and set them aside in a pan of water to add to the broth later.

Soon, her kitchen was filled with the aroma of fish chowder, and she hoped Evan and Nina would like it. She added a dash of sherry, a quart of milk, two cups of half and half, and a dash of salt and pepper to finish it off, then let it simmer on a low flame to give the flavors a chance to blend.

After cleaning up the kitchen, she went to the living room and looked out the picture window. Snow flurries were falling,

Gail Lowe

and off in the distance a group of children were playing on a hill. Watching them brought her back to another time and another place. Nicole had loved the outdoors, and on cold days Emily would bundle her up and take her to Hollyhock Hill. John had made a toboggan out of birch in his workshop one fall, and they had given it to Nicole for Christmas. That winter was especially snowy and the family gave the toboggan a good workout. Emily often invited Nicole's friend, Michelle, to go along for the fun, and after an hour or so of sliding down Hollyhock Hill, they went inside the lodge at the base of the hill and drank hot chocolate in front of a roaring fire. Her only unpleasant memory involved an accident with the toboggan when Nicole fell off, hit a tree, and sliced her hand open. Fortunately, Martin Jackson had been covering the emergency room that day and stitched Nicole's hand.

Nicole had been eight years old when the accident happened, and Emily was still in counseling with Reverend Lord. Progress was slow but it was being made because John had joined in the sessions, and though he acknowledged that he had been wrong in blaming Emily for Becky's death, the issue still hung between them like the sword of Damocles. But as feelings were being discussed, Emily was beginning to feel more comfortable around Nicole. Still, she was a long way from being the mother her child needed. She continued to be annoyed when Nicole made a mistake or said something that displeased her, but Reverend Lord assured Emily that Nicole's behavior was common among children her age. He suggested that she apologize to Nicole when she scolded her for something minor and give her a hug, and she had done that with good results. But the question he had foremost in his mind was whether Emily had properly bonded with her child. He decided to ask Emily if she would mind if he and a psychologist talked with Nicole alone.

After Emily and John gave him permission to call in a psychologist, Reverend Lord phoned his friend, Dr. Harriet Mackey, and asked her if she would sit in on a session with Nicole. After the meeting, Dr. Mackey shared her findings with Emily and John and Reverend Lord. First, she said that Nicole seemed more subdued than other children her age and had not been able to make good eye contact. She had questioned Nicole, asking her about her life at home and whether she was happy. She sat Nicole down at a child-size table in one of the Sunday school rooms and, after giving her a sheet of paper and a box of crayons, asked her to draw a picture of her family. When she was finished, Nicole handed the picture to Dr. Mackey, and she was not surprised at what she saw. Nicole had drawn ears on the child but not on the mother and father figures in her drawing. Dr. Mackey could clearly see that Nicole was trying to show through her art that no one in the family listened to her. After studying the picture, both Dr. Mackey and Reverend Lord had probed a bit more, asking if Nicole found it easy to talk to her mother. Sometimes, she said, her mother would tell her to be quiet when she was trying to read or watch a television program. And what about her father, Dr. Mackey had asked. Nicole had said that her father was rarely at home and when he was, he went to his workshop in the garage to make things out of wood.

Reverend Lord had shared Dr. Mackey's findings with Emily and John, and they agreed to take time out of every day to truly listen to Nicole, talk with her, and ask her questions about what interested her.

"Emily, and you, too, John," Reverend Lord had said, "listening to your child is the most important thing you can do. It's what God does with us when we pray. He listens. Take time with Nicole to really listen to her. Put down your book and turn off the television. And John, come out of your workshop. If you continue to tune her out, one day she will do the same to you."

Over the past twenty years, Reverend Lord's words had come back to haunt Emily again and again. She had followed his advice. She had learned to look for the good in Nicole and had taken a sincere interest in whatever it was she was doing. She had given her daughter every opportunity, from overnight summer camp to piano lessons, but always in the back of her mind was the ghost of Becky. And Becky was never coming back.

Gail Lowe

At breakfast Sunday morning, Emily found Tess sitting at the table alone. She guessed correctly that Tess would offer an apology for what she'd said the day before.

"Emily, I never meant to hurt you," Tess said. "Please accept my apology."

"I do accept your apology, Tess. But please, from now on keep your comments to yourself. I'm well aware of how I look when I don't get enough sleep."

"I will, and I'm sorry I ever said anything."

"Let's forget it now. You're forgiven. I haven't had a chance to talk to anyone about the trip to Maine. Have you heard anything about it?"

"Barbara went. So did Dan and Robert. They all had a good time, though the bathroom on the bus was out of order, so they had to make extra stops."

"Well, then, I'm glad I didn't go, aren't you?"

"Yes, I am. But I'm thinking that next time a trip comes along I'll sign up."

"Me, too. I'll go with you."

Tess began to tell Emily a story about what she had heard from their friend Barbara about the dinner in Portland. The group had stopped at a new restaurant on Market Street and there had been a mix-up in the orders, but she was only half listening. Instead, Emily was looking over Tess's shoulder toward the bank of dining room windows. It was sleeting heavily, and she was beginning to worry that a storm might interfere with her dinner plans. Evan would not start his shift until the noon hour so she had no opportunity to ask him if he and Nina would still be able to come that night if the bad weather turned into a major storm. He had recently changed his cell phone number and had forgotten to give it to Emily so she had no way of reaching him, either. She turned her attention back to Tess and heard her say something about a trip to Pennsylvania that was being planned for the Fourth of July.

"Really? Now that sounds interesting." The last time Emily had been to Pennsylvania was with John and Nicole the year she turned twelve. She had suggested they celebrate the Fourth of July in Philadelphia with side tours to Gettysburg and Dutch

Former Things

Country. The trip had been a five-day excursion, and though it had been enjoyable it did little to bring her and John any closer.

The family had stopped for an overnight stay at a romantic mountaintop retreat called The French Manor. The chateau looked out over a valley in the Pocono Mountains, and the view had been beautiful. The owners did everything they could to make their stay special, from providing thick terry robes to leaving chocolates on their pillows at night. The following day, the bus took them on a tour of Dutch Country with a stop at a pretzel factory and smorgasbord dinner at an Amish restaurant. The final stop was Gettysburg, with a guided tour to the battlefields. At night when Nicole was finally asleep in their hotel room, John had reached out for Emily in the dark, but she had turned her back to him, saying she was too tired for lovemaking after a long day of sightseeing. She also didn't want to risk another pregnancy. One child was more than enough.

"So what do you think? Would you want to go?" said Tess, bringing Emily back to the present.

"Maybe. I'll have to see what else is on the agenda, if anything," she said. "I've heard rumblings about a trip to the Hudson River Valley. I've never seen the Aerodrome in Rhinebeck or the Vanderbilt estate."

Alice and Rita came into the dining room while they were talking about their future travel adventures and sat down. "That's a pretty sweater you're wearing, Rita. Is it new?" Emily commented.

"An early Mother's Day present," she replied, picking imaginary lint off the right cuff. "It's cashmere. From my two daughters. I've always wanted a cashmere sweater, and now I've got one. It's so warm and cuddly."

Mother's Day had always been the most difficult holiday for Emily, and she forced a smile now. "Well, the raspberry color is beautiful. It looks lovely with your hair and skin," she said and meant it.

"Thank you."

"Dan said he saw you leaving Farmland yesterday," Tess said, changing the subject. "A chilly day to be out and about."

"I'm having company for dinner tonight and needed some things."

"Who are you entertaining?"

"Evan and his girlfriend, Nina."

Emily's revelation was met with silence. "Evan? You mean Evan Pierce? The young man who works here?"

"Yes. That Evan. And his girlfriend Nina."

"Well, that should be interesting," she replied. Her crisp tone did not escape Emily's attention.

"I'm sure she's a lovely girl. Evan tells me she recently got a job working in the kitchen with him."

"Is that so? What are you having for dinner?"

"Lobster."

"Now that's what I call a treat," Alice chimed in.

"One night I told him about my trips to Prince Edward Island. Churches there put on lobster suppers, you see. When I mentioned this to him, his eyes lit up, and I thought it would be fun to have our own version of a PEI lobster supper."

"And this girl . . . what's her name?" It was Tess again.

"Nina. I'll meet her for the first time tonight. She's a journalism student like Evan."

Mikayla appeared at the table then with her water pitcher and greeted the women. "Looks like we've got some bad weather out there today."

"Appears that way. Has Evan called?" Emily asked.

"Not that I know of. He's scheduled to work the afternoon shift, though."

"I know. I'm hoping the snow doesn't stop him from getting to work." Or to dinner tonight, she thought.

A few minutes before seven o'clock, Emily heard a knock at her door. So, Evan and Nina had made it after all, in spite of the weather. He hadn't called to let her know they weren't able to come, so she'd gone ahead and started preparing dinner. She could hardly wait to meet Nina and learn more about her.

Former Things

When Emily opened the door, she saw Evan standing next to a petite young woman with a full head of long dark frizzy hair. Nina's small face was lost in the wilderness of her locks, and Emily immediately wondered how much time it took every day to maintain such a hairstyle.

"You must be Nina. I'm glad you could come," she said, offering her hand.

When Emily took Nina's hand into her own, she couldn't help but notice that it was cold and limp. The girl gave a short laugh and mumbled something inaudible.

"Well, you must be hungry. Come on in."

"We are," Evan said, giving Emily a hug.

Emily ushered them inside and hung their jackets in the hall closet. Then they followed her into the living room.

"Something smells good," said Evan, rubbing his hands together.

"Probably the chowder. I hope you like it. Help yourself to the cheese and crackers on the coffee table. What can I get you? A soft drink? Apple cider?" she asked, moving toward the kitchen.

"Cider, please," he answered for both of them.

Emily poured two glasses of apple cider and carried them to the living room where Evan and Nina were seated on the couch.

"Evan tells me you're a journalism student, Nina. When will you graduate?"

"In two years."

"Do you have career plans?"

"No, not yet. I haven't decided."

"Do you think you'd like to be a news reporter like Evan? Or a magazine writer? Or are you leaning toward broadcast journalism?"

"I'm not sure," she said, lowering her head to examine her fingernails.

"Journalism is a fascinating line of work. Evan has mentioned he'd like to do some travel writing but says the field is very competitive. Is that what you think, too?"

"Probably."

Gail Lowe

Emily paused before continuing. "Do you enjoy traveling yourself?"

"Not much."

The room went silent as Emily tried to think of more topics to talk about. She supposed she could comment on the weather, but she was sure the girl was interested in far more important things than that. "You're a home body then? Do you like to cook?"

"Not really. I can hardly boil water."

"Well, then, do you enjoy sewing or some other type of handcraft?"

"I tried knitting one time, but I was all thumbs. In the last election, I campaigned for George Bush," she said, suddenly enthusiastic. Emily blanched at Nina's admission. "I belong to the Young Republicans Club at school."

"You do? Evan, I thought you were a democrat," Emily said.

Evan held up his hand like a stop sign. "Don't look at me, Emily. I am a democrat. Nina and I get into some pretty heated arguments about politics."

"I guess you must. I've always wondered how James Carville and Mary Matalin get along behind closed doors."

"Maybe it's all an act. Or maybe they just agree to disagree and don't discuss politics at home."

"Still, it makes you wonder."

Emily was uncertain how to keep the conversation buoyant and fun. It was becoming clear to her that she would have little in common with Evan's girlfriend, and she wondered what on earth they would talk about. She turned from politics to safer ground by asking where Nina came from.

"Keene."

"Oh, yes, Keene. I know the city well. I lived there once myself when I was a teenager. On weekends my friends and I used to hike Mt. Monadnock. Have you ever done that?"

Instead of answering, Nina shook her head no.

"Well, then, do you see your family often?"

"About once a month."

She waited for Evan to jump in. When he and Emily were alone, the conversation always flowed so freely, but when

Former Things

he didn't say anything the room went silent again and Emily began to wonder how the girl would ever make a living as a journalist. She certainly hadn't learned the art of conversation, and she didn't seem to be interested in Emily, not that she needed to be the center of attention. Emily thought that maybe Nina was just shy, or maybe she felt uncomfortable being there in the first place. Whatever the problem was, Emily was beginning to wish she hadn't invited Nina at all. She soon realized that she should have kept her friendship with Evan just between the two of them. They always had so much to talk about. Where Evan was outgoing and personable, Nina was closed off and almost unfriendly. Then again, what was it they said about opposites attracting? If that were true, then it was plainly evident in this young couple. Emily tried one last time to get the conversation going.

"Did Evan tell you we're having lobster?"

"Yes."

"Well, I hope you like it. I have a summer cottage on PEI. When I'm there I always make it a point to go to at least one lobster supper. Lobster suppers are PEI's version of an old-fashioned New England bean supper. Have you ever been there?"

"Once. With my family."

"And did you like it?"

"I liked the beach."

"And the red sand?"

"There's red sand? I don't remember that."

It was going to be a long night. Emily knew that now. When Nina began to twist strands of her hair around her finger, she noticed for the first time that the girl's fingernails were bitten down to the quick.

"There are some magnificent rock formations on the island. One is called Elephant Rock. It's on the west side of PEI, and the profile looks just like an elephant. I heard recently that the trunk was taken down by a storm. It completely spoiled the formation—sort of like what happened to the Old Man of the Mountain. You know . . . in Franconia Notch."

"That's too bad."

Gail Lowe

Up to that point, Evan had remained a quiet observer, but he suddenly rose to his feet and took Nina by the hand. Emily was grateful for the sudden rescue.

"Come here. I want to show you some pictures," he said, moving her toward the piano.

While he told her who was in each of the photographs, Nina stood beside him, continuing to twist her hair round her finger. "Oh . . ." was all she had to say.

Exasperated, Emily turned and went to the kitchen to check on her rice and start cooking the lobster. Secretly, she couldn't wait for the evening to end. She only hoped that she was good at hiding her feelings. She wouldn't want to hurt Evan for the world.

After dinner, they returned to the living room. To pass the time, Emily offered to play some tunes on the piano.

"Do you play a musical instrument?" she asked Nina before striking the first notes of *Clair de Lune.*

"Flute. For about a year. When I was eight."

"And you stopped?"

"I really didn't have any interest. It wasn't my thing," Nina said, sloughing off Emily's question. "We have to go soon," she added suddenly. "It's a school night."

"Yes, of course. But have some dessert first." Emily had made a blueberry pie from scratch and had paid dearly for the blueberries, which were out of season, but to her a lobster dinner just wasn't a lobster dinner without blueberry pie. She served it warm with vanilla ice cream, and for the first time that night Nina spoke first.

"It's delicious."

"I'm glad you like it," Emily said, careful not to mention anything about coming for dinner another time.

"Evan, do you think we could play chess next Sunday night after you finish work?"

Evan glanced at Nina and then looked at Emily. "It's going to be an exhausting week," he said, "Mid-terms are coming up."

"Well, then, how about if we wait and see."

Former Things

Nina looked at Evan. "We have plans that night."

"Oh, well, then, I wouldn't want to interfere," Emily said.

"We didn't have anything definite planned," he said, turning to Nina. "We don't even know if we can get tickets."

"But I thought . . ." Nina began.

Evan saw the confusion on Emily's face. "There's a rock concert at school," he explained. "A group from New York. Nina wants to go, but I don't care one way or the other." His words were measured and tight.

Nina sat there, scowling.

Evan got up from the table and said it was time for them to leave. He and Nina followed Emily to the front hall and after handing them their jackets, she opened the door and cautioned them to drive home safely. She watched as they walked down the hallway toward the elevator, and just before they turned the corner Emily could have sworn she heard Nina ask Evan why he would rather play chess than go to a concert, but then they were gone and she had no idea what Evan said in response. The comment had hurt Emily, and she hoped that she hadn't been pressuring Evan to spend time with her. From now on, she would let him make the first move.

On their way back to the dorm, Evan took the back roads, driving in silence most of the way.

"Like, what's the matter with you?" Nina asked.

"Nothing."

"Well, you're awfully quiet for nothing being the matter." She turned in her seat to look him full in the face.

He was seething inside, furious at Nina's rude behavior while visiting Emily.

"Maybe I should be asking you the same question."

"What do you mean?"

"You know what I mean. You weren't exactly nice to Emily tonight."

"Well, like, I don't understand why you want to spend time so much time with some old lady."

Gail Lowe

"Emily is not some old lady," he said. "She's my friend."

"She's, like, old enough to be your grandmother."

"So what? She's fun and exciting and she's one hell of a chess player. I love her company."

"And what about mine? We don't have enough time to spend together as it is. Like, I hardly ever see you."

"What are you talking about? We see each other every time we work at Emerald House. Plus Saturday nights."

"At work doesn't count, Evan. We're working, not on a freaking date."

There was nothing he could say that would change her mind. He'd been dating Nina for four months now, long enough to know that once she made up her mind there was no going back. He was growing tired of her demands, her possessiveness, and now this. Even the guys in his dorm thought he could do better. His roommate didn't like her and had called her a bitch. He felt terrible, knowing that Emily had gone to a lot of trouble to make a nice dinner for them, and Nina had hardly given her the time of day.

"I think we should take a break," he said suddenly, surprised at his own words.

"A break? You're breaking up with me? Like, no way."

"No, I'm not breaking up. I just said we should take a break. It doesn't mean I won't see you again. Or maybe it does. I don't know."

"Fine," she said, pouting. "What about the concert?"

"Find someone else to go with."

"But you promised!"

"Nina, I never promised you anything. Look, you might come from a wealthy family, but I don't. I need every dime I can get my hands on to get through school. I would never promise something I wasn't sure I could afford."

Evan let her off at the women's dorm without giving her a goodnight kiss. She opened the door and got out, slamming it hard. That did it. He knew he would not be calling Nina again anytime soon. He'd see her at work and be cordial, but as far as keeping her as a girlfriend? No way. She was history. He only hoped she'd get the message when he didn't call. He didn't want to have to spell it out for her. As for the leather jacket, he'd give it back to her. He didn't need it. Suddenly, it felt one size too small.

Back in her room, Nina found her roommate studying at her desk. She whipped off her jacket and flung it onto the bed. "Whoa . . . what's the matter with you?" Elizabeth asked, turning around. "You and Evan have a fight?"

"You could say that," Nina said, flopping onto the bed. "Evan is such a loser. I don't know why I bother. Our one night together and he takes me to some old lady's apartment for supper."

"Didn't you see Evan last night?"

"Yeah, but we hung out in his dorm. It was nothing special."

"Don't worry. Everything will be fine tomorrow."

Yes, it would. If Nina had anything to say about it, Evan's relationship with his beloved Miss Emily would soon be a thing of the past, and she knew exactly how to make that happen. She was not about to compete for Evan's attention with some old bag. No one was going to take her place. She would see to that. The old lady was about to become history.

In the morning, Emily watched while Nina placed carafes of coffee on the dining room tables. Odd. She had thought Nina had classes, but maybe they were scheduled for later in the day. After she and Evan had left last night, Emily thought about Nina and her relationship with Evan. Surely it wouldn't last. She hoped not anyway. She thought the two were a poor match, if ever there was one. From what she had read in articles in today's women's magazines, young people's romances were here today and gone tomorrow. Men and women liked to experiment now, the writers of the articles said, and rarely settled down with high school boyfriends or even the people they met in college. No, today's young people were apt to marry later, even in their thirties, before settling down and

Gail Lowe

having children. She was sure Evan would be single for quite some time. As far as she could see, Evan had little in common with Nina.

When Nicole was Nina's age—she guessed Evan's girlfriend to be about eighteen—she was in college, too. Nicole had had a difficult time getting through high school, and at one point Emily thought she might have to repeat her junior year. Something had been bothering Nicole, something that Emily hadn't known about, and it pulled her grades down. There had been a boyfriend—Gary—and Nicole was with him night and day. Emily worried that Gary was taking up too much of Nicole's time and that her schoolwork was suffering, but Nicole refused to listen to her mother, refused to curtail the time she spent with him. Emily feared that the more she tried to keep them apart, the more Nicole would defy her and run after him.

Gary was part of the problem, but there was something else. Emily recalled the day she had done the laundry and had found a soft-cover turquoise diary in the left-hand corner of Nicole's bureau drawer when she was putting her clean underwear away. She fought the temptation to take it out of the drawer and read it and instead concentrated on the task at hand. Emily finished putting the laundry away and turned to leave, but something stopped her. Nicole would never know Emily had read it. What could be written on the pages of the diary that was so secret anyway? She already knew everything about her daughter. Nicole was a good girl and was only going through a rough patch in her adolescence. She had nothing to hide. Or did she?

It was one-thirty, a full hour before Nicole was due home from school. Emily went to the bureau and eased open the top drawer. The diary was lying there, enticing as a new library book begging to be read. A tiny brass key was in the lock, and when she reached inside the drawer she was careful not to disturb it. She took the diary from its hiding place and went to the living room to read.

The unlined pages were thin, like onion skin, and they had a satin finish. There was a date at the top of each page. She turned to the second half of the book and was surprised to see that the

Former Things

first entry was made on September 1, the date of Becky's birthday. Curious now, Emily read:

No one talks about what happened on this day so many years ago. And neither will I. But I know. Mom and Dad think things can be hidden, but they cannot. Like cream, the truth always rises to the surface. I wonder why they don't talk about her. I would like to ask but I don't dare. I will always wonder about her, but I might never have an answer.

Emily had expected to read entries about Gary, but there were none. What had Nicole been thinking when she wrote the entry on the day of Becky's birth, Emily wondered. The writing unnerved her, and when Nicole came home from school she looked at her in a different light. What did she know? And if she knew about Becky, how had she found out? She thought about Nicole's words—*Mom and Dad think things can be hidden, but they cannot. Like cream, the truth always rises to the surface.* Had she intended for Emily to read that entry?

Hiding the truth could be a terrible burden. Emily knew that for a fact, since she had carried the secret of Becky's short life for many years. She'd hidden the fact that Nicole was no longer in her life, too, from the women she dined with every day. Sometimes she found it exhausting to pretend that Nicole was busy with work or that she was away on a business trip or on vacation. At times she thought it would be just as easy to tell the truth. One day she was bound to let it slip. She found herself having to constantly guard her words, lest she reveal her secret.

My daughter disowned me twenty years ago, she would confess. *She wanted her inheritance when her father died, and I told her no. She became angry. And then she left.*

She left? Tess might ask. *Over money?*

Yes, she left. Just like that.

She imagined what they would say when she was out of earshot.

There must be more to the story, one of them might say. *She must have done something wrong. Grown children don't just*

87

abandon their parents for no reason. Maybe she abused her daughter. You never know. Maybe her daughter had a valid reason for leaving. It'd be interesting to hear her side of the story. There are always two sides, you know.

While it was true that she had had a hard time recovering from Becky's death, Emily knew in her heart that she did not deserve Nicole's condemnation. She had not been a perfect mother—and she had acknowledged this to herself and to Reverend Lord many times. But she doubted that any mother could claim to be perfect. Not Althea, and not Alice. Her own mother had not been perfect, either.

More than once, her acknowledgement of the truth about Nicole had been on the tip of Emily's tongue, but she did not want to be fodder for anyone's gossip or the object of pity or scorn inside or outside of Emerald House. She wanted nothing more than to reconcile with her daughter, but while she waited for that day to come, she did not want people talking behind her back so she said nothing.

She'd hinted at the truth when Evan asked her about Nicole the first night they played chess, but he hadn't mentioned her since. One day she might tell him, but only if he promised to keep it their secret. And she knew he would. He was becoming more and more of a friend to her as time passed, and there was a solid loyalty building between them, a bond that she treasured. She knew he enjoyed her friendship, too. Once he had brought her a small bouquet of flowers. Another time, he had brought her favorite hazelnut flavored coffee. In Emily's book, that said a lot.

Yes, one day she would tell him about Nicole. Just not yet.

Emily heard Alice, Rita, and Tess chattering as they approached the dining room for breakfast. No sooner were they seated at the table than Alice broke the news about the death of one of the residents. "You remember Harold," she said. "A tall, good-looking man who had that really nice smile. A real gentleman. It's a shame."

Former Things

Emily knew the man Alice was talking about. Once he had been her partner at a whist game, and she found him to be good company and expert at playing cards. "What happened to him?" she asked.

"His heart. It was very sudden, from what I hear. They took him out in an ambulance late last night and he died on the way to the hospital."

"He was a widower, wasn't he?" Emily asked.

"Divorced. He was married to a much younger woman and once she knew he was coming here to live, she decided to look for greener pastures," she said sadly.

"I didn't know that. It's too bad. Did he have children?"

"Two. A daughter in Portsmouth and a son who lives in California. She's works for a financial planner. The son works in Silicon Valley, I think."

"Well, surely he'll come for the funeral."

"One would hope."

Emily sat quietly while the three other women talked about how quickly life passed by and how thin the line was between life and death. They talked about the importance of family and how some children offered more support than others. They discussed their own situations and how they had better live each day to the fullest, grab onto every opportunity for enjoyment while they could. *You never know what's going to happen next,* said Alice. *Darn right,* agreed Rita. *You have to be prepared for anything,* commented Tess.

"What do you think, Emily?" Alice asked.

What she thought would astound them all. What would they think if they knew about Becky, or Nicole, or John, or Dr. Martin Jackson? All she'd told them was that she'd been a nurse and that she had dedicated her life to her career. At least for now she planned to keep it that way.

"I think all three of you are right," she said.

CHAPTER TEN

After breakfast, Emily went to see Donald Magnuson in the property management office at Emerald House. He had left a message on her answering machine saying that he wanted to discuss something important with her and that it would only take a few minutes. She wondered what the call was about. Maybe her rent was going up. She'd heard on the news that the cost of living was increasing. Maybe everyone was facing a rent increase. But if that were true, wouldn't Mr. Magnuson simply send a letter to all the residents announcing the change? No, it couldn't be that. Besides, if the rent was going up, Alice and the others would have mentioned it. What, then, did he want to talk to her about? When Emily arrived at his office and his secretary announced that she was waiting to see him, he came out to greet her.

"Mrs. Preston, please come into my office and have a seat. I'd like to talk to you about something." Emily followed him inside and sat in a chair opposite his desk. He cleared his throat before speaking. "I'm afraid someone has registered a complaint," he said, folding his hands and leaning toward her.

"A complaint? What kind of complaint?" Her mind began to race. What could she possibly have done that would have offended anyone?

"Please don't misunderstand me, Mrs. Preston. It's my job to ensure that everyone living at Emerald House is happy. And that includes you. But, I have other people to consider as well, which is why . . ."

She waited for him to continue and when he didn't, she said, "Mr. Magnuson, I've done nothing to offend anyone. Who registered a complaint? And what is this all about?"

Former Things

Donald Magnuson was a middle-aged man with a stomach as big as a punch bowl, and he had a row of silver hair circling his bald head. It was his job to oversee the property, hire and fire the staff, and ensure that all the apartments stayed rented. He'd had a string of bad luck with his previous jobs, having been fired from one when a secretary accused him of sexual harassment and laid off from another when the economy went sour. He was determined to keep his current job, and to make sure things were running smoothly he'd developed a reputation for being a martinet. Evan had told Emily while they were playing chess one night that Donald Magnuson ordered the kitchen staff around like they were his own personal servants. "A little Napoleon" was how Evan had described him. She faced him now, hoping that she hadn't done anything to incite his wrath.

"We have an unwritten policy at Emerald House, Mrs. Preston," he said finally, meeting her gaze. "The rule is that the people who live here must not fraternize with the help."

"Not fraternize? I don't understand . . ."

"The point is, someone came to me and said that you and Evan Pierce are—how shall I put this—close friends."

"Evan? Why, yes, Evan and I are friends. We play chess together on Sunday nights after he finishes work, but not while he's on the job," she said, bewildered.

"Yes, I'm well aware of these facts. What I need to tell you is that your friendship with Evan will need to cease. You see, it just doesn't look good."

"What do you mean, it doesn't look good?" Who had complained? Alice, Rita, Tess? She thought a moment and concluded that it could only be Tess, most likely getting back at her for the confrontation they'd had a few days ago. "I assure you that Evan and I are only friends. We play chess and that's all we do. Frankly, I'm insulted."

"Mrs. Preston, your relationship with Evan is causing a bit of gossip and unrest at Emerald House."

"Who is gossiping and who is not at rest, as you put it?"

91

Gail Lowe

"I am not at liberty to say." He gave her a quick smile, revealing a row of crooked teeth. "I promised not to reveal my source."

"So, what you're telling me is that I can no longer be friends with Evan? That I have to pretend not to know him? What do you think? That we're lovers?"

"No, I don't think that," he said, hiding a smile behind his hand. "Please try to understand my position. I don't make the rules here. The board of directors does."

"But you said it was an unspoken policy, not something that's written in stone. Further, why should it be anyone's business what Evan does when he's not on the job? Or what I do in my own apartment? Why is an innocent game of chess on Sunday nights frowned upon?"

"We encourage the people who live here to have company, of course—just not the hired help. It sends a message, Mrs. Preston. A message of favoritism."

She couldn't believe what she was hearing. "Mr. Magnuson, in case you don't know it, I have very few visitors. I'm a widow, and my one daughter . . . she lives far away. And now you're telling me that Evan can't continue to visit me?"

"I'm afraid so. That's right."

"I beg to differ. That's wrong. That's very, very wrong."

He stood then and came out from behind his desk, an expanse of mahogany almost as wide as the man himself. "Whether right or wrong, it is Emerald House's policy, even though it's not spelled out as such in the residents' handbook."

"Then I'll have to think about whether or not I can continue to live here."

"Now, Mrs. Preston, surely you don't mean that." His tone was patronizing, and it irritated Emily.

"I most certainly do. I won't have anyone telling me who I can and cannot be friends with or who I can entertain."

"I wouldn't exactly put it that way."

"And how, may I ask, would you put it?"

He could see that he was getting nowhere. That morning when he had been told about Emily's friendship with Evan, he

Former Things

knew right away he had to take action. This was not what he had expected to happen. He expected Emily Preston to be reasonable and understanding, and she was far from either, in his opinion.

"Mrs. Preston, think about how it looks to the other residents. I mean, for Evan Pierce to be singling you out smacks of favoritism."

The informer had to be Tess, Emily decided, suddenly angry. Alice and Rita would never in a million years object to Evan visiting her apartment.

"What would you like me to do?" She gritted her teeth, and her words were measured and tight.

"Refrain from inviting him to your apartment. What you do outside Emerald House is your business, but what you do inside is mine."

She got up, avoiding his eyes, and turned to leave. "Mrs. Preston, I have many people to satisfy, including you. I don't wish to hurt anyone. My job is to create an environment at Emerald House where everyone lives in harmony."

She left his office without another word and returned to her apartment. As soon as she closed the door, she went to the phone and called Tess.

When Tess picked up her phone, Emily counted to three before she spoke but she was so angry she launched right in. "Tess, how could you . . ."

"Who is this?"

"Emily Preston. That's who," she said, a tremor in her voice.

"What's the matter with you, Emily. What have I done?" Tess said, gripping the phone. She had just awoken from a nap and had not been expecting any phone calls, least of all from Emily.

"You know very well what you've done. You told Donald Magnuson about my friendship with Evan. And not only that, you told him about the dinner I served Evan and his girlfriend last night."

Her words were met with a marked silence before a flabbergasted Tess finally answered. "Emily, I promise you I never said a word. I don't care if you feed him three meals a day. It's not my business what you do. Believe me, I couldn't care less."

Emily stopped and thought before continuing. "If not you, then who?"

"I have no idea, but it wasn't me. To even think of accusing me is . . . well, you're just way out of line. And don't point the finger at Alice or Rita, either. Neither of them give a damn what you do. None of us do."

Emily paused before continuing. "Then who complained? If not one of you, who would have gone to Mr. Magnuson? No one else knows about my relationship with Evan."

"That's not quite true. I can think of one other person who knows."

"And who's that?"

"Evan's girlfriend. Nina."

Nina. The girl's face suddenly loomed into Emily's consciousness, and her thoughts went to the night before when she and Evan had come for dinner. Had Nina gone to Mr. Magnuson this morning when she got to work? She certainly had been less than friendly and enthusiastic at dinner, and she recalled what Nina had said to Evan when they were walking down the hallway toward the elevator. Suddenly, it was clear to Emily that Nina considered her an intruder.

"I'm sorry for accusing you, Tess. Really. I'm truly sorry."

"It's okay. But next time, don't go accusing anyone until you know all the facts."

Emily kept to herself what Mr. Magnuson had told her, hoping that Tess wouldn't open her mouth and make it a topic of conversation at lunch. She hoped her apology would be enough. She wanted to put the whole incident with Donald Magnuson behind her. She wouldn't say a word to Evan, either, and if the matter of a chess game came up again, Emily would suggest that they meet at The King's Rook, a small tavern a few miles down the road from Emerald House. She knew they could linger over a cup of coffee there and not be asked to leave. In fact, the owner encouraged his patrons to read newspapers and play board games. If Evan asked about the change in venue, she'd simply tell him that she needed to get out of her apartment once in a while. "It'll do us both good," she would tell him if he asked.

Her thoughts about Nina throughout the day were less than kind, and she thought the girl cruel to have said anything to Donald Magnuson. She also considered confronting her, but to do so would put Evan in the middle and that was something she didn't want to do.

It galled her to think that she'd built up a solid friendship with Evan, only for Nina to tear it down by going to Mr. Magnuson. She knew she wouldn't be able to avoid the girl forever, at least not while she was working at Emerald House. Emily thought that maybe the best thing to do was to extend her hand in friendship to Nina and win her over to her side. But hadn't she tried doing just that by inviting her to dinner? She'd have to think things through before coming to a solution. She couldn't risk alienating Nina *and* Evan. Then she would be back to square one. She didn't want to lose Evan's friendship. If that happened, she would find herself alone all over again.

At dinner that night, Emily saw Evan approaching her table from the opposite end of the dining room. With only a few seconds to think about what she wanted to say, she gathered her thoughts quickly, practicing the words in her head. *I enjoyed meeting Nina last night. Such a nice girl. I hope she'll come again.* No, she didn't want to lie or be disingenuous. Yet, she couldn't come right out and say anything negative about the girl that would put Evan on the defensive. She decided to say nothing and let Evan carry the conversation.

"Hi, Emily."

"Hello, Evan. How are you tonight?"

"Still full. That lobster last night was delicious."

They chatted away, as they always did, then Emily spotted Donald Magnuson standing at the kitchen door watching them. "I think your boss might want you," she said, nodding toward the door.

"He can wait a minute. I just wanted to thank you for dinner last night. It was awesome. And when we play chess next Sunday night, I want to . . ."

Emily interrupted him and said she meant to talk to him about that very subject and asked him to stop by her apartment when he finished his shift. He looked at her, puzzled, but she said she would tell him later what she wanted to talk to him about.

"Mr. Magnuson is waiting for you, Evan." He turned then and saw his boss glaring at him.

"Gotta go," he said. "See you tonight."

At six-thirty she heard a knock on the door and opened it to find Evan standing there in his work clothes.

"Come on in," she said.

He came inside the apartment and stood in the hallway facing Emily.

"So what did you want to talk to me about? Is anything wrong?"

"No, I was just thinking that the weather would be getting warmer soon. It's already the middle of April and I wondered if you'd like to play chess somewhere other than this stuffy old place."

"Like where?"

"You know The King's Rook down the road? The owner encourages people to play board games. He has a lot of popular games on a shelf behind the bar, and I've seen people playing cards and reading newspapers and books while eating. We could play there. What do you think?"

"I've always liked your place, but if you want a change of scenery, it's fine with me."

"Good. It's settled then. We'll go out on Sunday nights from now on."

On the way back to the dorm, Evan wondered about Emily's sudden change of heart but attributed it to nothing more than a woman who felt cooped up. She was probably tired of looking at the same old four walls. Nothing unusual about that, he supposed. Sometimes he felt that way about his dorm room.

CHAPTER ELEVEN

The King's Rook was as silent as a library the following Sunday night. One man sat in a corner reading the *Boston Globe*. Another man seated at the bar was poring over the front page of the *Portsmouth Herald*. Emily also noticed a couple seated next to the wall playing a game of gin rummy. She picked a table near the fireplace where it would be warm and away from cold drafts blowing through the front door. Though it was already April, the weather still had not turned spring-like. The tavern was dim, with lots of exposed brick and heart pine floors, and the sturdy, antique wooden tables and chairs were the kind found in old New England one-room schoolhouses. Each table had a single lit candle in its center, and wall sconces hung on the beams, giving off enough light for Emily and Evan to play their chess game. Before setting up the board, they ordered cups of hot chocolate with marshmallows and two blueberry muffins. After all the chess pieces were in place, Evan told her to make the first move.

"White before black," he said, and Emily complied, advancing a pawn two spaces.

While Evan was contemplating his move, the front door opened and a middle-aged woman stepped inside the tavern. When Emily saw the woman, her breath caught in her throat and she gasped.

"What's the matter?" Evan asked, turning toward the doorway.

"It's nothing. I just thought . . ."

"What?" He turned around completely and saw a dark-haired woman standing there in a short red jacket and a white scarf draped across her shoulders.

Gail Lowe

"The woman who just came in," she whispered. "She's a dead ringer for my daughter."

Evan studied the woman before turning back to Emily.

"Is it Nicole?"

"No, but she looks a lot like her. At least she looks like Nicole did twenty years ago."

Evan had wondered about Emily's daughter since the first night he had visited her apartment. He hadn't wanted to intrude on her privacy, but now he found it as good a time as any to bring up the subject. "Don't you think it's time you told me about her, Emily? I mean, we're not exactly strangers anymore. You know more about me than I know about you. How come Nicole doesn't come to see you?"

It was then that Emily told Evan about Nicole's disappointment and anger after John died and how she'd quit her job and left town. "I have no idea where my daughter is, and that's the truth of the matter. It's hard for me to talk about because I never know if people might think I was a terrible mother. You can understand that, Evan, can't you?"

He thought for a moment before answering. "Yes and no. I understand why you would keep it to yourself," he said, "but I don't understand how you could think that anyone would judge you, least of all me. If I didn't think you were a good person, believe me, I wouldn't be sitting here with you right now. To be honest, I thought that maybe Nicole was mad at you over something. Otherwise, why wouldn't she visit you? I've never even heard you talk about her, and I've always thought that was strange."

"Thank you for understanding. It was never my intention to hurt my only child."

"I'm sure you did nothing to hurt her. Or, if you did, it wasn't intentional. Have you ever looked for her?"

"In the beginning, yes. I went to the police and then hired an investigator. Neither of them could help me."

Evan sat there in silence for a long moment, then he stood up and told Emily he'd be right back. On the way into the tavern he'd noticed a sign in the window that read "Free Wi-Fi! Ask

Former Things

about borrowing one of our laptops!" He asked the bartender for one of the computers and when he handed Evan a laptop, he carried it back to the table where Emily sat waiting.

"What are you going to do with that?"

"We're going to look for Nicole."

"What do you mean? How?"

"I know how to do a people search over the Internet. Modern technology is really cool. Wait till I show you." He picked up all the chess pieces and folded up the board and put the game away before opening the laptop. "We can play another time. This is more important."

Emily watched while he booted up the computer. A few seconds later, the monitor's screen lit up and when he pressed the IE icon the front page of the *New York Times* popped onto the screen.

Emily watched, fascinated. Emerald House had a computer room but she had never ventured inside because she had no idea how to use a computer. Evan showed her how to enter a site address into a line at the top of the screen and then waited for the computer to do its work.

"Now watch what happens," he said.

In a matter of seconds, a people search page opened where a person's name, city, and state could be entered into an address line. "We'll start by typing in Nicole's name and using New Hampshire as her home state. Is it Nicole Preston?"

"It was last time I knew. She may have married, though."

He typed in Nicole's name in the appropriate spaces and added Rye, New Hampshire.

A few seconds later, a page showing the search results came onto the screen with a long list of people whose names were Nicole Preston. "Now watch as I scroll through the listings. How old is she?"

"Forty-seven."

There were dozens of Nicole Prestons listed on the page, and Evan scrolled down until he found Nicole Preston, 47, Rye, New Hampshire. "Look here . . . it says she's lived in all these places."

Gail Lowe

Emily studied the column where it showed the various places Nicole had lived.

Beverly, Massachusetts
Sachem, Connecticut
Hoboken, New Jersey
Elkhart, Indiana
Willowdale, Illinois

She could hardly speak, so stunned was she to learn about the multiple locations where Nicole had lived over the past twenty years. She wondered what Nicole had been up to. She also wondered if Nicole might have thought to look her up, as well. "How does the computer know where Nicole has lived?"

"Government data. Employment records. Motor vehicle registries. We have no privacy anymore. They know everything about us."

"Does this mean that Nicole lives in Illinois now?"

"It's hard to say. They might not list the places she's lived in chronological order. She could be in any one of those places." He hesitated before continuing. "Or, she could have moved on. The government might be behind in updating their records. One thing is clear, though."

"What's that?"

"Nicole never married."

"How do you know that?"

"Because she's still listed as Nicole Preston. Unless, of course, she divorced and took back her maiden name."

Evan explained that though Nicole hadn't left a paper trail of her own, the government had been tracking her every move. While Emily continued to study the cities and states where Nicole had lived, her eyes wandered to another column where she saw her own name.

"Look here, Evan. There's my name . . . and John's . . . and Rebecca Preston." She stared at the name, curious. Rebecca Preston. Why would Becky's name be listed there? She had died years ago. "Can we look up Rebecca Preston? See what it says about her? I'm not sure who this is."

Former Things

Evan returned to the people search home page and typed in "Rebecca Preston." A new screen popped up, and he scrolled through all the Rebecca Prestons until he found an entry that linked her to Nicole. "Here it is. It must be her. See? She's also listed as having lived in Connecticut and the other places. Now it looks like she lives in Illinois. She's a little younger than me. Twenty-one."

Emily stared at the computer screen. Could Rebecca be her grandchild? A grandchild she had not known about?

Evan read the confusion on Emily's face. "Do you know who she is?"

"I have no idea. Maybe Nicole has a daughter." She hadn't told Evan about Becky but decided to tell him now. "There's more to the story I haven't told you, Evan. You see, two years before Nicole was born I had another child. Her name was Rebecca. Becky, we called her. We never told Nicole about her." She told him then about Becky's death and how deeply she had grieved the loss of her baby.

"Nicole knew nothing about her sister?"

Emily looked at Evan and attempted to explain. "I had my suspicions that she found out, but it's not something we ever talked about." As she spoke, the memory of the day she discovered Nicole's diary came into her mind. Maybe Nicole did have a daughter whom she had named for her dead sister. A granddaughter? The very notion both excited and angered her. If Nicole had kept her child a secret all these years, she had deprived her daughter from an important relationship, and her, too.

Evan closed the laptop and returned it to the bartender. Unanswered questions hung in the air between them. Questions that Emily now wanted answered.

They drove back to Emerald House in silence, Emily lost in her own thoughts, Evan in his. When they said goodnight, Emily went to her apartment with a heavy heart after realizing, once again, that she'd missed out on twenty years of Nicole's life. Her only daughter had lived in a half dozen places and Emily hadn't known about any of them. Sometime during those twenty years

Gail Lowe

it was very likely that Nicole had given birth to her granddaughter. Worse, somehow Nicole may have learned about Becky's life and death, even though she and John had never told her.

Before she went to bed, Emily went to the phone and picked up the receiver. She'd promised herself that she would never disturb Evan in his dorm, but decided that what she had to say was too important, so she called him.

He picked up on the first ring.

"Evan, it's Emily."

"I know. I've been thinking . . ."

"Thinking about . . ."

"Well, a lot of things. Let's meet tomorrow night. At The King's Rook. We may be able to find out more about Nicole. My curiosity is killing me."

"What time?"

"Seven. I'll meet you there."

She hung up, relieved that her burden of secrecy had been finally lifted. She hoped that Evan could help her learn more about Nicole.

CHAPTER TWELVE

The following night, Emily and Evan met again at The King's Rook. After setting up the laptop in their spot by the fireplace, Evan booted up the computer and went to a search engine. He typed in "Nicole Preston" and waited to see if there was any information about her archived on a website. A newspaper article published in May 1985 came onto the screen that said Nicole had been one of the members of the staff at The Boxcar Restaurant in Beverly, Massachusetts who had raised funds for the local soup kitchen. Nothing was mentioned about Nicole in the article that Emily didn't already know, but at least it confirmed that she'd lived in Beverly twenty years ago. Evan checked a few more entries before finding a page about Nicole joining the management staff at Burlwood Casino in Sachem, Connecticut later that same year. There were no links to her in New Jersey or Indiana, but a few entries later they found a press release that announced she'd been hired at Erekson Publishing Company in Chicago. At the end of the article, it said that Nicole was a resident of Willowdale which, by checking a map, Evan discovered was a small suburb a few miles outside of Chicago.

"I wonder if she's still there," said Emily.

"Could be. But it seems that she stays in one place for a few years before moving on. Probably her modus operandi. I've forgotten . . . did Nicole go to college?"

"Yes," Emily replied. "Franklin Pierce. But she may have continued her studies after she left Rye. I just don't know. From what it says in the article, it looks like she may have developed an interest in publishing."

Gail Lowe

"There are more questions about Nicole than we have answers," he said.

"You can say that again."

CHAPTER THIRTEEN

Since their search for Nicole had begun, Evan thought that he might be cut out to be an investigative reporter. Sleuthing was something he enjoyed and was good at, and he was becoming more and more intrigued with the story of Nicole and the prospect of finding her.

Earlier in the week, Professor Grieg had taken Evan aside to ask if he had chosen a topic to write about for his feature writing term paper. Evan had told his professor he was mulling over an idea in his mind, but it was something he needed to flesh out and wasn't quite ready to talk about it. No, he wanted to bide his time, take a wait and see approach before talking about it with anyone, especially Emily.

The following Sunday night at The King's Rook, they continued to search the Internet for several hours until the manager told them the tavern was closing for the night. Emily wondered if she should buy herself a laptop computer and mentioned it to Evan. Now that she had learned about Nicole's movements, she was hungry for even more information. She'd had no idea that the Internet was such a great resource of information.

"We'll go shopping soon," he said. "See what we can find."

Before his class with Professor Grieg on Monday, Evan asked if he could meet with him privately. "It's about the topic I'm thinking about for my term paper," he said.

"And what is that?"

Evan told the professor about Emily and how Nicole had disappeared from her life twenty years ago. "I did an Internet search for Emily and found that her daughter has lived in five

Gail Lowe

different places. I'd like to help Emily find her. I know it would mean a lot."

"And how would you go about doing that?" The professor regarded Evan. He was a topnotch student, one he had great hopes for, and was eager to hear what he had to say.

"I'm thinking about taking the summer off and proposing that Emily and I rent an RV and go on a search to find Nicole. We'd map out a route and stop in the cities and towns where Nicole has lived and visit police stations, libraries, churches, and other places where she might have been. Maybe we'd stay a week in each place, pass out fliers with Nicole's picture on them. Talk to people. See if anyone remembers her. Then I'd write about the trip for my term paper. I'd position it in such a way that it would be an investigative piece as well as a feature. All the better if we find Nicole. What do you think?"

"Sounds a little like Charles Kuralt with a mysterious twist." Professor Grieg was intrigued by Evan's plan and wondered if it might be feasible. The work Evan proposed would certainly encompass a magnitude none of his students had ever thought to tackle before. He knew Evan's father and wondered if the man knew how creative his son was. "I'd have to talk to my department head to see if we can extend the due date for your paper."

"I'm thinking long term. This could be a steppingstone to an investigative reporting career," said Evan.

"You could be right. If you can work out all the details and you can get your friend to agree, then I would say your idea is a good one—if your deadline can be extended. But how do you plan to convince your friend? I'm sorry . . . I don't believe you mentioned her name."

"Emily Preston. She lives at the place where I work part time. When she was younger, she loved to travel. She'd probably jump at the chance to go on a road trip."

"And have you thought about practical matters, such as how you would pay for an RV?"

"I think Emily may have some money. Her husband left her pretty well off. At least that's my impression. Emerald House is not a cheap place to live."

"Then all you can do is ask. If Emily really wants to find her daughter, she may decide it's worth every penny."

After Evan left his office, Professor Grieg went to his desk and thought about Evan's proposal. He knew that one day the young man would make a name for himself. He wished more of his students demonstrated such initiative. He finished the last of his paperwork and went to sit in his leather wing chair. He rested there a while and thought about his own son. It had been four years since he had last seen Garrett, and he wished he had the nerve to do what Evan was going to propose to Emily Preston.

The remainder of Evan's day passed in a blur, so preoccupied was he with the possibility of an RV trip to find Emily's daughter. First, he would have to present the idea to her. If she agreed, the next step would be to visit an RV dealer to see what size vehicle they'd need and how much it would cost. Next, they'd have to study a map and figure out a route. Then they'd have to decide on a date of departure and approximate return. The possibility of a road trip with Emily was becoming more and more real to him, not to mention exciting. He could hardly wait to see her again. Instead of waiting until their next chess game, he decided to call and ask her to meet him at The King's Rook later that night. A smile played on his lips when the thought occurred to him that the bartender might be wondering what was up with them. He might even be thinking that he was dating a woman old enough to be his grandmother. He laughed out loud at the very thought then picked up the phone and called her.

CHAPTER FOURTEEN

Emily wondered all afternoon what was on Evan's mind. He'd called soon after she returned to her apartment from lunch, and he wanted her to meet him again at The King's Rook. It probably had something to do with Nicole, she supposed. Maybe he'd found more information that he wanted to share with her.

She met him in the parking lot later that night, and when they went inside the tavern the bartender reached for a laptop and handed it to Evan without being asked. "Must be something mighty important you're looking at online," he laughed.

"You could say that," Evan replied, smiling.

When they were seated at their table, Evan turned to Emily and asked her how serious she was about finding Nicole. "Very," she answered. "I've never wanted anything so badly in my entire life except, of course, that Becky had lived."

"Then how about setting out to find her. And I don't mean over the Internet."

"And how do you suggest we do that?"

Evan outlined his plan. He explained to her that an RV trip would give them the freedom and flexibility to stay in one place for a week or two, ask around about Nicole, and post fliers in public places. He also told her it would be a perfect topic for his term paper and that he was considering pursuing investigative reporting as a future career. Going on such a trip would help prepare him for that. All they would have to do was rent an RV, map out a route, and visit the places where Nicole had lived. "We could set aside June and July and even part of August to find her," he suggested.

"It sounds like it might be the adventure of a lifetime," she said, "but, well, I don't know."

Former Things

"What don't you know?"

"What if we don't find her?"

"Then we don't find her. But at least you can say you tried. It's a risk but one you might not want to pass up."

Emily thought about Evan's proposal a moment before responding. "Where would we get an RV?"

"We'd rent one. There's a big dealership on Route 125 in Kingston."

"Who would drive it?"

"I would. And you could take over on the highway, if you want. They're not much different to maneuver than a car. Only bigger. On long stretches of road, it wouldn't be a problem for you. And if we have time, we could take in a little sightseeing. Turn it into a working vacation."

Emily remembered the summer she had taken Nicole to Prince Edward Island and how much fun they'd had. The prospect of a trip that would take up most of the summer appealed to Emily. She had not had anything as exciting to look forward to for a long time, and the last time she'd been away was three years ago when she went to Lenox near the New York border for a jazz festival with Mary Ellen.

Money was certainly no object. She had plenty to spare and no one to leave it to unless, of course, Nicole came back to her. No, money wasn't a problem. What, then, would stop her? She still had her health, and her apartment lease didn't come up for renewal until the end of August. She also enjoyed Evan's company and wanted to do what she could to help him move forward in life. In a roundabout way, she would be helping him to write his paper.

"Well, there's no harm in finding out about renting an RV. Why don't we go to Kingston sometime later this week? Maybe we could kill two birds with one stone. We were going to shop for a computer for me anyway."

Evan agreed and felt more and more excited by the minute. "I don't have any classes on Friday and I'm not scheduled to work. How about heading to Kingston late in the morning. We could have lunch and then go to a dealership."

Gail Lowe

"Yes, and why don't we start out by having lunch out. We'll go to my old favorite haunt in New Castle. Have you ever been to Wentworth-by-the-Sea?"

"No."

"Well, you're in for a treat."

Emily told Evan about the 1874 hotel and how she and John had dined there countless times while they were married. "You're going to love it," she said.

CHAPTER FIFTEEN

The week passed slowly, and Emily kept busy by making a list of all the things she'd need to do to prepare for a summer on the road while Evan mapped out a plan for how he and Emily might locate Nicole.

On Friday morning, Emily put on a navy blue pantsuit, white camisole, and a gold choker Nicole had given her for Mother's Day one year. She wanted to dress up enough for their lunch at Wentworth-by-the-Sea, but not so dressed up that she would feel uncomfortable shopping for an RV rental.

Just before eleven, Evan knocked on her door and she opened it to find him standing there in a pair of chinos, blue plaid shirt, navy blue sports jacket, and penny loafers. She thought him handsome and wished fervently that she had a grandson just like him.

Half an hour later, they were driving along Route 1A toward New Castle in Evan's old blue Plymouth. The day was sunny and the Isles of Shoals were clearly visible from the roadway. While driving along, she watched the fishing boats toss and dip in the late April wind. The waves were rolling in, long and lazy, like old men with nothing to occupy their time. She asked Evan to drive past her old house and was amazed to see that the Sterlings had changed the exterior color from its original pale gray to yellow. She reveled in the drive along the Rye coastline and marveled at the high waves crashing over the rocks. The sky was a startling shade of crystal blue, a color so sharp it looked as if the sky could break into a million pieces. They drove over a tiny bridge in New Castle and

Gail Lowe

off in the distance Wentworth-by-the-Sea rose up in front of them, big as a cruise ship. Emily thrilled at the sight of the old hotel, now refurbished to its former glory. The last time she'd had dinner or even lunch there was with Mary Ellen when they celebrated the sale of Emily's house.

"Wow . . ." was all Evan could say.

"She's a beautiful old girl, isn't she?" said Emily, eyeing the place. "I'm only glad they didn't tear the building down. That was the plan before she underwent restoration."

Evan parked to the far right of the hotel and together they walked to the front entrance where a doorman stood waiting for guests to come inside. He held the door for them and they entered the lobby. An oversized vase of exotic flowers placed on a round table stood in the middle of the room and blue and rose upholstered sofas and chairs circled a fireplace.

They climbed the stairs to the restaurant on the second floor and were greeted by a maitre d' wearing black pants and white shirt. "Do you have a reservation?" he asked.

"Yes. Emily Preston."

"Right this way."

Once they were seated, Evan took in his surroundings. "It's pretty cool to be on the receiving end for a change," he said. "Thank you."

"You deserve it," she said, handing Evan his menu. "Order anything you like. My treat. The baked stuffed sole is excellent."

"I'm looking at that lobster roll. Everything looks good."

"Well, we might as well get our fill of seafood now. If we do go on a trip, we won't be finding good old New England fish on any of the menus. At least not fresh out of the ocean."

Emily ordered shrimp cocktail and the stuffed sole and Evan ordered a lobster roll with French fries and cole slaw. While they ate, they talked about possibilities for their trip. Emily suggested they visit Mark Twain's House in Hartford, and Evan said he'd like to explore New York City. Emily suggested that if the trip took them as far as Chicago they should make a point of going to The Art Institute.

Former Things

"Whoa . . . I'm living on a waiter's salary at the moment."

"Never mind. If we do decide to go, it'll be on my expense account, not yours," Emily laughed. Then she was serious. "I have no one else to spend my money on and I'd be delighted to spend it on you, Evan. Believe me when I tell you that you have enriched my life beyond anything I could have possibly hoped for. This is my way of saying thank you."

For a moment, Evan was speechless. "I'll make it up to you. I'll do everything in my power to help you find Nicole."

"You know, it hasn't been easy for me all these years. There are some things money can't buy, and the love of your child is one of them."

"I'm sure that's true."

Thoughts of Nina came to Emily then. "We haven't discussed Nina. What will she think if you go off with me for the summer?"

Evan hesitated before answering. "I haven't seen Nina. Actually, I broke up with her."

"Really? I'm sorry to hear this," she said, but she was not surprised at all.

"Nina has a lot of growing up to do. I know I do, too, but at the moment she and I just aren't right for each other. I saw how rude she was to you last Sunday night."

"I wouldn't think much about it, Evan."

"Well, I do. You went out of your way to cook us dinner, and all she did was sit there like a stick of wood."

Emily wondered if she should mention the incident with Donald Magnuson but decided to keep it to herself. Some things were best left unsaid, and this was only one of them. As long as she and Evan could continue to meet at The King's Rook, it no longer mattered one way or the other. Her problem with Donald Magnuson had been solved.

"It's really okay. Nina may not have felt comfortable, that's all."

"Whatever. Let's change the subject. I'm done with her."

"Okay. How about dessert? Vanilla ice cream and hot fudge sauce?"

"Absolutely. What else is there?" he teased.

On the way to Kingston, they passed fields still patched with snow and narrow streams flowing alongside the road. Soon, the trees would begin to sprout buds on their branches and wildflowers would spring up in colors of purple, yellow, and pink. Emily longed for the warmth of summer the way she longed for reconciliation with Nicole—with a sense of urgency and importance. Life, she knew, was not always patient, and not always long enough for goals to be reached. In fact, so preoccupied was she with thoughts of Nicole that she found herself lost in a daydream while Evan talked excitedly about types of RVs they might rent and road maps and provisions they would need for their trip. She wondered what would happen if she and Evan were successful in their search for Nicole. What if, after all their planning, Nicole had no interest in reconciling with her? What if she told Emily she'd never been happier now that she was free of her? There were so many "what ifs" to consider.

"Everything okay?" Evan asked, glancing at Emily.

"Oh, I'm fine . . . just doing a little wool gathering."

"About?"

"Just thinking of all the things I'd have to do if I left home for a few months."

"For instance?"

She thought quickly. "Well, I'd have to pay my rent ahead of time. Shut off my phone. See that the post office held my mail, make arrangements for the cat . . . practical things like that."

"Don't worry. You'll have plenty of time. I'll help you."

Emily was silent for a moment then spoke.

"Evan?"

"What?"

"What is it about me?"

"What do you mean?"

"Why do you bother with me? I'm an old woman. Why do you want to go on this trip with me?"

Former Things

"Because I think you're a lot of fun and looking for Nicole will make a unique topic for my term paper," he said, reaching across the seat for her hand. "I need a mother figure in my life. In a way, you're a replacement for the mother I lost. My father and I have never been close, but my mother and I were. She's the one who encouraged me to pursue a writing career."

"I had no idea. Tell me about her."

"There's not much to tell. She was pretty and smart and loved Pablo Neruda's poetry. She taught me to read before I even went to school. She read to me a lot."

"A mother who read to her child," she mused.

"Comic books were my favorite, of course. Spiderman, Batman . . . you know, all the stuff kids like."

"I've never read them myself but, yes, I do know. Tell me more. Did she work?"

"She was an editor at a publishing company. After I was born, she worked part-time."

"Did she write, too?"

"Only poetry. I still have her journals. Actually, one of her poems was picked up by *The New Yorker.* It's hard to say what she might have done with her writing had she lived."

"How wonderful! I'm sure you'll always treasure her journals."

"I certainly will."

"Speaking of books and journals, we need to stop at a bookstore to buy a road atlas. We'll need one in case we go."

He looked her square in the eye then. "In case we go? I think the time has come, Emily. We have to go."

CHAPTER SIXTEEN

The blue and white sign for Anderson's RV Sales and Rentals towered over Route 125 in Kingston. Underneath the name of the company in smaller letters were the words "No one beats us in price. Anderson's—the RV dealer with special deals."

Evan slowed as he approached the turnoff from the road into Anderson's parking lot and saw a man wearing a red plaid woolen jacket and a pair of jeans bending over and looking at the tires on an RV. He wondered if the man might be Mr. Anderson himself. He parked the car and he and Emily headed for the sales office. No one was there but a few minutes later, the same man wearing the red plaid jacket came inside.

"Howdy-do, folks, what can I do for you?" he asked.

"We'd like to take a look at your RVs," said Evan. "Nothing too big. Probably a Class C motor home is what we'd be interested in. To rent, not buy."

"We have a few on the lot. Cal Anderson's the name," the man said, taking off his hat and running his hand through his salt and pepper hair. "How far you plannin' to go?"

"From here down to Massachusetts, then Connecticut, New Jersey, Indiana, and Illinois," Evan replied. "We haven't figured out the route or approximate mileage yet. Maybe two thousand miles round trip, give or take. Does that sound about right to you?"

Cal Anderson ran his hand over the stubble on his face while figuring the mileage in his head. "What I usually tell folks is to plan on doublin' the amount of miles they think they'll drive. So, I'd put a sure bet on maybe four thousand, more or less." He eyed Emily and Evan and figured they were probably grandmother and grandson. He wondered who else was going along

116

Former Things

for the ride and asked. "Just the two of you goin'? Or are there more in your party?"

"Just us," said Emily.

"Hmm . . . when you fixin' to get on the road?"

"The first week in June. Probably be back late July, early August. Something like that."

"We get busy late May. Better reserve one now if you're gonna be on the road this summer."

"Can you show us a rental? Something in a Class C?"

"Sure. Got two on the lot right now. Both in good shape." He held the office door open and a gust of wind blew in. "Follow me," he said.

Emily and Evan followed Cal to a silver and blue motor home at the end of the lot. "This is probably the better of the two," he said. "Eight hundred a week is my usual price, but I can let you have it for seven-fifty if you reserve it now."

"Can we see the inside?"

Pulling a ring of keys from his belt loop, Cal went through them one by one until he found the right key. "Here we are," he said, jiggling the key in the lock and opening the door.

They stepped inside and marveled at how roomy the interior was, in spite of how small the RV looked from the outside.

"This here's the kitchenette," said Cal, demonstrating how a fold-up table could be pulled out from the wall. "And up top here, above the cab . . . that's one bed. And these couches pull out. There's another bed in the back and so is the head. Shower, toilet . . . everything you need. Plus a microwave oven, TV, and DVD player. You have to bring your own towels and sheets. Before you leave, I'd show you how to set the thing up, hook up the water . . . all that practical stuff. And I'll give you a directory of campgrounds. A home away from home, you might say. That's what I tell my customers. Cheaper than one of them flea-bag motel rooms, and cleaner, too, I don't mind adding."

Evan checked out the sleeping quarters above the cab and went to the rear of the RV to have a look at the bathroom. When he came back, he looked at Emily. "Well, what do you think?" he said.

117

"I don't know . . ."

"Look, if seven-fifty is a little too much for your wallet, I'll let it go for an even seven. Believe me, if you think you can get anything like this for less, you're sadly mistaken. There isn't another dealer within a hundred miles of here that'll give you a better deal."

"Can we talk about it in private?"

"Sure. I'll be back in my office. Look, I'll even throw in a pair of bikes you can ride while you're on your trip."

Cal left them alone, and Evan turned to Emily. "Should we do this or what?"

"Life's short. Let's do it. What do you think?"

"No doubt in my mind. I think we're in for one hell of an adventure if we go."

"Then let's go see Cal."

Back in the sales office, Cal prepared the paperwork and Emily wrote a check for seven hundred dollars. "Believe me, you're gettin' a steal of a deal . . . isn't any dealer within a hundred miles . . . I already told you that, didn't I? Well, it's worth repeatin'. Make sure you tell your friends. Send 'em on down. Tell 'em I got a deal waitin'. Isn't any better advertisin' than word of mouth. No, suh. That's the way to go. Word of mouth."

On the way back to Emerald House, they stopped at Staples and bought a road atlas and brand new laptop computer for Emily. Now that their road trip was turning into reality, they talked about what they'd need to do before setting out—figuring out a route, targeting towns and cities where Nicole had lived, and making up fliers with her picture to post in libraries, post offices, and police stations in the towns. They also planned to visit hair and nail salons, churches, coffee shops, and restaurants where they'd show the flier and ask shopkeepers to hang them in their windows.

Emily was tired on the way home, and though she didn't mention it to Evan, after lunch she felt as if she was coming down with the flu. Her muscles ached, her chest felt tight, and her face was flushed when she looked in the mirror on the car's visor, but Evan had been so excited about renting the RV and buying the computer and atlas that she didn't want to put a black mark on the day by complaining. She would rest when she got home. If she was coming down with the flu, there was nothing she could do about it or prevent Evan from catching it. She hoped it was nothing more than a case of exhaustion. Thoughts about the trip had kept her awake the past few nights, and she'd found herself tossing and turning. Yes, that was it. She was just overtired. When she got home, she would draw a nice warm bath and throw some lavender-scented crystals into the water, relax for a while, and then wrap herself up in her favorite pink bathrobe and take a nap. Tomorrow she'd make an appointment to see Dr. Talbot. Just to make sure everything was working the way it should be.

It was late afternoon when Evan pulled into the parking lot at Emerald House. He parked Emily's car in its usual spot, then walked her to the front door. Emily looked around to see if Donald Magnuson was anywhere in sight, but no one seemed to be around. She breathed a sigh of relief.

"Do you want me to set up your computer now?" Evan asked.

Immediately she thought of Mr. Magnuson. "No. I'll bring it with me Sunday night. We're playing chess, aren't we?"

"Sure. Same time? Same place?"

"Yes. You can teach me all the ins and outs of my laptop. Or at least the basics."

"The basics. It takes time to learn all the ins and outs."

He held the door while she carried her bags inside. "Need any help?"

"No, I can manage," she said quickly. "Why don't you go along. I'll see you later." Emily did not want to take any chances that Donald Magnuson would see them together.

CHAPTER SEVENTEEN

When they met on Sunday, Evan showed Emily how to turn on the computer and how to navigate the Internet. She marveled over the fact that she had an entire encyclopedia at her fingertips and that she could travel anywhere in the world by simply clicking the mouse. Before shutting it down, they looked for more information about Nicole and Rebecca Preston but only found one mention on the American Red Cross website that a Rebecca Preston of Chicago, Illinois had worked as a volunteer at a blood drive. Since her name was not connected to Nicole's in any way, she continued to remain a mystery.

Evan closed the computer and took the atlas from a paper bag and set it on the table. "Let's see if we can estimate distances," he said.

He turned to a page displaying the entire United States and pointed to New Hampshire. "This is our starting point here in Kingston and this is our ending point in Illinois," he said.

Emily stared at the map. "How many miles do you think?"

"From Kingston to Beverly, I'd estimate about forty miles, give or take a few," he said, studying the map. "We're looking at about 1,300 to 1,500 miles one way total. We have five locations to cover, and if we count in a few sightseeing trips we should probably plan on staying for at least a week in each location. What do you think if we plan on being gone for about two months?"

"I think we've got ourselves a plan. Now, how about a game of chess?"

120

Former Things

At breakfast the following morning, Emily was feeling much better. She'd had a good night's sleep, and her flu symptoms from the day before had all but passed. When Alice, Rita, and Tess joined her, she could hardly keep her travel plans to herself. She wondered what they'd think if they knew she had rented an RV and was going off on a trip with Evan for part of the summer. She wondered, also, what Nina would think. She saw the girl now at the back of the dining room putting fresh fruit in a bowl on a shelf. As if on cue, she turned and glanced at Emily, a half smile on her face. Yes, she was certain now that it had been Nina who had gone to Donald Magnuson. But what good had it done? Not only had she already lost Evan, she'd also failed to accomplish her mission. She felt sorry for Nina. Maybe, like Nicole, she had a troubled spirit. She hoped for Nina's sake that she would one day look inside herself and get the help she so desperately and obviously needed. Emily turned her attention back to Alice and the others and listened while they discussed their plans for the day.

"I'm headed to Portsmouth," said Rita. "Would anyone like to join me?"

Since she'd been out the day before, Emily declined the invitation. She had plans of her own—to play with her new computer. "Sorry. I was out all day yesterday. Think I'll stay put today," Emily said.

"That's right . . . we missed you, Emily. Where were you?"

She didn't want to lie but telling the truth was not something she wanted to disclose just yet, either. "I had a few errands to run. The bank, grocery store . . . things of that nature."

The other two women jumped at the chance to go along for the ride to Portsmouth and started chatting about what they'd do once they arrived. She thought about her own outing with Evan yesterday and smiled about the secret she was holding inside. If they only knew what she was up to. Eventually, she would have to tell them that she was leaving for most of the summer, but she wanted all her plans firmly in place before she let the cat out of the bag. There was nothing much to tell anyway. Not at this

Gail Lowe

point. All she could say at the moment was that she and Evan had rented an RV and they were going on a road trip. She didn't want to be barraged with a long list of questions that she wasn't prepared to answer. The time would come when she'd have to reveal her plans, but it would not be today.

CHAPTER EIGHTEEN

Back at her apartment, Emily sat at the dining room table and opened the road atlas to the state of Massachusetts. She ran her finger along the coastline until she came to Beverly. She'd been there once before when John was building his business. He'd invited a client to dinner and she'd gone along to keep the client's wife company. The restaurant had been near the railroad station—The Boxcar—but what she remembered most about the dinner was the client's wife. Natalie had talked on and on about people Emily didn't know and she'd complained bitterly about her children, calling them ungrateful brats. She shook her head, remembering that she couldn't wait for the night to end. On the way home, she'd told John that it would be the last client dinner she would ever attend and she'd kept her word.

She wondered what had taken Nicole to Beverly. A job? A friend Emily hadn't known about? She was looking forward to visiting places where Nicole might have passed through. The library, for instance, or a movie theater. Maybe she and Evan would even have dinner at The Boxcar.

She went to the chest in her bedroom where she kept all her old photograph albums to look for pictures of Nicole. What she needed was a close-up that would show Nicole's facial features. She realized that her daughter was twenty years older now, but people didn't change that much, did they? Maybe a little gray hair, a wrinkle here and there, but most women covered over the gray and some signed up for anti-aging treatments. While she was looking at the photographs, she came across Nicole's birth certificate. Had she ever needed a copy for some reason? If she had, what had she done to get it? Had Nicole called City Hall in Portsmouth?

Gail Lowe

She sat thinking about these things and wondered what she would say to Nicole if she came face to face with her. A dozen scenarios had crossed her mind since yesterday, ever since they signed the rental paperwork for the RV. She imagined Nicole living in a high-rise apartment building. If that were the case, Emily would have to go inside the lobby and look at names on a printed list. Maybe they'd be listed alphabetically. She'd search all the names beginning with P, and there, near the end of the listings would be Preston. Nicole Preston.

She envisioned herself pressing the buzzer for her apartment and waiting for someone on the other end to answer.

"Who is it?" Nicole would say.

"It's your mother, Nicole."

There would be a pause, perhaps a long one. Then Nicole would say, *"My mother? Who is this?"*

And Emily would answer, *"Nicole, it's me. Your mother. Please let me in."*

And then what would Nicole do? Tell her to go away? Buzz Emily in? Would she come to the lobby? Would she even answer the buzzer? Or would she say, *"My mother is dead. Go away."*

Maybe Nicole lived in a house that had a fence around it and a back yard and garage. Emily imagined herself walking along the sidewalk toward Nicole's house. She'd open the gate in the fence and climb the steps leading to the front door. She'd ring the doorbell and wait on the front porch. Maybe Nicole would peek out the window while hiding behind a sheer white curtain and see her standing there, bouquet of roses in one hand, pocketbook in the other. Would Nicole rush to the front door, swing it wide open and hug her? Would she welcome her inside?

It was possible that Nicole would simply open the door and stand there, arms folded, her face as blank as a sheet of unlined paper. *"What are you doing here? How did you find me? You are not wanted here."* Maybe that's what she would say. Would she be that cold-hearted? Emily wondered.

What would happen if Nicole wasn't home? Would she leave her a note, asking that she call her on Evan's cell phone, only to wait and never hear from her? Maybe she would see Nicole on the

Former Things

street or at a store. Would they even recognize each other? What if Nicole had changed so much that Emily wouldn't know her own daughter? Emily had no idea what the future held, but now that she'd thought of all the possibilities she was beginning to fear the outcome. Nevertheless, before closing the album she chose two photographs of Nicole. The first one showed her standing next to the brand new silver Audi John had given her for her twenty-fifth birthday and the second was a close-up of Nicole sitting in a lounge chair by the swimming pool in the back yard.

Rockport, Massachusetts was one place Emily would want to visit while in Beverly. She'd read about the history of suffragist Hannah Jumper and looked forward to visiting the art galleries and boutiques on Bearskin Neck. Maybe she and Evan would walk along the jetty and view Motif #1, an old fishing shack an artist had immortalized in a painting.

Searching for Nicole would be a pleasurable experience when they weren't focused entirely on the outcome, but it would also have its intense moments, she knew. Visiting Rockport and other beautiful places would take the edge off. She'd suggest to Evan that they stop at Woodman's in Essex for lobster. Or someplace in Ipswich for fried clams.

If they didn't find Nicole in Beverly, they'd leave for Connecticut to continue the search. Nicole had never been a gambler, at least to the best of Emily's knowledge, but she thought she might enjoy visiting the casino and hotel at Burlwood. Maybe a famous comedian or singer would be in the entertainment line-up. Someone like Bill Cosby or Natalie Cole. Maybe she'd spring for tickets for herself and Evan. Why not? Life was short. She had the money. Why not spend a little? And if they still didn't find her in Connecticut, they'd move on to New Jersey. Parking the RV there would likely be tricky, but maybe there'd be a Wal-Mart nearby. She'd read in a magazine that the retail chain allowed people traveling in RVs to park in their lots. Good for business, the article had explained about Wal-Mart's outreach to travelers. It made plenty of sense to Emily. Maybe they'd stock up on provisions while they were parked there. Might as well thank Wal-Mart in some way.

Gail Lowe

Emily saw on the map that Hoboken, New Jersey was a stone's throw from New York City, making it easy for them to take a bus or train into Manhattan. The Guggenheim would be a must-see and Ground Zero, too. Maybe they'd do some window shopping on Fifth Avenue. And she'd see about getting tickets to Radio City Music Hall.

Stops in Indiana and Illinois might include a visit to the Indiana Dunes National Lakeshore before continuing on to Illinois. Willowdale—their final stop—was a small town where the people lived close to one another. Surely, someone there would know who Nicole was.

Emily picked the best of Nicole's photos to include in the fliers. She'd ask Evan to write a description of Nicole under the photo, then have copies made so they could be distributed. With less a month to go, time was running short. In twenty-seven days they'd be on the road.

CHAPTER NINETEEN

May was one day after another of bright sunshine, warm breezes, azaleas in full bloom, and leaves the color of limes. Every day Emily used her time to shop for food and other necessities, pay her bills ahead of time, and update the trip schedule. She also went shopping for casual clothes to wear on the trip and used the Internet to jot down in her notebook addresses of libraries, police and gas stations, and coffee shops in each of the five locations. She didn't want to waste even one minute of precious time while they were on the road because she had failed to organize and plan ahead. She also saw Dr. Talbot, and she'd declared Emily healthy, though she wanted her blood tests repeated in three months because of a high cholesterol count.

At breakfast that morning, Emily finally decided to let the others in on her plans. Alice, Rita, and Tess listened quietly and with sincere interest while she told them about her mission. "I've never told any of you that I have a daughter," she said. "It's something I've kept to myself. In fact, very few people know about her, but it's time to let go of secrets. We've been estranged for twenty years, and Evan has proposed that we try to find her."

"Why would you keep something like that to yourself?" asked Alice.

"I suppose I've been afraid of being judged," she said.

"We would never judge you." Alice said, looking from Rita to Tess.

"Just the other day I was watching Oprah, and her guest said that family estrangements have become an epidemic. She said it's a hallmark of this generation. It's happened in my own family so I know this is true," said Tess.

Gail Lowe

"It happened to you?" Emily asked.

"No, to my sister. She hasn't seen her son in years. And you're right, Emily. It's a subject no one wants to talk about because who in their right mind would walk out on their own mother?"

"Unless the mother is abusive or neglectful," said Tess.

"I promise you I was neither of those things," said Emily, reaching for the salt and pepper. "I was loving but firm. Nicole simply wanted what she wanted when she wanted it. There's no other way to explain it. And believe me, I tried to make things right between us, but she wasn't willing to have any of it."

She then told the women about Nicole's demand for money after John died and how she had told Nicole she'd have to wait. "But I also told her she'd never want for anything, either."

"Money," said Alice. "It causes so many problems in families. Greed is a terrible thing."

"Isn't it one of the seven deadly sins?" asked Tess.

"Yes, I believe it's called avarice in the Bible."

"Well, whatever it is, I call it the 'great divider,'" said Emily.

They talked among themselves about how money was viewed as being the root of all evil, and as they talked Emily felt the great burden of secrecy being lifted from her shoulders.

"You'll be gone the entire summer?" Alice asked.

"We aren't sure, but just in case, we've rented the RV until the end of August. If we find Nicole at the beginning of the trip, then we'll just come home."

"What if you do find her? What do you think will happen? Do you think you'd move closer to where she lives?"

"I'm not sure what her reaction would be, but I probably won't move. I like Emerald House—it's my home now. If Nicole wants to visit me, I have a pull-out sofa."

Evan approached their table with his water pitcher, and Emily gave him a wink that said, "I've told them."

"So, what's new ladies?" he asked, picking up Rita's water glass.

"What's new?" they responded in mock surprise. "You tell us!"

Former Things

He laughed and joined in their conversation about the trip. "Did Emily tell you I'll be writing about the trip?"

"Yes," said Alice. "And have you thought about selling your work to a travel magazine?"

"I haven't thought that far ahead. My professor would probably help with that. Which reminds me, Emily. He wants to meet you. I have to see him tonight. How about coming with me?"

Emily told Evan she'd meet him at The King's Rook and they could drive from there. All day long she thought about Professor Grieg and what he might want to talk to her about. She was an open book now. There was nothing left to hide.

That night, Emily and Evan drove to the UNH campus and parked in front of a brick building where Professor Grieg had an office. They climbed a flight of stairs and went down a dark corridor to a small room where a light was burning. Professor Grieg was known to work long hours, and he often stayed late at night to grade papers and prepare for the next day's classes.

"Have a seat," he said when Emily and Evan came into his office.

Emily took note of Evan's professor. A slight man with a trim silver beard and hair pulled back into a short ponytail, he was dressed in a burgundy long-sleeve shirt, jeans, and loafers. He had a quiet, reserved manner that spoke of a sturdy classical education, perhaps from one of the Ivy League colleges.

"Can I get you anything? Water? Tea? Juice?"

"Nothing, thanks," said Emily.

"Well, then, I'll get right to the point. I wanted to meet you, Emily, because I'm curious about your adventure." He leaned forward in his chair and fixed his gaze on her. What she was doing was admirable, in his estimation, and took a great deal of courage. "Evan tells me you have a daughter you've not seen in some years. Is that correct?" he asked gently.

"Yes, it's true. When I told Evan about my estrangement from Nicole, he suggested we rent an RV and set out to find her.

Gail Lowe

He managed to convince me when he told me about the paper he wanted to write."

Professor Grieg turned away from Emily and looked toward the window. A new moon had risen in the sky, a silver wafer so close it seemed to be within reach. He thought for a long moment before speaking again. "This is a topic I'm greatly interested in personally," he said. "You see, I have a son."

"Oh . . ."

"A son I have not seen in four years. His name is Garrett. He was a promising student . . . a gifted boy, really. Anyway, his mother and I . . . we did what we could to help him along. Only . . . " he said, hesitating. He rarely mentioned Garrett, even when he was among his closest friends.

"Yes . . . well."

"He . . . in hindsight my wife and I were able to see the signs. He announced one day that he was gay. Janice—that's my wife—she went to pieces. He was our only son, you see, and we had hoped that one day he would give us grandchildren. His announcement was devastating. Janice and I tried to accept his lifestyle, but Garrett knew we didn't approve, so he moved away. Like you, I have no idea where he is now. That's why when Evan told me your story I was touched in a personal way. I wanted to meet you in person, not just read about you. I hope you understand."

Evan looked at Emily and then spoke. "I had no idea, Professor Grieg. I'm so sorry," he said, for the first time noticing a photograph on the second shelf of a bookcase behind the professor's desk. The picture was of a young man in a blue cap and gown, and Evan assumed it was Garrett.

"I suppose it's why I've taken such a keen interest in my students. It's not that any of them could ever replace Garrett, but they fill a vacuum in my life. I miss him terribly. I miss my son."

"Of course you do," said Emily. "I understand fully. Have you ever tried to locate him?"

"Yes, many times. I think he might live in the San Francisco Bay area, but I have no address or phone number for him. I think he has chosen a lifestyle he knows his mother and I would not think is best for him. I read in the *San Francisco Chronicle* a year ago about a group of activists who were promoting gay marriage. His name was mentioned in the article. I don't know if he's married or is in a partnership of some kind. Mind you, I am not close-minded at all. It's just that I think his life will be difficult. Intolerance is an ugly thing. And his mother . . . well, she's another story altogether."

So Alice had been right about estrangement being common. She'd had no inkling that Evan's professor might suffer, too, from a child lost to him, but there it was. Professor Grieg knew exactly what estrangement was all about. Now, more than ever, she was determined to find Nicole. Doing so might give the professor hope.

After Emily and Evan left, Professor Grieg sat in his office alone thinking about his son. His bookshelves were lined with volumes containing philosophical wisdom passed down through the ages by the great thinkers, but in spite of all his studying and knowledge he had failed to hold on to his own son. He took the same framed photograph Evan had noticed from his bookshelf and studied it. As he recalled his conversation with Emily, he wished he had the nerve to do what she was about to do. If only he could gain Janice's cooperation. But he knew that was wishful thinking. He supposed he should go home and get some sleep. He glanced at the clock. Ten o'clock. For three hours he'd sat talking with Emily and Evan. Amazing, he thought, how time seemed to slip away when people talked about something they had in common. He looked out the window and saw that the moon had risen high in the sky and, unlike earlier in the evening, it seemed so out of reach. Just like his son. He placed Garrett's photograph back in its spot on the shelf and picked up his keys. Twenty minutes later, he stood at the front door of his house. Turning the key, he unlocked it, went inside, and turned on the hall light. A small stack of mail sat on a table beside the door, and he noticed his wife's coat hanging on a hook in the hallway. He hung his own jacket next to hers, then climbed the

Gail Lowe

stairs. Exhausted and empty, he put on his pajamas and went to Garrett's old bedroom. It had been a long time since he and Janice had slept together. Not since Garrett had told them he was gay. Now and then a co-ed at school tempted him, but he was a professor and he knew his place. He did not need a scandal or a divorce. Bad enough that he had lost his only son.

CHAPTER TWENTY

The day before they were to leave for their trip, Emily reviewed her list and checked off each task to make sure she had taken care of all her affairs. Her bills had been paid ahead of time, she'd made arrangements at the post office to have her mail held for the summer, and Alice, Rita, and Tess had agreed to take turns watering her plants and taking care of her cat. Evan had dropped off the box of fliers and it sat next to her front door, waiting to be loaded into her car along with her luggage. She'd told Donald Magnuson she would be gone for most of the summer, and Evan had given notice as well. In due time, he'd no doubt learn about the RV trip she was taking with Evan from Nina or Alice, Rita, or Tess. Emily wondered what he'd think when he found out. As far as she was concerned, it was none of his business.

Her final task had been to put a copy of her new will in her bedroom safe. The week before, she'd made a last minute appointment with Attorney Bramhall to bring it up to date, and she'd left his office, comfortable with his advice and suggestions.

The plan was to leave at eight o'clock Monday morning and head straight for Kingston to pick up the RV. Cal Anderson had told Emily she could leave her car on his lot while they were gone, and they'd made arrangements to spend the first week of the trip in a campground a few miles west of Beverly.

Emily flushed with excitement and anticipation while she packed her new jeans, Dockers, polo shirts, sweaters, and walking shoes. She thought to also pack a bathing suit and cover-

Gail Lowe

up, sandals, sun visor, and camera. After filling her cosmetics case with soap, shampoo, conditioner, moisturizer, and other toiletries, she slipped her renewed nurse's license in the zipper compartment of her purse and called Evan to tell him she was all set to go.

He answered on the first ring. "What's up, Em? Change your mind about going away with me?"

"Not on your life," she laughed. "Just wondering if I should go to the grocery store to buy cold cuts and bread . . . you know, for lunch."

"Sure, why not? We can stock the refrigerator before we leave."

"Good. I'll see you first thing in the morning."

Emily had difficulty getting to sleep that night. Her mind was filled with thoughts of Nicole and what steps they would take to find her. If they did find her, it would be a miracle. All she could do was hope for the best.

Nicole

CHAPTER ONE

The day Nicole stormed out of her mother's house and sped down the driveway she had no idea what she would do or where she would go. The only thing she did know was that she had to get away. What had just happened in her mother's kitchen was the final chapter in a long, disturbing family saga, in her estimation. She gripped the steering wheel, a blind rage sweeping over her like an out of control fire, and headed for Poor Man's Pub across town. The name, she thought, ironically suited the occasion. What better place to drown her sorrows than a pub for poor men—and women, too.

Around five o'clock a few of Nicole's co-workers from the insurance company wandered in, and she waved them over to her booth when she saw them come through the front door. Nicole ordered a round of beer for everyone, then another and another, and soon she was laughing and joking with her friends, all but forgetting about the confrontation she'd had with her mother a few hours earlier. At eight o'clock they called it a night. She stumbled toward her car, got inside and pulled out of the parking lot, barely missing slamming into the car in front of her. She was on the highway for ten minutes when she saw the flashing blue lights of a police car in her rear view mirror. Fumbling around inside her purse, she found a breath mint and popped it into her mouth before pulling to the side of the road. With blurred vision, she watched as a police officer approached her car.

"I'm sorry, officer. What did I do?" she said, lowering the window, oblivious to the fact that she was slurring her words.

"You were all over the road," he said. "I saw you cross the center line at least twice."

Gail Lowe

"I can explain. You see, I dropped something on the floor and was trying to find it. That's why I . . ."

"License and registration, please," he said, dismissing her attempt at an explanation.

Nicole opened the glove box and rummaged through papers, napkins, maps, and an owner's manual until she found the car's registration. She handed it to him with her driver's license.

"Step outside the car, please."

"But officer . . ."

"I need you to step outside your car. Be a good girl now and cooperate with me."

Nicole opened the car door, got out, and stood shivering on the pavement next to the police officer. The January night was freezing cold and she had not zipped up her jacket.

"Ever been arrested for drunk driving before?" he asked, eyeing her.

"No, never," she said. A bit unsteady on her feet, she leaned against her car.

"By the looks of you, you are about to be," he said, taking note of her glassy, red-rimmed eyes.

After giving Nicole a field sobriety test, he asked if she would submit to a breathalyzer test.

"What happens if I say no?"

"You'll face some mighty stiff fines and I'll suspend your license right now."

The officer, whom she estimated to be a full foot taller than herself, was old enough to be her grandfather. She knew she'd have to take her lumps and decided not to argue with him. Instead, she gave in and he handed her the breathalyzer. She hoped the reading wouldn't indicate the number of beers she'd polished off.

She handed it back to him when she was finished. ".10 percent," he said, shaking his head. "That's above the legal limit. Do you know how much black ice there is tonight? One false step and you could have killed someone, including yourself."

"Officer, please. I know I had one too many drinks tonight, but this is highly unusual. I had an argument with my mother and I was upset and . . ."

Former Things

Ignoring her, he read her Miranda rights, allowed her to get her jacket, and put her in handcuffs. Then he maneuvered her into the back seat of his cruiser. Minutes later they arrived at the police station where she was photographed, fingerprinted, and booked. "Do you want to call anyone?" he asked. "A family member? An attorney?"

She was shaken to the core. Who could she call? It was almost ten o'clock at night, and she wasn't about to call any of her friends and certainly not her mother's attorney or even her mother, for that matter. She could hear her mother now, "How could you do this to yourself? To me? Your father would roll over in his grave," she would say.

"No, there's no one," she said.

"Come with me, then. I'll have to arrange for your car to be towed."

The officer led her down a long corridor and up a flight of stairs to a block of cells, none of which were occupied. He opened the cell on the far right, number four, and told her it would be her home for the night. "Toilet, bed, blanket—everything you need right here. You'll be arraigned in Portsmouth District Court in the morning. I suggest you sleep off the booze. You'll need to be alert."

After she was inside, he locked the cell door and she studied her surroundings—light green cinderblock walls with a video camera mounted in a corner of the ceiling, white porcelain sink and toilet, cot and a dark green scratchy blanket. She sat down, placed her head in her hands, and cried. How had her life come to this? She didn't deserve to be treated this way. She was a good person. A hard worker. Her mother was to blame and she'd had enough. After she went before the judge and was released in the morning, she'd quit her job and go somewhere to start a new life. She didn't care where she went. She simply had to get away. It was the first of the year, a perfect time to start life over. At that moment she didn't know what she'd do or where she'd go but one thing she did know was that she hated everyone, including herself.

ℒ❤

139

Gail Lowe

Nicole opened her eyes around seven o'clock, hung over, and sick to her stomach. At first, she couldn't remember where she was, but then events from the night before came back to her in brief flashes. She only nibbled at the corners of a piece of toast and took a few sips of coffee before putting them back on the tray a security guard had brought her. Exhausted and spent, she lay back on the bed and tried to sleep but all she could think about was getting out of town.

At eight-thirty, another police officer came to the cell door and said he'd drive her to the Portsmouth Courthouse. There had been a snowfall during the night, and Nicole nearly froze while seated next to the police officer in the cruiser. Soon, they were in downtown Portsmouth, driving past trendy boutiques, restaurants, and bars.

A few minutes later, she found herself inside the courthouse standing in front of a court officer.

"Do you want your own attorney or one that's court-appointed?" he asked.

"Court-appointed," she said.

"Have a seat on that bench. You'll have a pre-trial conference with Attorney Michael O'Brien. Then you'll see the judge."

Michael O'Brien was a tall, barrel-chested man with silver hair that fell almost to his shoulders. Nicole thought he might have been a hippie during the 1960s. "I can probably get you off this time and save your license, but if you get caught driving drunk again, you're looking at not only losing your license but paying some heavy fines. And some judges impose jail time," he warned.

Nicole was frightened when she heard this. The last thing she wanted was to spend another night in some godforsaken jail cell. She nodded that she understood and sat with him on a long wooden bench with six other people who were also waiting for their cases to be heard. A scruffy looking man sat next to her, his navy blue jacket filthy, his hair so stringy and greasy it looked

Former Things

as if it hadn't been washed in weeks. Across from her, a teenage boy sat straight as a yard stick while an older woman, maybe his mother, tugged on his arm while whispering angry words in his ear. A man and woman sat next to the teenage boy, both of them silent. A young girl, perhaps eighteen years old, was with a man who might have been her lawyer. Every now and then he'd lean toward her and say something, and she would nod.

She wondered why they were there. Drugs? Domestic violence? Theft?

At promptly nine o'clock the courtroom doors opened and they were told to come inside. The courtroom looked no different from what Nicole had seen on television. Long wooden tables, an American flag, raised judge's bench, a juror's box. While she was surveying the courtroom, she heard her name called. A sudden, anxious feeling took hold of her and she thought she might vomit on the spot. "Please approach the bench," she heard the judge say.

Attorney O'Brien pleaded guilty on Nicole's behalf and asked for lenience since it was her first drunk driving offense. The judge pondered the attorney's request and studied the paperwork in front of him while Nicole shifted her weight from one foot to the other. He recognized Nicole's name and knew she was the daughter of John Preston, a man he used to play golf with at his country club.

"Against my better judgment, I'm going to give you a warning this time, young lady. Drunk driving in the state of New Hampshire is a serious offense that requires forfeiture of a driver's license. I could also order you to attend Alcoholics Anonymous and a series of classes on alcohol abuse. But since this is your first offense, I'll let you go this time, but I never want to see you in my courtroom again. Do you understand?"

"Yes, your honor."

"Case dismissed. Next."

Nicole was shaking while Attorney O'Brien led her out of the courtroom. "I don't know how to thank you," she said.

"You can thank me by promising never to see me again."

Nicole knew it was one promise she'd never break. "It's a deal."

As soon as she was back in her car, she made a mental list of things she needed to do. First, she had to call her boss to let him know she wouldn't be coming back. No, better not do that, she decided. She owed him nothing. But she did need clothes. She'd go to her apartment, pack her suitcase and leave. She owed rent, but tough. The place was a dump anyway and not worth the money she paid every month. She needed cash so she'd have to go to the bank and draw out what she had saved over the last few years. Before noon she'd be on the road.

CHAPTER TWO

Later that morning while Nicole was driving south along Route 95 from Portsmouth she wondered if Paul LaScola still had his house sitting job in Beverly, Massachusetts, a city twenty miles north of Boston. The city was known for its excellent live theater, fine dining, and a wealthy neighborhood along the coast. She'd met Paul in college and remembered that every year around this time he took care of a waterfront Victorian home in Beverly while the owners vacationed at their chateau in the south of France.

While in college, she'd visited Paul at the house on weekends, and they'd had parties the entire time she was there. The closer she got to Beverly, the more she wondered about Paul. She exited the highway toward Beverly and drove through the downtown area until she came to Route 127. When she passed the big yellow house with the wide porch and turrets, she saw him at the rear of the driveway shoveling snow. He was dressed in a navy blue pea coat, jeans, and construction boots, and his cheeks were red from the cold. Paul smiled broadly when he saw Nicole and waved her into the driveway. After catching up on the news, Nicole told Paul about the fight with her mother and, taking pity on her, he insisted she stay for the weekend. One weekend turned into two, then three, and before either of them realized it, six months had passed. Living together benefited both of them, as it turned out. Paul had someone to cook and clean for him, and Nicole had a roof over her head that cost her nothing. Paul wouldn't hear of taking as much as even one dime from Nicole.

She got a job as a waitress at an Italian restaurant on Cabot Street and saved almost every penny she earned. Not once did she think to call her mother to let her know she was in Massachusetts. For one thing, she was too busy working and having fun with Paul. For another, she was still furious about being left out of her father's will.

Over the Fourth of July weekend, Paul invited a group of friends to a cookout on the front lawn. One of his acquaintances was Christopher Silva who lived a few miles away in Marblehead. Chris owned a sailboat and made a handsome living chartering the boat for deep-sea fishing trips from June to the end of August. A golden tan set off his aquamarine eyes, and the shock of sand-colored hair that fell across one eyebrow made Nicole think of a young Robert Redford.

Chris and Nicole took an instant liking to one another, and later that night when the fireworks exploded over Beverly, another kind of fireworks ignited between them while they were lounging on a blanket spread on the front lawn. All night they had joked with each other and flirted, and the attraction between them continued to grow after they had a few glasses of wine. Later that night, the cool breeze coming off the water chilled the air, and Chris placed his arm around Nicole's shoulders and pulled her close to him. He smelled of suntan lotion, salt air, and musk and when he ran his fingers over her upper arm she shivered, but not because she was cold. He continued to stroke her arm and nuzzle her neck until she was fully aroused. She took a final sip of wine before getting up from the blanket. She looked down at Chris, and when he looked up she locked onto his eyes. He read the intent in her half smile before she turned and walked toward the house. A few minutes later, he followed.

Once inside the house, he called for Nicole. "In here," she answered. He walked through a maze of rooms and found her standing at the base of a winding staircase that led to the second floor.

He came to her then and kissed her softly. She took him by the hand and led him up the stairs, their passion building as they climbed each one. Once they were inside Nicole's bedroom

Former Things

and the door was closed behind them, she raised the window shade next to the bed to let in the light of the fireworks coloring the night sky. He moved toward her and lifted her white cotton sweater over her head, tossing it onto a nearby chair. Next came her bra, then her pink shorts, and finally her bikini underwear.

He moved her toward the window so he could take in the sight of her nakedness. Holding her close, he kissed her throat and then her breasts. She allowed him to make love to her, caress and kiss her for a long time before they moved toward the bed. His words were soft and warm, like summer rain, and she felt as if she were evaporating with every touch.

She opened up to him and allowed herself to enjoy the wonder of the experience, the completeness of his lovemaking. He was a practiced and experienced lover, and she'd never felt such intensity with any man. So engrossed was she in what they were doing, and perhaps because she was slightly drunk, that not once did she think about birth control.

Nicole pulled down the bed covers while Chris removed his shirt, pants, and sandals and she took note of the ripple of his chest muscles and the bulk of his arms and legs achieved from the demands of sailing. She settled on the bed, and in an instant he joined her, stroking and kissing her, and telling her how beautiful she was. She drank him in, absorbing and savoring each moment, recognizing for the first time how starved she was for love—any kind of love. Chris controlled his every move, bringing her in and out of ecstasy again and again, and when he finally brought her to the brink, she held onto his hips and rode the waves of orgasm.

When it was over, he was out of the bed and back into his clothes before she had a chance to catch her breath. "Everyone's probably wondering where we are," he said, his voice suddenly anxious. "We better get back to the party before they start looking for us."

Nicole wanted to coax him back into bed but thought better of it. She was disappointed, but what could she expect? She reminded herself that they barely knew each other, only having met that very night. Surely he'd want to see her again. Maybe even

145

over the weekend. He'd take her to dinner, then for a sail on his boat. There'd be a moon, and they'd make love again. He'd make plans with her before the night was over. Of course he would.

But an hour after the fireworks finale, people started to pack up and leave the party. Nicole hovered near Chris while everyone was saying goodnight, but he moved away from her to speak to a tall dark-haired man with a mustache. She waited for Chris to return, but all he did was glance at her and give her a military salute before climbing into his black BMW convertible and speeding off into the night. She returned a weak salute and then went inside to help Paul clean up.

The following morning over coffee, she brought Chris up in conversation.

Paul looked at Nicole, a quizzical look on his face. "Chris? You mean Chris Silva? He's a pothead. Do yourself a favor and don't get mixed up with him. The only reason he came last night was because he knew there'd be free food."

And free sex, she thought, but she wasn't about to tell Paul that.

Nicole moped around for days afterward, going through the motions of working at the restaurant and cooking and cleaning for Paul, but nothing could erase the memory of what she'd shared with Chris. He left her feeling that she'd been used and cast aside like yesterday's newspaper.

By the end of August, Nicole knew she was pregnant. To confirm her suspicion, she bought a home pregnancy test kit at the drug store and used it as soon as she got home. When the paper test strip turned pink, she had her answer. In September, the owners of the house called to say they were coming home, and Paul locked up the house and made plans to go back to Boston. She had no idea where she'd go next, but one thing she did know was that she would not terminate her pregnancy. No, she was not about to travel that path again. She'd done it once while in college, but never again. To this day she could still recall the events leading up to her abortion.

Former Things

She had called on a Saturday morning to tell her mother that she was pregnant.

"Is everything okay, Nicole? Are you all right?" her mother had asked.

"I guess . . . but . . ."

"But what?" There was a silence, then her mother guessed the reason for the call. *"You're pregnant."*

"How did you know?"

"A mother always knows. I could hear it in your voice."

"I've scheduled an abortion," Nicole had said flatly.

"An abortion!"

"Yes, an abortion. I want you to come with me."

"Nicole, please . . ."

"I've made my decision. I'm going through with it. I'm not ready to have a baby, and I'd make a terrible mother."

"There are other alternatives."

"What? Adoption? Raise a kid alone? No thanks. As far as I'm concerned, those are not options. Will you come with me or not?"

"Who's the father? Have you told him?"

"Some guy from New York. An investor. I met him a few months ago, and we spent the weekend together . . . do I have to give you every single detail?"

"No, you don't have to give me every detail, but have you told him?"

"No, there's no point in telling him. He's married. I'm having an abortion and I'm having it with you or without you."

"Nicole . . . please, won't you reconsider?"

"No, I've made up my mind."

"When is the appointment?"

"Tuesday. I have to be at the clinic at eight o'clock in the morning."

"What do you want me to do?"

"Pick me up at seven-thirty. The clinic is only a few blocks away from school. And whatever you do, don't tell Dad."

Her mother had gone along with the plan, even though she hadn't wanted to, and the day for both of them had been long,

Gail Lowe

emotional, and exhausting. Half an hour after the abortion, Nicole found her mother waiting for her in an outer hallway at the clinic. She went to Emily and stood there. *"You're okay?"* her mother had asked, reaching for her.

"I'm fine, Mom. I just want to go to bed."

Emily had taken Nicole back to her dorm and stayed with her for the remainder of the day. At lunchtime while Nicole was resting, her mother walked to a Chinese restaurant around the corner and returned with hot and sour soup for lunch. After eating, they were exhausted and spent, and Nicole lay on her bed with her mother cuddled up next to her. Five minutes later, they were both sound asleep.

No, she would never have an abortion again. After making her decision, she quit her job at the restaurant, packed up her clothes, and headed for the highway.

CHAPTER THREE

With no particular plan in mind, she allowed the car to take her where it wanted to go. She passed a sign pointing to Rhode Island and New York but by-passed these exits and instead crossed the state line into Connecticut. Nicole had heard about a casino ninety miles away that had opened the year before in Sachem. Maybe she'd make a pit stop there, play a few of the slots, get a bite to eat.

She tuned in to an oldies station and let the music blare inside the car. Paul McCartney was singing about Eleanor Rigby, and her mind instantly conjured up a lonely old woman picking up rice inside a church. *All the lonely people* . . . Paul sang. The song saddened her, making her more determined than ever to have this baby come hell or high water, and give it a good home, even if she had to raise the child alone. For once, she'd have someone to love and someone who'd love her back. Maybe she'd have a son, or a baby daughter. She didn't care, as long as the baby was healthy.

She arrived in Sachem mid-afternoon. From the roadway, she could see the top floors of a resort hotel peeking over woodlands. She drove along a winding road that led to a parking lot, pulled into one of the spaces, and hopped aboard a shuttle bus that whisked guests away to the casino.

Most of the people seated at the slots appeared to be senior citizens, perhaps on some kind of field trip. That would account for the dozens of buses she had seen in the parking lot. She went to the cashier to change a fifty-dollar bill. If she lost that, so be it. She'd worked hard waiting on tables all summer and deserved to have a little fun. While she was playing poker at one of the machines, a woman with red hair and green eyes sat down

Gail Lowe

next to her. Soon, they were laughing and chatting and cheering each other on. Nicole got a royal straight flush after inserting a five-dollar bill into her machine, setting off a series of bells and whistles as the quarters spilled out into the silver tray.

"That was lucky. Are you from around here?" the woman asked. Her voice was warm and friendly, and Nicole liked her right away.

"No. New Hampshire," Nicole answered. "And you?"

"I work here. It's my day off."

"No kidding. What do you do?"

"Manage the sales and marketing department."

"So you look for ways to get people into the casino?"

"You got it. I'm Rayelle Johnson," she said, smiling.

"Nicole Preston."

"Nice to meet you, Nicole. Are you here alone?"

"Yup. Sometimes it's better that way."

"Don't I know it. I gave my husband the boot last year. Best thing I ever did."

"I don't have a husband, but I've got a baby coming . . . and no job." Nicole considered telling Rayelle about the argument she'd had with her mother, but decided to keep it to herself. "No family either."

Rayelle studied Nicole for a moment. She seemed vulnerable, as if she were carrying the weight of the world on her shoulders. She felt sorry for the young woman seated next to her. While working at the casino for the past five years, Rayelle had seen a lot of lost souls cross her path. Nicole was just one of many, but somehow she seemed different from the others. "And you're going back to New Hampshire?"

"No, I've had enough of the live free and die state. I think I'll head to New York. See if I can get a job there."

"What do you do?"

"Mostly administrative work."

"How would you like to work here?"

"You're putting me on."

"As a matter of fact, I'm not. I've been on the hunt for an assistant, to tell you the truth. Where do you work now?"

Former Things

"I left a job in January. A friend needed me to help him out while he was house sitting an estate in Massachusetts while the owners were in France. I needed a change so I said I'd do it. He's gone back to Boston now, and I decided to move on. I just stopped here to have a little fun. It seems like a good place to set down roots, though. I like the idea of living in the country. And having a casino nearby. There'd probably be lots of action, you know?"

"Yes, I do know. If you work at the casino, you automatically get to live on the property. Management sets aside a block of hotel rooms for select employees. You would qualify because you'd be working for me. You'd be able to use the pool and exercise room, too. Would that interest you?"

What Rayelle had just told her seemed too good to be true. Maybe she had misunderstood. "You mean I would get housing in addition to a salary?"

"I know it sounds unbelievable, but it's part of our employment package. And you get big discounts on restaurant food. Do you know how to use a word processor?"

"Yes."

"Do you have a few minutes now? I'd like to interview you. See if you might be a good fit." Rayelle had always prided herself on being able to read people. Intuitively, she knew Nicole would be a good addition to her staff.

Nicole had come to Sachem, not once giving a single thought that she might strike it rich, but not only had she just won a jackpot, she might have a job offer in the palm of her hand. Maybe she could stay put long enough to have her baby. Not having to pay for housing and a huge grocery bill would mean she could save a good chunk of her salary.

An hour later, Rayelle had already talked to Paul LaScola, who gave Nicole a good reference, and put her on the payroll. She also showed Nicole a suite of rooms she would call home for as long as she held her job. "Starting Monday, you'll be working from nine to four-thirty with a half hour for lunch. You can move your things in today if you like. Get the lay of the land. Do a little shopping. Have a little fun. You'll be working hard for me."

"And I'm up for it."

"Good. Then I'll leave you now to get settled. Just come to the marketing office Monday morning. First floor. In back of Americana . . . it's one of the restaurants. Ask for Jan. I'll meet you there."

Rayelle left then and as soon as she closed the door behind her, Nicole flopped onto the bed and pinched herself. Sure enough, lady luck had come her way.

Nicole moved what she had brought with her into the tenth floor suite of the hotel and settled in. Everything she needed was already there—towels, sheets, even maid service. Every day she took her meals in one of the five restaurants inside the hotel. As her pregnancy progressed, she became more and more tired and found that she needed a nap in the afternoon. Rayelle knew what it was like to be seven months pregnant, having had three children herself, and told Nicole to take an hour for lunch so she could rest.

She enjoyed her job in the sales and marketing office, and her relationship with Rayelle went beyond that of boss and employee. On weekends, Rayelle invited Nicole to go shopping and on occasion they went to see a movie or out to dinner. Nicole was grateful for Rayelle's friendship, since she'd left all her old friends and co-workers behind in Rye.

When she was eight months along, Rayelle suggested they go shopping for the baby. They drove to Hartford and found a store specializing in baby equipment and clothing and toys, and before they left to return to Sachem Nicole had spent more than four hundred dollars.

Rayelle knew Nicole didn't earn a lot of money and held a baby shower for her. Patty from the accounting office was there. So were Melanie, Kathy, Carol, Shirley, Marilyn, Jan and Marcia. They all chipped in and bought a crib for the baby, and management at the casino gave her a gift certificate for a stroller.

Since Nicole planned to breast feed, she set up the crib next to her bed so she could just reach for the baby in the middle of the night when it was hungry. Now and then, she thought about her mother and wondered what she would think if she knew she was about to become a grandmother, but then dismissed the thought from her mind. Her mother would probably look at her in disgust if she knew that the father of her child was a complete stranger. No, it was better that her mother didn't know. She had better things to do than risk her mother's wrath and judgment.

On March 31, Nicole got up, noticing that her lower back hurt but never once gave a thought that she might be in labor. But after work when she got inside the elevator and was on her way to the tenth floor a pain, deep and low, suddenly struck, nearly taking her breath away. It had passed by the time the elevator doors opened, but she was suddenly alert. Her due date had been sometime in mid-March, but she knew that babies arrived on their own schedule. Another pain struck an hour later and by nine o'clock her pains were coming every fifteen minutes. Just as she was stepping into the shower to get cleaned up and wash her hair, her water broke. Nicole called the front desk and asked if someone could drive her to the hospital. She was not about to take any chances. She had no intention of giving birth on the highway.

A few minutes later, there was a knock on the door. Malcolm Waterman, the night manager, told her to meet him in the lobby. He would drive her to the hospital. On the way, she thought to call Rayelle. It was doubtful that she'd be in work tomorrow. From what she'd read about giving birth, she didn't think this was false labor. She smiled when she realized her baby would probably be born on April Fool's Day.

Malcolm helped get her into the hospital, and a man working in the transportation unit came by and got her into a wheel chair and took her to the maternity ward on the second floor. She told Malcolm not to bother staying around. "I'll be okay," she said. "I'll call the hotel and let the front desk know when the baby arrives."

"Do you have any family you want us to call?"

"No. I'm on my own. I'll be fine."
"You're sure?"
"I'm sure."

Malcolm was reluctant to leave Nicole all by herself, but there was nothing more to be done. Besides, he needed to get back to the hotel to make sure things were running smoothly. He wondered where the father of Nicole's baby was. What a life, he thought. About to have a baby and no one to celebrate with. It just didn't seem right.

Rebecca was born the following morning at 10:42. At eight pounds and twelve ounces, she was a sturdy baby with a head full of dark hair. When the doctor put Rebecca on her chest, Nicole wished her father were still alive. He would have loved knowing he had a granddaughter. To be fair, Nicole knew that her mother would have been thrilled, too.

Nicole struggled with child care and her full-time job at the casino and as Rebecca grew, so did the cost of raising her. The hotel offered an on-site day care center, a godsend, since Nicole had no one to watch Rebecca during the day while she was at work. She'd had no idea that raising a child could be so expensive. Even though she had a suite of rooms to live in and food discounts, her child had needs that cost a small fortune. Between clothing and doctor visits and prescriptions for multi-vitamins, Nicole had little money left over at the end of the month.

She'd been working at the casino for six years when she discovered an opportunity to increase her salary without asking for a raise and wondered why she hadn't thought of it before. Rayelle had become so confident in Nicole's ability to attract new customers to the casino that she'd promoted her to assistant manager of the sales and marketing department. Part of her responsibilities were to think of new ways to bring in people who were willing to part with their hard earned money at the craps and poker tables. At night while she was watching television with Rebecca, she worked out plans in her head and the

Former Things

answer to getting people into the casino seemed to always come around to one simple word: money.

Money, Nicole knew, motivated people more than anything else. In fact, it was money that had caused the separation between herself and her mother, when she thought about it. She wondered how she could get people into the casino by offering them money on top of money. How could she offer them extra cash that would eventually end up in the slot machines and on the gaming tables?

One night after she put Rebecca to bed, an idea suddenly started to gel. All she needed was a single piece of blank letterhead with Rayelle's signature at the bottom. Once she had the letterhead in her hand, she would write a letter to corporations offering them free play coupons that their employees could use at the casino. Companies, she had learned over the years, often held their sales meetings and retreats in Las Vegas, Reno, and Atlantic City. Maybe they'd consider Sachem. If she could get them to buy in, the casino would rake in millions of dollars in new revenue.

When she told Rayelle that she was working on a special project to increase business, Rayelle told her to go ahead. "You have my blessing, Nicole. Just do what needs to be done."

Nicole contracted with a local printer to print thousands of coupons worth one hundred dollars each that would be mailed with the letter to corporations from Rayelle. For every thousand coupons, Nicole kept one hundred for herself that she later sold to people at half price. All she really needed was an extra few hundred dollars every month, and she knew she could make that easily enough by selling the coupons. It was a plan that benefited everyone concerned, including her.

Nicole realized that what she was doing amounted to stealing, but she went ahead with the plan anyway, figuring that no one would ever be the wiser. If she were found out, her defense would be that she had brought in a ton of new customers. How could Rayelle argue with that?

When Nicole started selling the coupons and pocketing the money, a feeling of exhilaration and power came over her. Now

Gail Lowe

she was able to go shopping not only for Rebecca but herself. She loved the powerful feeling of being able to shop in the casino's boutiques and pay cash for designer pocketbooks, shoes, jewelry, and clothing. Nicole's "second job," as she had come to think of it, was working well until she sold six of the coupons to Rayelle's cousin, Mike. She had no idea who Mike was until Rayelle called her into the conference room a few days later. Nicole sat across from Rayelle, her back to the door. The serious look on Rayelle's face told Nicole that something was very wrong. When Rayelle wouldn't make eye contact with Nicole, she knew she was in trouble.

"Do you know a man whose name is Mike Cutler?" Rayelle asked.

"The name doesn't sound familiar," said Nicole.

"Well, maybe you'll recognize the face. Mike, please step inside the room."

Nicole turned toward the door and saw the man she had sold the coupons to a few days before standing there. "Got any more coupons to sell?" he said. "I'm Rayelle's cousin."

She stared at him, devastated that lady luck had quit on her.

"Thanks, Mike. I'll talk to you later," Rayelle said. "Please close the door behind you."

After he left, Rayelle turned her attention back to Nicole. "What were you thinking, selling those coupons?" she asked. Her expression was grim and her disappointment in Nicole clearly showed in her eyes.

"I didn't think I was doing anything wrong. I mean, those coupons brought in millions of dollars," Nicole said innocently. "I figured it wouldn't hurt to sell a few and keep the money. I thought of it as a little bonus for myself."

"A little bonus for yourself? Have you ever heard the word 'theft'? That's what this amounts to, Nicole, and I can't have someone on my staff who steals."

"What are you telling me?"

"That you're dismissed. I'm sorry it's come to this, but you've put my job on the line for doing what you did. I want you

Former Things

to clean out your desk and your hotel suite. You'll need to be off casino property in one hour."

Nicole sat there, stunned.

"Rayelle, I had no idea you'd think of this as stealing. Really. Trust me when I tell you that I thought of it as a little side job."

Rayelle fixed her eyes on the 14 karat gold bangle bracelet Nicole was wearing on her wrist. The black cashmere sweater. The Prada shoes. She shook her head sadly and looked at Nicole. "Trust you? I could never trust you again."

Nicole leaned toward Rayelle and pleaded with her to reconsider. "I have nowhere to go. You know how hard I work here. I need this job. Please, Rayelle."

"You should have thought of that before you helped yourself to those coupons. Look, I've enjoyed you as a friend, not only an employee, Nicole, but what you've done is a major breach in trust. Do you realize I could bring criminal charges against you? As a matter of fact," she said, reaching for the phone, "I should call the police."

Nicole stared at Rayelle, sudden fear taking over her. "Please, Rayelle. Think of Rebecca and what it would do to her. I'm sorry," she said, beginning to sob. "I'll do whatever it takes to save my job. Please don't fire me and don't call the police."

"I'm sorry. I have no choice but to let you go." She hesitated before continuing. "I won't call the police because of Rebecca, but I need you off hotel property. Now please go get your things. I want you out of here in one hour. And if you're not, then I *will* call the police."

Nicole stared at her boss for a moment, then got up and ran out of the conference room to her office, passing the desks of her confused co-workers. Once she boxed up her belongings, she went past the elevator and instead took the stairs two at a time all the way to the tenth floor.

"Why are you packing up our things, Mommy?" Rebecca asked when she saw her mother throwing clothes and toys into suitcases.

"We're leaving. I don't like it here anymore."

"Why? I don't want to leave."

Gail Lowe

"Rebecca, put a lid on it. Now help me by getting your things together. And no whining."

An hour later Nicole and Rebecca were on the road. "Where are we going, Mommy?" Rebecca asked.

"I have no idea," she said as she pulled into the parking lot of the bank where she had deposited her savings. "But first Mommy has to take care of some business."

CHAPTER FOUR

Nicole had managed to save more than ten thousand dollars from her winnings at the slots, poker tables, and coupon sales and figured it would see her through until she could find another job. She put a makeshift bed together for Rebecca in the back seat of her car and headed west toward New York, driving through Wilton, Fairfield, Greenwich and other tony communities before crossing the state line into New York.

When she arrived in Hoboken, New Jersey an hour later she parked in a supermarket lot, put her seat in the reclining position, and fell asleep. When the sun came up in the morning, Rebecca was awake. "I'm hungry, Mommy," she said, poking her mother's shoulder.

"Hmm . . . when the stores open in a little while I'll buy you something to eat. How's that sound?"

"Okay, but where are we?" she said, looking at the unfamiliar surroundings. "Why are we here?"

"We're in a brand new place near New York City. I got tired of living in a hotel, sweetie, and my job . . . well, I was tired of that, too. I'll find a new one and an apartment for us. And you'll have a whole new set of friends. You'll see."

"But I liked the hotel. Will our apartment have a swimming pool like the one at the hotel?"

"I can't promise that, but I will promise that life will be good."

Nicole broke her promise almost as soon as the words were out of her mouth. She heard a tap on the driver's side window, and when she turned she saw a man's nose pressed against the glass. His face was unshaven and dirty, and when he asked for a dollar she saw that most of his teeth were missing. Startled, she

Gail Lowe

quickly locked the car doors, turned the key in the ignition, and sped out of the lot.

"Mommy, that man scared me."

"Me, too, sweetie. Me, too."

Nicole had no idea what to do next. She knew she had to find lodging, but where? A seedy hotel? A roach-infested apartment? She kicked herself now for not being more careful about selling the free play coupons. She should have asked if they had any connections to the casino. A "yes" would have made all the difference. Next time she came up with a plan to make extra money she'd be more cautious and much smarter. No one could be trusted. She had learned that lesson the hard way.

She stopped at a real estate office, hoping that a sales agent might know of a rental. Something clean but cheap and already furnished. When she and Rebecca approached the reception desk, a young woman with lazy brown eyes and long blond hair parted in the middle looked up from her crossword puzzle.

"Can I help you?" she said.

Nicole explained why she was there and the woman told her to take a seat. "Renee Schofield will help you. I'll let her know you're here as soon as she's off the phone."

Rebecca tugged at Nicole's sleeve. "I'm hungry, Mommy."

In her haste to get out of the parking lot, she had all but forgotten to feed Rebecca. "As soon as we're finished here, we'll go get you something to eat at Burger King. I saw one right up the street. How's that?"

"Okay."

A few minutes later, a stout, middle-aged woman with black hair and too much makeup strode into the reception area. "Renee Schofield," she said. Her voice was husky, and Nicole thought she was probably a smoker. "Caroline tells me you're looking for a rental."

"Yes," Nicole said, rising to her feet. "Small, furnished, clean, and inexpensive. That's my short list."

"I may have just the thing."

Former Things

They drove in Renee's Volkswagen to a small street lined with trash barrels fronting tall, narrow brick-front apartment buildings. "I've got something to show you on the corner of this street. There's a neighborhood school your daughter could go to. What's your name, honey?"

"Rebecca."

"Well, there are lots of children in this neighborhood for you to play with. I'll bet you'd like that."

"Uh-huh."

Renee squeezed into a parking space, and they walked to a tidy walk-up with a front porch outfitted with a pair of rocking chairs. Already, Nicole liked what she saw. Once inside, she found the apartment small but adequate for their needs. There was a hall closet, living room with outdated wallpaper, small eat-in kitchen with only two cupboards, tiled bath, and bedroom she and Rebecca could share. The furniture looked fairly new. "I can't stand bugs," she said.

"Not to worry," said Renee. "The landlord can't stand them, either. He lives on the fifth floor. A great view of the Hudson River up there. He makes liberal use of the pest control people."

"How much?"

"Three and a quarter a month. With utilities."

"I'll take it."

"I'll need a reference."

Renee saw the crestfallen look on Nicole's face. "If I pay cash, will you still need one?"

"I'll have to check with the owner. Let me call him."

Renee used the wall phone to call the landlord and smiled at Nicole when she hung up. "Can you pay two months' rent in advance?"

"Yes."

"Then you've got yourself an apartment."

They went back to the real estate office where Nicole signed a one-year lease and gave Renee a roll of bills.

"I need a job. Any ideas?"

"What are your skills?"

"Office. Administration. A little accounting. Marketing."

"There's a temp agency across the street," Renee said, looking out the window and pointing to a two-story building. "Why not try there? It's a start."

"I have Rebecca . . ."

"She can stay here if you want to take a walk over there now. I'm not busy this morning."

Nicole looked at the child who was staring up at her. "I won't be long, sweetie. I'll hurry back as soon as I can. Then I'll get you something to eat."

Nicole left then and went across the street to Temp-Aid. An hour later, she was back at the real estate office to get Rebecca. "How did you make out?" Renee asked.

"I start Monday. A law firm on Fifth Avenue. Receptionist. It's temporary, but it's a start." Thank goodness she'd been able to reach Paul LaScola. Count on him to give her a glowing recommendation.

"Well, congratulations. Looks like today's your lucky day—a new apartment, a new job."

Renee handed Nicole the keys to her new apartment, and she and Rebecca left to get some breakfast.

Now all she had to do was find someone to watch Rebecca before and after school. That wouldn't be so easy.

"You're a big girl, now," Nicole told Rebecca on Sunday night. "I'll show you how to lock the door on your way out in the morning. And when you get home from school in the afternoon, stay inside until mommy gets home from work."

"But I want to play with the other kids."

"And you can, but not until I get home from work."

"I want to go back to the hotel."

"We can't. This is our new home, and you'll just have to get used to it," Nicole said firmly. She felt bad for letting Rebecca down. If only Rayelle's cousin hadn't opened his mouth, Rebecca would probably be swimming in the hotel pool right now. Some friend Rayelle turned out to be. If only she'd been understanding, none of this would have happened.

"I want to go swimming. Why couldn't we find an apartment with a pool?" she said, as if reading her mother's mind.

"Because we're in the city now. And there are no pools."

Before leaving for work on Monday morning, she instructed Rebecca not to let anyone inside the apartment while she was gone. On Friday, she'd enrolled Rebecca in the Thomas Jefferson elementary school around the corner, and Nicole was grateful there wouldn't be any busy streets to cross and that Rebecca could eat her lunch in the school's cafeteria. She'd worry about what to do over the summer months later. With a new job in a new city she had enough to think about for now.

They settled into a daily routine of work and school, and by the end of their first month in Hoboken they knew their way around. On Saturdays, Nicole took Rebecca on the bus to Manhattan. FAO Schwarz was always a favorite stop-off. So was Central Park where Rebecca could run and play, roller skate, and visit the zoo animals.

It was while they were at the zoo that Nicole met Danny. He was there with his eight-year-old son, Michael, and while the children were roller-skating, she and Danny struck up a conversation. Danny was tall, like her father, and she thought him good looking with his dark eyes and curly hair, bushy mustache, and football player build.

Before an hour passed, Danny had asked Nicole for her phone number. She'd given it freely and hoped he'd call soon for a date. She didn't have long to wait. That night, the phone rang and when she picked it up on the first ring she heard Danny's voice on the other end of the line.

He took her to dinner in Little Italy the following Saturday night while Rebecca stayed behind in the apartment. "I won't be late, sweetie. Just stay inside and watch television. And don't let anyone in. I'll call you later to check on you," Nicole told Rebecca.

Her date with Danny was better than anything she could have hoped for. They ordered shrimp scampi and Chianti and talked and laughed their way through dinner. And when he asked to see her again on Sunday, she said yes. This time, they included Rebecca and Michael and went to Central Park so the children could play while they got to know each other better. Later, they bought hot dogs and ice cream from a vendor.

Soon, they were seeing each other every weekend and on occasion Danny and Michael would have supper at Nicole's apartment after she came home from work. He always brought a bottle of wine, and it would be gone by the end of the evening.

Six months after Nicole met Danny, he asked her to move in with him. His apartment on the Lower East Side off Canal Street would be much closer to where Nicole worked, he said, convincing her to make the move. She accepted his offer, and after giving her landlord a month's notice and subletting the apartment, she and Rebecca moved in with Danny and Michael.

His apartment was larger than the one she left behind, and Rebecca now had her own bedroom. The law firm offered her a chance to make extra money by having her work at the reception desk to greet after-hours clients. Two nights a week she got home at nine o'clock, but she didn't have to go back to work until ten the following morning. She liked sleeping in those two days. Danny got Rebecca off to school, and she considered that another bonus.

As happy as she was, Nicole barely noticed that Rebecca was not. One Saturday morning she came to her mother while Danny was out on an errand and looked up at her with sad eyes. "What is it, Rebecca? You look like you're about to cry."

It was then that Rebecca told her mother what went on at night when she was working. After supper, Danny went to the living room and turned on the television, she said. Only it wasn't the news he was watching. It was pictures of naked ladies. "He makes me sit on his lap. And then he kisses me. I don't like it when he puts his tongue inside my mouth."

Former Things

The anger rising inside of Nicole turned to rage as Rebecca's story unfolded, and when Danny came through the door an hour later with Michael she confronted him.

"Rebecca and I had a little chat while you were out," she said, her voice as sharp as a straight-edged razor.

"Oh, yeah? What about?"

So enraged was she that she picked up a book from the coffee table and threw it at him, hitting him in the chest. "You've been raping my daughter when I'm at work! And exposing her to porn!"

"Nicole, calm down. She doesn't know what she's talking about." He picked up the book off the floor and went to put his arms around Nicole, but she pushed him away.

"Don't you tell me to calm down. I could have you arrested. Tomorrow, I'm out of here. We're leaving!"

"I'm telling you, she's making it up."

"Really?" she said scornfully, opening a table drawer next to the couch. "What's this then?" She reached in and pulled out a video. "What? I'm not enough for you?" She tore open her blouse then, ripping the buttons off and exposing her breasts. "Blazing Bed Buddies doesn't sound like a kid's cartoon to me!"

"Nicole . . ."

In the next room, Rebecca heard her mother and Danny fighting and she heard her mother say they were leaving. Where they would go, she didn't know, but she was glad that Danny wouldn't be coming with them. She'd miss Michael, but not Danny. Not one bit.

In the morning, Nicole got Rebecca dressed and took her to work. She packed a bag full of coloring books and crayons and paper dolls that would keep Rebecca busy while she worked. There was a conference room with a small television set right behind Nicole's desk and she would set up Rebecca in there. She'd take her to the company cafeteria for lunch, treat her to an ice cream cone for dessert, then they'd walk to the bank and she'd withdraw all the money she'd saved over the past year.

Gail Lowe

As soon as she was finished for the day, she'd go back to the apartment and pack their clothes and gather up their belongings before hitting the road. She and Rebecca would be gone by the time Danny got home from work. She felt guilty about not giving the law firm any notice that she was leaving her job, but she had to do what she had to do. And that was to protect Rebecca.

CHAPTER FIVE

After the car was packed, she headed north, then west across the state of New York, stopping long enough to have supper at a hamburger joint and bedding down for the night inside the car. Nicole wanted to preserve every cent she had, and she was not about to spend it on some fleabag motel. No, better to conserve her money. She had no idea where they'd end up, but she needed money for her next rental.

In the morning, she headed south and drove a short while through Pennsylvania until she crossed the Ohio state line, stopping in Canal Fulton to get gas. The village was small enough to get lost in, and she thought about staying for a while but decided that job prospects would not be good. She'd probably have to commute to Akron, and she didn't want to tack on an extra hour to her work day. No, she needed to be in a location where she could find work close to where she and Rebecca lived. Canal Fulton was not the answer.

She continued on until she reached the Indiana border. She had read in the travel section of the *New York Times* about the Indianapolis 500 and wondered what it would be like to live nearby. Maybe she'd have her pick of men who came to the speedway to watch the races and drive their muscle cars. She thought about checking out the city until she made a pit stop in Elkhart. The city was small, but not too small. She liked the friendliness of the people who waited on them at a roadside diner and the land was flat enough to enjoy a bike ride.

One of the first things she wanted to do was buy Rebecca a bike. The child had been clamoring for one for months, but living in New York City was not the best place for bike riding, so Nicole had always said no to Rebecca's pleas.

167

Gail Lowe

If she lived somewhere in Elkhart, then maybe she'd be able to get her a bike for Christmas. She drove along the St. John River until she came to a sprawling RV dealership. Curious, she pulled into the parking lot to take a closer look.

The RVs came in all sizes and some were as big as ranch-style homes. Holding Rebecca's hand, she approached a salesman and asked if they could take a look at one. Al Burney wondered what Nicole would want with an RV and doubted she'd buy something on the lot, but he decided to humor her. A good-looking woman could always wrap herself around his finger. "What's one of these cost, anyway?" she asked.

"They range in price. Anywhere from $1,200 for a small used pop-up to $100,000 or more for one of the big ones," he said. "You're not from around here, are you?"

"No . . . New England."

"Maine? Massachusetts?"

"New Hampshire."

"You just passing through, or are you looking to settle someplace?"

"Not sure yet. I don't know. We just got here today."

"Well, I know a place where you can stay, if you have a mind to."

"Where?"

"Maddie Hathaway's place down the road. She bought a dozen of these RVs and rents them out to people who need temporary housing. I know she could use the business. And living in one for a while would give you a better idea if you'd like to own one."

Nicole thanked him for the tip, and he showed her around the lot. She was surprised to find that they were like homes on wheels and wondered what it would be like to live in one. "Are these a lot of work to set up? I mean at a campground."

"Not at all. It only takes a little getting used to. After a few times on the road, it gets to be a piece of cake."

"I'm not interested in buying right now, but you never know."

Al handed her his business card before Nicole headed back to her car with Rebecca. A few minutes later, she pulled into Maddie's RV park. Small children were playing jump rope in the

Former Things

middle of the dirt yard, and a few were riding their bicycles in circles. "Can anyone tell me where to find Maddie?" she asked a freckle-faced girl about ten years old. "Over there," the girl said, pointing to a sleek silver Airstream.

Nicole thanked the girl and she and Rebecca walked across the yard to Maddie's RV. When Nicole knocked on the door, she heard someone moving around inside. Seconds later the door opened and Nicole saw a black woman standing there, hands on her wide hips, eyes dark as kohl. "What can I do for you?" she asked.

"A salesman at the RV dealership down the road said you might have an RV for rent. I'm thinking about settling in Elkhart with my daughter. We'd need something just big enough for the two of us."

Maddie looked at Rebecca then back to Nicole. A single mother with a child. She knew what that was like. She'd raised five of her own without the benefit of a husband. Being a single mother was a hardscrabble life. She knew that for sure. Until Max had come along, she'd shouldered everything herself. "You got a job?"

"Not yet. But I have good skills and shouldn't have trouble finding one."

"How will you pay the rent until you find work?"

"I have savings."

Maddie considered her options. She could send the young woman and child on their way, but she'd also be letting one of her RVs stand empty. She knew she was taking a risk letting them become renters, but it was a risk she was willing to take. If the woman didn't pay her rent, she'd have to start the eviction process and that was one thing she never looked forward to. Still, she was willing to take a chance. "What's your name?" she asked, eyeing Nicole.

"Nicole Preston. This is Rebecca," she said, combing the child's honey-colored hair with her fingers.

"A small RV, you say?"

"We don't need much space. Someplace to put our clothes, a few toys. A place to eat and sleep."

Gail Lowe

"I might have something to suit you. A small Shasta. Wait here a minute while I get the keys."

When Maddie went back inside her Airstream. Nicole peeked inside and saw a nicely furnished living room and large modern kitchen. A soap opera was blaring from a wide-screen TV.

"I don't want to interrupt your TV program," said Nicole when Maddie came back with a ring of keys.

"Don't worry about that. It's almost over anyway, and tomorrow they'll do a recap."

Maddie led the way across the dirt yard to a small RV with Cape Cod curtains in the windows. "It's already furnished. Just in case you're wondering."

"That's what we need. We don't have furniture."

Maddie inserted the key in the lock and opened the door. The musty odor caused Nicole to sneeze. "Once it's aired out, that smell will be gone," she said. "I'll ask my husband to clean it up for you."

"How much would you charge by the month?"

"How much you willing to pay?"

Nicole had no idea how much to offer. She took a stab at a figure. "Two hundred and fifty dollars? Does that sound fair?"

"You got a deal. I'll ask Max—that's my husband—to get it ready for you. When you want to move in?"

"Today if at all possible."

"Not a problem. If you have errands to do, go ahead and do them. It'll be ready by four o'clock."

Nicole counted out the first month's rent and handed Maddie a wad of cash. Why wait until Christmas? Rebecca deserved to have her bike now. Before leaving, she asked Maddie if there was a Wal-Mart nearby.

"Sure is. Go there all the time myself. End of the road, hang a right. Go to the next set of lights. Take a left. Wal-Mart'll be right there in front of you."

An hour later, Nicole had a brand new blue and silver Schwinn tied to the roof of her car.

After they stopped for a bite to eat at a diner, Nicole opened an account at the Elkhart Savings & Loan and bought a load of groceries at the local supermarket.

By the time they were finished, it was almost four o'clock and Rebecca was anxious to try out her new bike. They arrived at the RV park a few minutes past four, just as Max was running a moistened paper towel over the kitchen window in Nicole's newly rented RV. She parked her car and headed over to Max. He came through the door and stood on the top step. "You Nicole Preston?" he asked.

"I am. And this is my daughter, Rebecca."

"Well, hello there, young lady," he said, reaching into his pants pocket. "A little treat for the little miss." Max handed her a lollipop with a loop handle.

"What do you say, Rebecca?"

"Thank you."

"I see you got yourself a bike. Need help getting it off the roof?"

"If you don't mind."

Max went to Nicole's car and untied the rope that held the bike in place. Minutes later Rebecca was trying to get the hang of pedaling while Nicole held up the rear. By five o'clock, she was riding around the dirt yard with the other kids, kicking up dust.

After a supper of fish sticks and French fries, Nicole wandered over to Maddie's Airstream and knocked on the door. "Anything wrong?" she asked when she saw Nicole standing outside.

"No, I just need to find out where I can enroll Rebecca in school."

"There's an elementary school a quarter mile from here," said Maddie. "You might want to talk to some of the other mothers whose kids go there. They know more than I do."

Maddie stepped outside and looked across the yard toward an RV where Nicole had seen a young woman hanging laundry

Gail Lowe

on a folding rack earlier in the day. "That's Nadine's place," said Maddie, nodding toward the RV. "She's got three kids in school. She can tell you what you need to know. She's probably home. Come on. I'll go with you."

Maddie knocked on Nadine's door, and a small boy about four years old with a dirty face opened it. "Your mother home, Andy?" Maddie asked.

The boy called for his mother, and she came to the door a few seconds later. "Nadine, this here is Nicole. She's just moved in today. The Shasta up back. She's got a girl about six. Needs to know about the schools. I told her you'd help her out."

Nadine glanced at Nicole and wondered where she had come from. She had an air about her that suggested she might be from the city. "Where you from?" Nadine asked.

"New Hampshire. Then I moved to New York."

So that explained it. Nadine envisioned Nicole shopping on Fifth Avenue and walking along Park Avenue. She wondered what had brought her to Elkhart.

"How old's your girl?" she asked, looking at Rebecca.

"Six, almost seven. She was in second grade in New York."

"That would be Mrs. Pomeroy's class at the Lincoln. There's only one class for every grade. Class size is pretty big, but they all seem to be learning."

"Who would I see about registering Rebecca?"

"Mr. Fogarty. He's the principal. Why don't I take you over there in the morning. No time like the present for the kid to start."

Inside Nadine's RV, Nicole could see two children sitting on a couch in front of a television set. A baby around two years old clung to her mother's leg. Nicole guessed Nadine to be about five months pregnant and she wondered if there was a husband in the picture. As if reading her mind, Nadine said, "My husband's not home from work yet. Should be here any minute. He can watch the baby while we're at the school tomorrow."

A few minutes later, a red pick-up truck drove into the park. "There's Troy now," she said.

Troy parked, swung down from the truck, and walked toward Nadine. Dressed in tight jeans and a white long-sleeve shirt and cowboy boots, he cut a handsome figure. And when Nadine introduced him to Nicole, she noticed he held eye contact with her a little longer than necessary. Troy's eyes were a startling shade of blue against his hair dark and he had a dimple in his right cheek when he smiled. A real hunk, thought Nicole.

"We've got ourselves a new neighbor," said Nadine.

Nicole stuck out her hand and Troy took it with a firm grasp. "Nicole Preston. And this is Rebecca."

"You just moving in?"

"Today. I've rented the silver and blue Shasta at the back of the park. Just big enough for Rebecca and me." Nicole noticed he raised an eyebrow and gave a secret smile when she failed to mention a husband.

Nicole and Nadine walked the children to school the following morning, and an hour later Rebecca was seated in the second row of Mrs. Pomeroy's classroom. On the way back to the park, Nicole asked Nadine when her baby was due. "The middle of January. I thought we might lose this one, but after a month of bed rest things got right with me. I hope we have another girl to balance out the family. Two boys, two girls. To me that's a perfect family."

Nicole envied Nadine's big family and wished that someday she could have a second child. She hated the thought of Rebecca growing up alone. Even now, Nicole regretted not having had a sister or brother. She remembered pleading with her mother about it, but no matter how hard she tried to convince her mother to give her a sister or brother Nicole remained an only child.

They went their separate ways at Nadine's RV, and Nicole went back to her place to shower and dress. She had to see about getting a job somewhere and she didn't have all day. She put on a blue denim skirt and white cotton sweater and slipped into her black suede jacket. On her feet she wore a pair of knee-high black leather boots. This time, instead of working in an office, she wanted to look for a job that would keep her on the move. Since she'd turned thirty-five she'd gained a few pounds and needed to work them off.

On the way to her car she saw Troy standing next to his truck talking to Max. When she drove past them, Troy winked at her and waved, and she waved back.

Nicole drove to downtown Elkhart and parked behind the five and dime. She stopped to buy the city's newspaper before heading for a small restaurant where the sign outside said that breakfast was served all day. Once she was seated at the counter, she ordered a glass of orange juice and turned to the help wanted section.

She read the general help wanted ads and found one placed by Encore, a restaurant on Bellevue Road. The ad said that the restaurant was Elkhart's finest. After finishing her juice she paid the bill and left a tip. Then she asked for directions from the clerk at the cash register and went to her car for the three-mile drive.

Encore was a low-rise steakhouse built on the banks of the St. John River with a wide deck out back that ran the length of the building. As she drew closer to the restaurant, she imagined herself serving meals to people in the summer months while enjoying the scenery. The building was made of logs and a plate glass floor-to-ceiling window was the dominant feature out front. Through the window, Nicole could see a massive fireplace in the center of the restaurant. Yes, she thought, working at Encore would suit her just fine.

She parked in the adjacent lot and went inside where she found a maintenance man running a vacuum cleaner over a royal blue carpet. She stood at the entrance, not wanting to interrupt his work, but when he turned to run the vacuum cleaner in the opposite direction, he saw Nicole and shut off the machine. "Can I help you?" he asked.

"I'm here to apply for a job I saw advertised in the Elkhart Courier. Is your manager here?"

"He's in his office. I'll go get him."

The worker, a skinny, light-haired man in his thirties, went off to find the manager and returned a few minutes later with another man behind him.

Former Things

"Tom Doyle," he said, approaching Nicole. "And you are?"

"Nicole Preston. I read in the paper that you need to hire a waitress."

"That's right. Why don't you come into my office where we can talk."

She walked alongside him, taking note of his highly polished cordovan loafers, navy blue pin-stripe suit, and starched white shirt. His irregular facial features didn't make him a handsome man, but he had a nice way about him, and Nicole liked that he whistled as they walked along. He led her to an office upstairs and motioned for her to sit in a captain's chair on the opposite side of his desk.

"You live here in town, Nicole?"

"Yes," she replied, being careful not to give an address. He'd find out where she lived soon enough if he hired her. She didn't want to give him the impression that she was a transient. Fair or not, it's how she viewed the people living in the RV park. "Just off the highway near Water Street," she said.

"What's your experience as a waitress?"

Nicole told him that she had worked at The Boxcar when she lived in Beverly seven years ago. "I enjoyed working with the people who dined there, and they seemed to like me," she said.

"So you're a people person. That's what I'm looking for. Tell me about your last restaurant job."

Nicole explained that she had enjoyed the atmosphere of The Boxcar and the people who came in for dinner. Many were local politicians and their wives, she said, and she had got to know what they liked to eat and drink. The tips were good because she learned early on what they usually ordered, and she'd memorized the specials of the day and kept a good distance from their tables so she'd be accessible but not intrusive.

"I like that, Nicole. I like how you operate. I've been trying to teach my staff not to intrude on diners for a long time, but they just don't seem to get it."

"Another thing I do is wait until everyone is finished eating before clearing the table. I think it's rude to take a dinner plate from the table when other people are still eating. It makes the

Gail Lowe

others feel rushed. At least that's how I feel when I'm in a restaurant. The Europeans have it over us when it comes to service in a restaurant. What do you think?"

She watched while he took notes on a small pad of paper. "I've never been to Europe, but I like what you just said. In fact, I'm going to insist from now on that the rest of the staff waits till everyone finishes before clearing. Listen, at Encore I pay minimum wage and you get to keep all your tips. There's no tip-sharing here. I believe that tips are earned and not to be divided up. Does that seem reasonable to you?"

"Yes, it does."

"I'd start you out on the lunchtime schedule and if you do well, I'll put you on the dinner shift in three months." He tapped his pencil on the desktop, waiting for Nicole to answer.

Nicole breathed a sigh of relief. With Rebecca in school until almost three o'clock, she would be home from work in time to meet her.

"Your hours would be from ten to two-thirty. You'll set up your station with dinnerware and glasses and be ready to wait on people when they start arriving at eleven-thirty. Most people are out of here by one-thirty. The last hour you'll clean up and help out in the kitchen, if it's needed."

"When can I start?"

Tom Doyle looked at Nicole and saw a go-getter. Just what he needed. Someone to spruce things up. Someone who wouldn't be afraid to take charge. "How about tomorrow?"

"Perfect. What do I wear?"

"White shirt. Black pants. We supply the black bow tie. No white waitress shoes or sneakers. Flat black dress shoes. Just make sure they're comfortable. You'll be doing a lot of walking."

"Got it."

He stood up, indicating that the interview was over. She followed him out of his office and down the stairs to the front door. "Tomorrow at ten, Nicole. When you arrive, ask for Jean. She's our head waitress."

Nicole got into her car and drove over to Wal-Mart to buy three white shirts and two pairs of black pants.

She found a pair of black flats, too. All on sale.

Two weeks before Christmas, Nicole and Rebecca went looking for a small tree. Nicole let Rebecca pick out the decorations, including a blue star tree-topper that blinked on and off. She also bought three packages of small red velvet bows, two strings of colored lights, a double strand of silver garland, and a tree stand.

On Christmas Eve she invited Nadine, Troy, and their three children over for hot chocolate and oatmeal raisin cookies. The little RV was crowded, but she wanted to offer some holiday cheer to her neighbors as well as to herself and Rebecca. For each of the children, she had bought a coloring book and box of jumbo crayons and while the grown-ups talked, the children sat on the floor coloring pictures.

Nadine was only a few weeks away from giving birth and her body was grotesquely swollen from the sixty pounds she had gained. Nicole thought her face looked like a blown-up balloon, but she would never tell Nadine that. "The doctor said I have edema," she explained, "and he put me on a water pill. I'm constantly in the bathroom peeing and I'm up and down all night long. I can't wait to have this baby. I hope it comes early."

Troy sat there quietly, but it was clear that he was anxious for the birth to happen, too. He glanced at Nicole, lowering his eyes to her chest. It was a suggestive look that made her slightly uncomfortable. Still, it had been a long time since any man had looked at her openly with lust and she secretly enjoyed it.

Nicole had been working on a knitting project—a yellow blanket for the new baby—and she handed the gift-wrapped package to Nadine. "It's not much, but I wanted you to have a little something for the baby."

With Troy looking on, Nadine carefully peeled away the gift wrapping and was overwhelmed by Nicole's generosity. "It's so pretty," she said. "I've always wanted to learn how to knit. Maybe someday you'll teach me?"

"Sure. My mother taught me when I was ten. It had been a while since I last picked up a pair of knitting needles, but it's something that never leaves you. It's like riding a bike. You never forget." The memory of herself and her mother sitting on the living room couch with a pair of knitting needles and ball of yarn suddenly loomed in Nicole's mind. She had not thought about her mother in months, and now she wondered how she was. While she was growing up, Christmas had always been an elaborate affair with a tree at least nine feet tall and a wide assortment of gifts for everyone in the family. There had been a turkey dinner with relatives around the dining room table, and her Uncle Ben always arrived in the afternoon with a handmade gift for her. One year he made a doll cradle. Another year he carved a set of nesting dolls out of solid oak. Nicole's friends were invited, too, and they all gathered around the piano while her mother played all the old Christmas carols. Rebecca's Christmas paled in comparison, but the child didn't seem to mind. At least she never complained.

After the first week in January, Tom Doyle approached Nicole and said it was time for her to work the dinner shift. She was elated to hear the news because she knew that her salary would almost double. Lunchtime tips were good, and those she got from customers who came at night would be two or three times as much.

The only obstacle in her way was Rebecca and what to do with her. She tossed around options in her mind until finally deciding that Rebecca was old enough to stay by herself. All she had to do was get something to eat, do her homework, and watch a little television. She could put herself to bed, and if a problem came up she could call Maddie or Nadine.

"Plan on working the dinner shift starting next Monday night," said Tom.

For the rest of the week, Nicole primed Rebecca for the change in her work schedule, quizzing her again and again about what she had been instructed to do. Never leave anything cooking on top of the stove. Clean up after yourself. Television off at eight-thirty. To bed no later than nine. In case of emergency, call Maddie or Nadine.

Nicole found herself getting home around ten every night. She was bone tired from being on her feet for five hours straight, but she had been right in guessing that her salary would at least double and the first week she saved half of what she earned. A little financial security went a long way. It had been ingrained in her since childhood. Two weeks after starting her new shift, Nadine called from the hospital to say she'd had a baby girl. "I'm thrilled to pieces," she said. "We've named her Julia Rose. What do you think?"

"A beautiful name. I can't wait to see her."

No sooner had she hung up the phone than a knock came at her door. She peeked out the window and saw that it was Troy. She opened the door and said, "I just heard the good . . ."

Nicole never had a chance to finish her sentence. In an instant, Troy was inside the RV and he slammed the door behind him. He moved toward Nicole and kissed her tenderly on the mouth. In spite of her better judgment, she found herself responding and kissed him back. Minutes later, they were in Nicole's bed, naked. "I've wanted you ever since I first laid eyes on you," he murmured in her ear. "You're gorgeous, Nicole. Do you know that?"

No, in fact, she didn't. Only then did she realize how hungry she was for a man's touch. He brought out passions that had been buried for a long time, at least since Danny. Then she thought about Nadine. Only this one time, she promised herself. Nadine would never need to know. "You have to go, Troy. Rebecca will be home from school any minute." He left then, both of them knowing they would meet in secret again.

Nicole had no idea what Troy told Nadine on the nights he visited her, but their lovemaking had become part of her weekly routine and she looked forward to seeing him. To cover

Gail Lowe

his tracks, on the nights he came to Nicole's RV he drove his pick-up out of the park and left it in a picnic area on the side of the road and walked the half mile back to her place in the dark, being careful not to be seen by any of the neighbors, especially Nadine. For five years they met three nights a week, but as Rebecca grew and stayed up later, they had to find places to meet outside of the RV park and their trysts became shorter and less satisfying.

Over coffee one morning Nadine asked Nicole why she didn't have any dates. Actually, she wasn't interested, not as long as she had a lover, but she wasn't about to tell Nadine that. Not when her lover happened to be Nadine's husband.

"You know, I've often thought about dating, but I just don't have the time. Maybe when Rebecca gets older. I'm just not all that interested, to tell you the truth," she had told her friend.

The year Rebecca turned twelve, Nicole confronted Troy about his intentions. "I know you don't sleep with Nadine anymore," she said. "She told me that herself. How long are you going to stay in your sham of a marriage?"

He looked at Nicole and longed to be with her, but he had four children to think about, not to mention child support if he left Nadine. "Nicole," he said, "you've got to understand what I'm up against. How can I up and leave Nadine while the kids are little? Imagine what that would do to my wallet."

"So, you're allowing money to rule you," she countered. "I thought I knew you better than that. Besides, if we were a couple, there'd be two salaries, not just one. And children do grow up, you know. Child support wouldn't be forever."

She had a point, and he knew it. Still, he liked the arrangement the way it was. Home cooked meals Nadine made every night. The company of his children. And a knock-out girlfriend on the side. Any man would envy him. Why change something that worked perfectly?

Sensing his inner thoughts, she said, "You don't give a damn about me, Troy. If you did, you'd make an honest woman of me. Furthermore, I'm sick to death of doing it in the back of your truck. " Nicole sulked then, and refused to have sex with him.

Former Things

For the first time, Troy felt himself caught up in something he hadn't bargained for. And that was a girlfriend who demanded more than he could give or was willing to give. Maybe it was time to look for a new woman. Someone who wouldn't make demands. There was a sharp-looking gal down at the Bluebird Diner he'd had his eye on. A petite blonde, shapely legs, perky breasts. Madeline was her name. She didn't wear a wedding ring, either. He wondered if she had a boyfriend. He had no idea but intended to find out.

The next time they were together, Troy told Nicole he wouldn't be able to see her on Friday night. "There's a meeting at work," he lied.

"On Friday night? What kind of meeting is that?" Nicole asked, suspicious.

"Just some of the guys getting together to talk about union stuff."

"Well, why don't you come over after the meeting?"

"Can't. Nadine would wonder why I'm getting home so late."

Nicole's intuition told her Troy was lying, but she said nothing. Better to keep an eye on the situation and see what happened, she decided.

From that point on, Troy always had one excuse after another for not being able to see Nicole on Friday nights. She suspected there was someone else, but she couldn't prove it. Not until the Friday night she was driving home from work and thought to stop at the Bluebird Diner to use the rest room. She had wanted to leave work as soon as she finished and didn't take the time to use the bathroom there, but as she drove along she knew she wouldn't make it home without stopping somewhere.

When she pulled into the diner's parking lot, she saw Troy inside talking and laughing with a young blonde woman. She also saw the woman reach across the table and take Troy's hand into hers. When she saw Troy lean over to give the woman a kiss on the lips she knew what was going on. Troy glanced around to make sure no one saw them, and when he looked toward the parking lot he saw Nicole inside her car staring right at him. Enraged, she started her car, backed up, and headed for home.

In her rear view mirror, she could see Troy standing in the road, trying to wave her down.

Her insides churned as she sped home. When she pulled into the RV park and stopped in front of Nadine's place, she got out of the car and marched to the front door. She knew she was banging on the door hard enough to wake everyone in the RV park, but she didn't care. When Nadine opened it and saw Nicole standing there, she asked right away if something had happened to Rebecca.

"No, this has nothing to do with my daughter and everything to do with your husband."

"Troy? What did he do?"

"In case you don't know, Nadine, your husband has been paying me visits three nights a week for the last five years. He's a cheat and a liar. Did you know that?"

Nadine felt stricken to the core. For a long time she knew her husband ran around behind her back, but never once did she think he'd do it with someone she knew. "Yes, I've known about his betrayal for a long time, but I never thought you'd be a party to it, Nicole," she said through her tears. Nicole then realized what she had done. She intended to hurt Troy to the core, not Nadine. She was the innocent one, only now it was too late.

Nadine screamed at Nicole and told her to get out. "I never want to lay eyes on you again, you tramp, and if it means telling Maddie about your disgusting behavior, then that's what I'll do!"

Nicole trembled with fear. Since coming to Elkhart, she'd made a life for herself and Rebecca. She had a job. Rebecca was getting along well in school, and she'd had Troy to fill in for the husband she didn't have. She knew she couldn't stay in the RV park, not after what had just happened, but she didn't want to move to town. Word had a way of getting out, and she didn't want to be involved in some kind of ugly scandal. She'd have to move on, take Rebecca out of school, find a new place to settle down. Next time she'd be smarter. Next time she'd know better than to get involved with a married man.

Former Things

The following morning, she told Rebecca the news. "My job isn't going well," she lied. "There's more work in Chicago. Higher class restaurants. The tips at Encore aren't as good as they used to be. I think we'll go there."

"But Mom, I'm happy here. I don't want to leave my friends. There's the school play and . . ."

"Rebecca, no guilt trips, please. I am doing this for your good, not mine. Before you know it, there'll be college bills to pay. I can't send you to school on my waitress salary. Well, at least not in Elkhart. We have to go. You can always make new friends."

Rebecca cried and pleaded with her mother to stay in Elkhart, but when Nicole didn't respond she knew her mind had been made up. There was no sense talking to a stone wall.

Nicole went to tell Maddie they were leaving, and when she came back she told Rebecca it was a good thing they were getting out of there because Maddie had been mean to her and called her names. "The sooner we leave, the better," she'd told Rebecca. "Hurry up, now. Let's get our things into the car so we can be on our way."

CHAPTER SIX

By the afternoon they were on the road, this time bound for Chicago. Rebecca sulked most of the way. She was sick of moving and longed to settle down in one place where she could make friends who would be here today and not gone tomorrow. In fact, this morning she hadn't even gone to school to let her teachers know she was leaving. Her mother had made her stay home to help pack.

The terrain between Indiana and Illinois was pretty with rolling hills and estuaries, and the bucolic scenery lulled Nicole and Rebecca into a false sense of well being. Soon, Rebecca fell asleep. Her dreams took her to places she'd never been before. A cave where bats flew around her head. A lake where a speed boat was coming straight toward her. A school where all the kids pointed at her and laughed.

When Nicole hit a pothole in the road, Rebecca awoke with a start. Nicole announced that they had just crossed over into Illinois, and she hoped her tire wouldn't go flat because of the pothole. Rebecca wished she could take over the wheel. She hated the way her mother drove. She couldn't wait until she turned sixteen. Then she'd get her driver's license. She'd borrow her mother's car and chauffeur her friends around the way the teenagers in the RV park did. She wondered who her next set of friends would be. She wondered where she'd go to school. She wondered all these things while her mother wondered aloud why her life seemed to always go wrong. Nothing seemed to be fair in life, her mother said. Not one thing.

♥

184

Former Things

The city of Chicago loomed off the side of the highway, its magnificent buildings and bridges rising tall over Lake Michigan. Nicole congratulated herself on choosing to come to a city where she was sure she would settle for good. She'd always thrilled to the hum and pulse of city life, and every time her mother took her to Boston on a shopping trip she hated going back home to Rye. "Someday I'm going to live in a big city," she'd told her mother and Emily had smiled and said, "I'm sure you will one of these days."

She was here now, and her number one priority was finding a place to live. She knew that housing in the city would be too rich for her pocketbook, so instead of heading into Chicago she took an exit off the highway and found herself in a small town called Willowdale.

The place radiated with charm. The word "quaint" came to Nicole's mind, and she delighted in the fact that it had its own movie theater and a number of chic clothing boutiques and bistros. The town seemed small yet big enough to get lost in, but it had a big city vibe. Best of all, it was a stone's throw from the main attraction—Chicago.

Nicole pulled up beside the visitor's bureau and told Rebecca to wait inside the car while she asked for information. A few minutes later, she returned with a packet of pamphlets and brochures. "There are tons of rentals," she said. "And the rents are reasonable. No more RV parks. Things are looking up. Yes, baby, just like The Jeffersons—we're movin' on up."

"Who are the Jeffersons, Mom?"

Nicole looked at Rebecca and laughed. "An old TV show, sweetie. It was very funny."

Rebecca smiled inside. Maybe things *were* looking up. She hoped so for her mother's sake and her own, too.

Nicole drove to a real estate office on Main Street the woman at the visitor's bureau had told her about and saw apartment listings taped to the plate glass window out front. After parking her car, she and Rebecca went inside and approached a receptionist with short red hair and a rose tattoo on her wrist. When the receptionist looked up from the book she was reading, Nicole asked to speak to a rental agent. "That would be Joyce," the receptionist said, reaching for her phone. Nicole noticed the black polish on her fingernails. "I'll let her know you're here."

A moment later, Joyce came out of an inner office to speak with Nicole. Unlike the woman in New Jersey, the rental agent was wearing no makeup and was plainly dressed in a long red jumper and white blouse with a ruffled collar. "Were you interested in a condo? An apartment in a multi-family dwelling? A small house?" she asked, her pen poised over a pad of paper. "And what would be your price range?"

Nicole thought about each question before answering. A condo might have its own swimming pool. That would be good for Rebecca. An apartment might be a good choice, too, because she might be able to rely on her neighbors to keep an eye on Rebecca. A small house might be nice, as well, for its privacy. "What do you have in the way of a small house? I'm thinking in the six hundred dollar range, maybe a little more."

"Oh, that's just what I hoped you would say. I have a darling little two-story brick cottage on Garfield Street—it's named after President Garfield. I think you'd absolutely love it. The place has the sweetest little kitchen and bath and a fireplace in the living room. Plus, it has all natural woodwork that never needs cleaning and two small bedrooms. Perfect for you—that is, if it's just for you and your daughter. The owner has moved to Florida and didn't want to sell right away. He decided to rent it instead. There's a neighborhood school, too. It's just a short walk away. Would you like to see it?"

Nicole looked at Rebecca. "I'd like to, Mom."

The little brick house was in a neighborhood only a short distance from downtown. On the drive over, Nicole asked Joyce where she should look for a job.

Former Things

"Most people who live here work in Chicago," said Joyce. "There are lots of jobs there. Publishing companies, pharmaceutical firms, law offices. You name it, they have it."

Prospecting for a job would have to wait until Monday. Right now she and Rebecca needed a place to live. She gave Joyce Paul LaScola's name as a reference, explaining that she had lived with him one summer and had helped him house sit. Nicole crossed her fingers, hoping that Paul still had the same phone number. Otherwise, she might not be able to rent an apartment, let alone a house.

Joyce made the call while Nicole and Rebecca sat in her office. He answered the phone while in the middle of eating his lunch. "Paul here," he said, swallowing a bite of his tuna sandwich.

Joyce wasted no time introducing herself. "I'm Joyce Petro and I need to speak with Paul LaScola. It's about Nicole Preston."

"Nicole Preston? Is she okay?"

"She's sitting right here in front of me," she said. "She gave me your name as a reference so she can rent a home here in the Chicago area."

"Well, well . . . I wondered where she'd taken off to. I can vouch for her. Can I speak to her for a minute?"

Joyce handed the phone receiver to Nicole. "Hello, there . . . long time, no talk."

"What? It's only been about ten years."

"More like twelve going on thirteen. Ask me how I know."

"How do you know?"

"My daughter is almost thirteen. I had her the year after I left Beverly."

"Wow. Who's the dad?"

The dad? She hadn't thought about Chris Silva for a long time. She wasn't about to tell Paul about her passionate encounter with Chris that Fourth of July night, but maybe she could get around to asking about him and Paul's other friends in a general way.

"A man I met after leaving New Hampshire." It wasn't a lie. She had met Chris after leaving New Hampshire.

187

"Still in the picture?"

"No. It didn't work out. I haven't heard from him in years. By the way, staying with you that summer was so much fun. How is everyone? Patrick Ryan . . . Bill Doane . . . oh, and what was his name . . . Chris something . . ."

"Chris Silva? He's married with two sets of twins. Last I heard he and his family were living in Hawaii. Ended up being a millionaire selling pharmaceuticals for some big corporation."

Nicole wished she hadn't asked. Maybe she should have contacted him when she found out she was pregnant. She could have pressed him for child support. She could have kicked herself for being so stupid. Thousands of dollars down the drain. Men. They were the cause of all her problems, beginning with her father and ending with Chris. If her father had spelled out in his will what his intentions were regarding her inheritance, she wouldn't have fought with her mother in the first place. Then she wouldn't have left New Hampshire and she wouldn't have met Chris or Danny or Troy. And she wouldn't have Rebecca. Now she had a new chance at a decent life. A decent life in a decent place. If an attractive man happened to cross her path, she vowed then and there that she wouldn't give him the time of day.

Joyce was tapping her pencil against the pad of paper. She looked up at Nicole, hoping she'd get the message to end the call. "Well, Paul, I have to run. I need to get some documents signed. Thanks for the reference. How about if we talk again soon?"

"Sure, Nicole. Anytime. Take care of yourself."

I will, she thought, and that means you won't be hearing from me again. Paul, she now realized, was just another cog in the wheel of men who had caused her problems. No, Mr. Paul LaScola would not be hearing from her anytime soon.

As soon as the rental agreement was signed, Nicole and Rebecca were on their way. They stopped at a supermarket to shop for groceries, sheets, towels, and other necessities and started to settle into their new home a few hours later. After a supper of corn chowder from a can and a few crackers, Nicole suggested that she and Rebecca take a walk around the neighborhood to look for Rebecca's new school. Just as Joyce had said, it turned out to be a short walk only a few blocks away. While exploring the grounds, Rebecca noticed an Olympic size swimming pool at the rear of the school. The thought of being able to use it lifted her spirits and she began to look forward to registering on Monday.

It was the beginning of April. That meant only two more months of school before the start of summer vacation. Rebecca was still a little young to stay by herself all day while Nicole worked, but she would have to deal with that problem later. While on their walk, Nicole picked up a copy of the *Chicago Tribune* to look at the help wanted listings. The publishing field intrigued her, especially where newspapers and books were concerned. Maybe she'd go back to school and learn something new. Studying the humanities had been interesting when she was in college, but maybe it was time to expand her horizons. She'd had her fill of waiting tables, so getting a job in a restaurant was out of the question.

Later that night after Rebecca went to bed, she sat on the couch and read the newspaper cover to cover. Chicago was going to be a fascinating city to explore because of all its history. She was anxious to tour the city, see where the great fire had taken place, and walk along the sandy beaches fronting Lake Michigan. The list of things to do was endless, but first things first, she told herself. Her first order of business was to find a job. She turned to the help wanted pages and looked under the business section. Northwestern University was hiring a student newspaper advisor. A chemical company called PhenolGram was looking for a purchasing agent. Erekson Publishing Company needed an assistant for one of their book editors. She had edited papers while she was in college and loved playing with words. Maybe she'd go to the company on Monday and apply for the job. All that was required was a college degree in

Gail Lowe

liberal arts and one year of experience in publishing. She didn't meet the exact qualifications, but close enough. Working for a publishing company would definitely appeal to her. She went to get a pair of scissors from the kitchen and cut out the want ad along with two others.

***

On Monday, after seeing Rebecca off to school, Nicole dressed in a navy blue business suit she'd bought on sale at Saks when she lived in New York and slipped her feet into a pair of black patent leather pumps. She stood in front of a mirror and thought she looked every bit the businesswoman, and she hoped whomever she met today would think so, too.

Nicole was hopeful after talking to the personnel director at Erekson. The woman she met with, Cheryl Dixon, reminded her of her old boss and former friend at the casino. She wondered if Rayelle was still working there.

"We have a generous educational program in case you're interested in continuing school," Cheryl told Nicole. "Your application looks good. We'll just have to check your references."

She'd given Cheryl Tom Doyle's name, and a call from Cheryl came a few days later. "You got a glowing reference from Mr. Doyle, but I do have to ask why you didn't give him any notice when you left his employ."

Nicole thought quickly. "It was a medical emergency," she said and then to gain sympathy thought to add, "My mother needed me and I had no time to spare. She died a few days later."

The story worked. "I'm so sorry to hear that," said Cheryl. "You don't need to explain any further. My own mother died last year. I miss her more every day."

"I know just how you feel," said Nicole, without missing a beat. "My mother was my best friend. It's unbelievable how much I miss her."

***

Cheryl invited Nicole to Erekson to meet with the man she would work for. On the day of her interview with David Gately,

Former Things

she made sure that in addition to wearing her navy blue business suit she had her hair cut and styled. Nicole had hit it off with Iris, her new stylist, and the two laughed like old friends while Iris washed, cut, and styled Nicole's hair.

"So you're from Massachusetts originally?" Iris had asked.

"New Hampshire."

Iris told Nicole that she also lived in town. "On Burton Street. It's just off Main." She also told her that she was a single mother of a twelve-year-old daughter named Sara. "Our girls are probably in the same class at school," she said. "Why don't we make plans to get together after work some night?"

The two women became friends and the girls often played together, either at Iris's or Nicole's. Iris had a farmer's porch on the front of her house, and she and Nicole sat there on warm summer nights drinking strawberry slush laced with vodka.

One night Iris asked Nicole how she had come to live in Willowdale. "It's a long story," she said. "My mother and I came to blows over my father's will, and I wrote her off."

"Really? You wrote your own mother off?"

"I did. It was the final straw in a long list of insults."

"I'm sorry, Nicole. Me . . . I'm close to my mother. If not for her, I wouldn't have gone to hairdressing school. And she was always so good at watching Sara while I worked. I don't know what I'd do without her. She doesn't have much money, but she's always given us what she could."

"Well, if you had a mother like mine, you'd write her off, too."

"What do you mean?"

Nicole then told Iris about her childhood and how miserable she'd been. "My mother was not a nice person," she said. But when Iris pressed for details, she could not think of anything specific to say. "She was a witch. That's all I can say."

"Do you ever think you might one day want to see her again?"

"I've thought about it. I do have an inheritance waiting for me and I should probably check to see if she's still alive. I mean, for all I know her lawyer might be looking for me to tell me she died or something."

191

Iris listened to her new friend and wondered about Nicole's mother. "You know, Nicole, I've sometimes wondered what Sara will think of me when she grows up. I've made some real bloopers as a mother, and I'd hate to think that she'd reject me one day. You know what I mean? Being a single mother hasn't exactly been easy, and sometimes I run out of patience and lose my temper. It was worse when Peter and I were married—things were really bad then—but still, life hasn't been perfect by any means. It would kill me if Sara ever left. Maybe the bottom line is that no mother is perfect. Not me, not you, not anyone."

Nicole thought about what Iris said and pushed away any thoughts that she might have faults. "All I can say is I've done my best to be an excellent mother to Rebecca, and if that's not good enough, then that's just too bad. Let me tell you, Iris, my life has not been easy. I've had one problem after another and none of them have been of my own doing."

After their conversation, Nicole started to think up excuses not to visit Iris. The woman, she thought, had colossal gall to question her about her mother. Who did Iris think she was, suggesting that she had shortcomings when it came to raising Rebecca. Nicole obsessed about their conversation and a few weeks later decided it would be worth calling all the funeral homes in Portsmouth to find out if any of them had held a wake for a woman named Emily Preston. There was no sense in having money lying around unclaimed. She was, after all, her mother's only heir. When she made the calls a few days later, she learned that no one named Emily Preston had been waked at any of the funeral homes.

Nicole stopped making hair appointments with Iris, and instead started having her hair styled at a salon in Chicago a block away from where she worked. She told herself that it made more sense to have her hair cut on her lunch hour than wasting an entire Saturday morning at a hair salon in Willowdale, but when she was downtown shopping and saw Iris walking along the street, Nicole crossed to the other side so she wouldn't have to speak to her. She also encouraged Rebecca to make new friends.

"I hate to mention this, but I think I saw Sara looking through your top drawer when she was here this afternoon," she told Rebecca one Saturday night after supper. "She might have taken something, but I can't say for sure. Maybe you should check."

Rebecca ran to her bedroom, opened her top drawer, and rummaged through her belongings. "Mom! My silver bracelet is gone! My favorite one. Do you think Sara took it?"

"Maybe you just misplaced it, but if it's gone, don't worry. I'll get you another one. Rebecca, it's high time you learned that not everyone in this world is honest. Even your best friend is capable of stealing from you. Trust me. I know what I'm talking about. Why do you think I don't see Sara's mother anymore? I found out that she was dishonest, that's why." That people were dishonest was a lesson Rebecca needed to learn sooner or later, Nicole thought. In the following days, Rebecca went through her room, top to bottom, but she had no luck finding the bracelet. A few days later, Nicole handed Rebecca a small bag, and when she looked inside there was a brand-new silver bracelet just like the one that had gone missing. Rebecca would never have to know that it wasn't a new bracelet at all but the original one. Nicole had hidden the old bracelet in her own jewelry box until just the appropriate time. She believed that it was her responsibility to teach Rebecca about people's dishonest habits, and if taking the bracelet and casting a veil of suspicion on Sara was the only way to do it, then so be it.

After she had lived in town for almost ten years, Nicole congratulated herself for finally finding a place she could call home. She loved the idea of living in a town where everyone knew everyone else, but she also liked that she could spread her wings and live a little on the wild side in the anonymity of Chicago. While it was true that she hung around in the city's bars some nights during the week, most of the time she went home and ate supper while watching the news. Later, she would curl up on the couch with a good book before going to bed. When she first started staying in Chicago after work, she'd have a few cocktails and gossip with her co-workers before going home to feed Rebecca. Then as Rebecca grew older, Nicole decided she could fend for herself. The girl never gave her any trouble. She was an honor student, honest and polite. Much like her when she'd been a kid. Too bad her own mother hadn't appreciated her the way she appreciated Rebecca. Now that Rebecca had gone away to college, Nicole no longer had to concern herself with what time she came home, so she stayed in Chicago after work more often.

Wednesday, July 15, had been hot and humid and Nicole had stopped off at a hotel near her office after work to unwind with a few drinks before heading for home. She had struck up a conversation with a salesman from Boston, a guest at the hotel who was in Chicago on business. The man—she couldn't remember his name now—Gary? Gerry?—had plied her with multiple glasses of wine, and they'd laughed all the way to last call. Nicole had missed the last bus back to Willowdale, and he'd invited her to spend the night in his hotel room, but even though she was drunk she still had enough sense to know she had to get home. "Suit yourself," he'd said. "But you don't know what you're missing."

Nicole had hesitated. It had been a long time since she'd slept with a man. Not since Randall, a guy she'd met at her company's Christmas party two years ago. In some ways, she missed sleeping with a man, but her life was a busy whirlwind of work and play, and with Rebecca thrown into the mix, she had little time to think about much more than having an occasional fling. If she gave in to temptation tonight, she knew she'd be in no shape to go to work tomorrow. Besides, there was that customer service training her boss had signed her up for and it was scheduled for first thing in the morning. When she declined the man's invitation, he turned on his heel and left her standing alone on

Former Things

the dark street corner outside the hotel. *"Bitch,"* she heard him mutter as he walked away.

She knew the last bus to Willowdale had left more than an hour ago and the only way home would be by taxi. She walked toward the main drag, keeping her eyes open for a yellow cab. Fifteen minutes later, she spotted one coming toward her and waved down the driver. When he came to a stop, she leaned into the passenger side window.

"Where to?" asked the driver, a middle-aged bald man with a paunch that pushed against the steering wheel.

"Willowdale. 12 Garfield Street."

Nicole got inside the cab, suddenly dizzy and nauseous. Fighting the urge to vomit, she rested her head on the back of the seat and closed her eyes. The inside of the cab was quiet except for the crackle of the dispatch radio and the prattle of a late night talk show host chatting with a guest about the world economy and how the U.S. was headed for a fall just like the Roman Empire. The man's voice droned on and before long Nicole was nodding off. While she dozed, neither she nor the driver was aware that a tanker truck carrying nine thousand gallons of gasoline sped by on the highway toward Main Street in Willowdale where the manager of a gas station was waiting for a fuel delivery. The driver of the truck had no reason to believe that he would not meet his deadline. No, Jack McNulty was not worried at all.

When Nicole opened her eyes, she saw the familiar boutiques and restaurants along Main Street. There was LePetite Café where she bought bagels and muffins on weekends. Next came The Belle Shop. She enjoyed the store for its unique pocketbooks and shoes. And Common Scents where she liked to buy scented soaps. "Stop in front of that store," she told the driver. "I've changed my mind about going to Garfield Street. I'm going to walk the rest of the way home." She was still feeling the effects of the alcohol and walking home would help sober her up. What she needed was fresh air. Maybe she'd stop for a cup of black coffee at the cafe.

"Sixteen-fifty," he said, his voice flat.

"Here's a twenty. Keep the change."

Nicole stepped out of the cab and started walking along Main Street. When she turned the corner from Main Street onto Cedar, a red Mustang with its convertible top down screeched past with a bunch of teenagers hanging out the windows and hooting and hollering. *"Damn kids,"* she muttered. *"Gonna get themselves killed."*

Jack McNulty had been in a mood to celebrate that night. Earlier in the day, his union had negotiated a raise and additional health benefits for all the company's drivers. Even better, Jack's divorce from his ex-wife, Irene, would become final the next day. The judge had denied Irene alimony, and next week he'd make the final payment on his car loan. Life was looking up. Now he was free to ask Trish to marry him. He had an engagement ring in his pocket—a sweet little diamond solitaire he'd picked out himself at a pawn shop on his last trip to Elmwood Park. He knew she'd love it and couldn't wait to propose to her Saturday night when he took her to the Sunset Tavern for supper. He pulled from his jacket pocket the little black velvet box where the ring was hiding in secret and flipped the top open. Even in the dark cab the stone sparkled like a moonbeam. He wondered absently how the ring had ended up in the pawn shop. Probably some poor slob had bought the ring for his girlfriend only to be ditched by her later. As he was admiring the ring's beauty, he took his eyes off the road for a moment, and in that short span of time he didn't see the same red Mustang that only minutes before had sped past Nicole. The driver of the Mustang careened around the corner, not knowing that Jack's tanker truck was heading straight for him.

The crash caused Jack's truck to turn over onto its side, bursting the tank that held the gas. People living near the corner of

Former Things

Main and Cedar raced to their windows when they heard the ear-splitting sound of metal against metal and the screech of brakes. An ocean of fuel spilled into the street and ignited instantly when it poured into a manhole, causing a tremendous underground explosion. All five teenagers inside the Mustang were jettisoned into the air on impact, landing more than fifty feet away, while Jack remained trapped inside the truck's cab. Gas flooded the street and gushed down an incline into neighboring homes where it came in contact with a hot water heater and stove in a basement apartment. An old man two floors above was sitting in his favorite chair smoking a cigarette and watching the late news. When he heard the thunderous blast, he got out of his chair and went to the window. He looked out but didn't see anything out of order, then a second later he smelled a strong odor of gas. Alarmed, he moved toward his front door and that's when he saw tendrils of black smoke seeping through the jamb. He mistakenly opened the door, and a cloud of thick black smoke rushed at him. In a matter of seconds, the apartment was full of smoke, and he didn't know which way to turn. The old man finally made it to the window, but when he opened it the air fanned the flames in the hallway and in an instant the room turned into an inferno. Fire caught the hem of his pajamas, and in a panic he swatted it, but it spread up the back of his legs, searing his flesh while climbing up his torso. Screaming in agony, he hurled himself out the window, falling more than twenty feet to the pavement below. The man was later found burned over ninety percent of his body, and he was declared dead on arrival at the hospital.

Halfway down the block, a woman living in an apartment building had just gone to bed but got up and called the Fire Department when she smelled smoke. No sooner did she hang up the phone than her apartment building blew up. She was killed instantly and so were thirteen of her neighbors.

Around the corner on Burton Street three homes went up in flames. One of them was occupied by Iris and Sara. By the time they smelled smoke it was too late for them to get out alive.

Nicole, too, had smelled the gas, and a few moments after the crash she heard what sounded like ten thousand cannons

Gail Lowe

going off all at once. When she saw flames spreading to the little shops along Main Street she started running in the opposite direction, but in the dark she stepped off a curb and fell into the street, twisting her ankle and hitting her head hard on the pavement. The last thing she remembered seeing was a giant fireball rising in the night sky and then her world suddenly went black.

Emily and Nicole

CHAPTER ONE

When Emily and Evan left Kingston, it was raining so hard that Evan had to pull to the side of the road twice before continuing on. Not a good sign, thought Emily. But whether or not the sun was shining didn't really matter. There were few things in life that could be controlled, and the weather was one of them. By the time they arrived in Beverly an hour later, the rain had let up and the sun was breaking through the clouds.

They found the campground in Gloucester where they had reserved a space for the week, and while Evan was talking to the groundskeeper Emily called a car rental company to arrange for a small sedan. An hour later, an agent arrived with a small blue car and after taking him back to his office they drove to Beverly to start their search.

They stopped for dinner at a charming Italian restaurant on Cabot Street and Emily wondered if Nicole might have eaten there, though she knew that restaurants came in and out with the tide and it may not have even existed when Nicole lived there. Just in case, she brought one of the fliers into the restaurant with her. She showed it to the waitress when she brought menus to the table, and after taking it from Emily, she pulled a pair of glasses from her uniform pocket and put them on.

No, the waitress said, she'd never seen the woman in the flier before. She didn't even look familiar. "If I ever do run into her, I'll give you a call," she said, folding up the flier and sticking it inside her pocket along with her glasses.

✑❤

The following day Emily and Evan drove all over Beverly dropping off fliers at the library, police station, clothing bou-

Gail Lowe

tiques, restaurants, and marina. On Friday, they managed to squeeze in a ride to Rockport and stopped for lunch at the end of Bearskin Neck for a cup of seafood chowder. They lingered a while to watch the fishing boats sail by and gulls dive into the cold Atlantic in search of food. By Sunday, they were so tired they took the afternoon off and bought a pair of tickets to a live magic show at a theater in downtown Beverly.

When the show ended and Evan turned on his cell phone, there was one message waiting. A man named Chris had called to say he'd seen the flier with Nicole's picture and that he'd met her some years back—something about a Fourth of July party—but he hadn't seen her in about twenty years. He said he was visiting family in Beverly and lived in Hawaii now and would be flying back home tomorrow. A callback number didn't appear on the caller ID, so they had no idea who Chris was or how to reach him. They waited a few days to see if he'd call again, and they asked around if anyone might know who their mystery man was, but no one they spoke with could offer any information. The man named Chris didn't call again.

At least they knew now that Nicole had lived in Beverly, possibly right after leaving Rye. Evan was encouraged to think that the people search engine he'd used was more accurate than not, and he told Emily he believed they were on the right track.

CHAPTER TWO

On Monday morning, Emily and Evan sat down for a bowl of cereal, fresh strawberries, and coffee before they started out for Connecticut. On the way, they stopped in Hartford to tour the Mark Twain House. The guide took them through the property, a fascinating home made up of outside staircases and porches, indoor phone booth, fireplace mantle lined with figurines, and a billiards room on the top floor.

A few hours later they headed south and arrived in Sachem late in the afternoon. They parked in a Wal-Mart lot and for supper they cooked hamburgers on top of a small grill. Emily bought potato salad at a small grocery store and sliced some fresh tomatoes and cucumbers they bought at a farm stand. It was still light enough for a short bike ride, and they were grateful that Cal Anderson had provided a pair of Treks with the RV rental. Around eight o'clock, they settled in for the night and watched *Cast Away* with Tom Hanks on the DVD player.

Tuesday was another idyllic June day, and Emily wished they could spend more time outdoors bike riding. She mentioned it to Evan.

"Why not bike ride over to the casino instead of renting a car then?" he said. "It's only a few miles away."

Soon, they were riding along the pastoral country roads hugging the rolling hills, meadows laced with a bounty of yellow wildflowers, and streams running alongside the road.

They planned to go to the casino to see if anyone in the human resources office recognized Nicole. Emily knew that she might have left long ago—if, in fact, Nicole had even lived in

Sachem, but someone might have information that would lead them to her.

The casino was a flurry of activity with people crowding in at the gaming tables, slot machines, and bingo games. Bells rang, signaling lucky wins, and waitresses in skimpy outfits carried trays of cocktails and bottles of beer, serving them to thirsty customers.

The atmosphere crackled with excitement, and Emily and Evan had to shove their way through the crowd. They were jostled by patrons as they moved through the rooms until they spotted a security guard who stood at one of the casino's doorways. Evan asked him for directions to the human resources office. "Up that set of stairs. First set of doors on your right," the guard said, pointing the way.

Emily and Evan climbed the stairs and came to a set of locked double doors leading to a suite of offices. Evan pressed a doorbell on the wall to the left of the doors and waited. A woman wearing tortoiseshell glasses seated at a desk in front of a computer saw them standing in the doorway and buzzed them in.

"Can I help you?" the woman asked, moving her stack of paperwork to one side.

"Is the HR manager in?" asked Emily.

"That would be June McShane. Do you have an appointment?"

When Emily said they didn't, the woman said she would see if June was out of her meeting. She rose from her chair and went to one of the inner offices. A few minutes later, she reappeared and asked Emily and Evan to have a seat. "She'll be right out," she said before turning back to her paperwork.

June McShane appeared seconds later and invited them into her office. "What can I do for you?" she asked, once she was seated in her black leather office chair.

Emily took the flier from her purse and handed it to June. "This is my daughter, Nicole Preston. She's been missing for

Former Things

a long time, and I wonder if she may have worked here in the past."

"You know there are privacy laws forbidding us to divulge any information about our employees, past or present," June said, leaning back in the chair and crossing her arms.

"Yes, I do know that. I have no interest in breaching any confidentiality laws. I don't want to harm my daughter or anyone else," Emily said. Her hands felt clammy, and she suddenly wondered what had ever possessed her to look for Nicole, but it was too late now. "I just want to know that she's safe. And I'd like to see her again before . . . well, you know."

"You don't have to say anymore. I understand."

June took pity on Emily. Her own sister had not been in touch with the family for more than twelve years, and she knew the pain and suffering her sister's absence had caused her mother. She wondered what had happened between this mother and daughter but refrained from asking.

"I don't recognize her at all," said June, frowning as she studied Nicole's picture. "Wait here . . . I want to see if someone I work with knows her." She disappeared down a corridor and into another office and came back a few minutes later. "Rayelle—she's our marketing manager—remembers her. She said she left the casino about fifteen years ago. She'd have to look through our archived records for people who left around that time, but she's pretty sure she recognizes the picture. What's her name again?"

"Nicole Preston."

"I'll be right back." June went back to Rayelle's office again and returned minutes later.

"Rayelle confirmed that your daughter worked here at one time."

"Can we talk to Rayelle?"

"I'm afraid she wouldn't be able to say much more than that she knew your daughter. We're strict about giving out any information—even to members of the immediate family. All we can tell you is that she did work here many years ago. Even that

Gail Lowe

information is supposed to be confidential, but I trust you won't use it against us."

"Of course not. But you wouldn't consider bending the rules . . .?"

"I'm really sorry. I wish I could help, but there's nothing more I can do."

Emily thanked her and turned to Evan. "Well, at least we know she was here," she said. "We'll just have to keep looking."

After Emily and Evan left, June went to see Rayelle. "I hate to say it, but that woman would be a lot better off without her daughter. If she knew about the little stunt Nicole pulled when she worked for me, I think she'd be shocked," said Rayelle.

June nodded and said. "Maybe she would, and maybe she wouldn't. But I agree—she's better off without her."

CHAPTER THREE

On the way to New Jersey, Emily told Evan that even though they were still in the dark about Nicole's whereabouts she felt better knowing at least a little about her daughter's history, and she was confident that they were getting closer and closer to finding her.

Hoboken was almost impossible to explore because the city was so densely populated and there were few places to park the RV. Evan finally found a small supermarket and the manager gave him permission to park in the side lot while he and Emily made a whirlwind sweep of laundromats, women's clothing stores, coffee shops, restaurants, gas stations, library, small food markets, real estate offices and other places Emily thought Nicole might have been. They had no idea that Nicole had lived only a few months in Hoboken before moving to New York City to live with Danny. After a week of distributing fliers and talking to people who might have seen or known her, they took a few days off and rode the bus to New York City to visit the Guggenheim Museum, Rockefeller Center, and St. Patrick's Cathedral. On their final day in Hoboken, they boarded another bus to New York and wandered around Central Park, taking in the sights. Neither of them had a clue that they were walking the same route Nicole and Danny had walked with Rebecca and Michael.

CHAPTER FOUR

By the first week of July they were on the move again, this time passing through the state of Pennsylvania. On the way, they stopped long enough for shoo-fly pie in Pennsylvania Dutch country and took tours of cheese and pretzel factories. They also stopped in Gettysburg and took a bus tour of the battlegrounds and stood at the spot where Lincoln gave his address at the end of the Civil War.

Emily was grateful that the RV was air-conditioned as she maneuvered it along the highway. She popped a Willie Nelson CD into the player and sang along to *On The Road Again* while Evan sat next to her. He'd been right. The RV was almost as easy as driving a car—at least on a straight road. Over the Fourth of July weekend when they visited Gettysburg, the weather had been hot and humid. The temperatures climbed even higher when they left Pennsylvania and crossed the state line into Ohio. A few times they veered away from the highway, bypassing Akron and instead heading south toward Wooster in Amish country. They continued west, passing Columbus and Dayton, until they finally reached Indiana. Outside Indianapolis, they swung north on Route 89 toward Elkhart, just south of the Michigan border, and arrived in time for supper.

They were too late for the city's annual Rhapsody in Green festival and too early for the air show, but Emily and Evan found plenty to keep them busy while visiting the city. After passing out fliers at the usual locations, they spent afternoons on the city's riverwalk where children roller-bladed and bike riders whizzed by.

Former Things

For a week, they walked from one end of Elkhart to the other without even a tidbit of success until, on their last night, they had an early supper at Encore and sat on the deck overlooking the St. John River. Emily brought a flier with her and planned to show it to a man seated at the reception desk on the way out. The flier was lying face up on the table when their waitress stopped by to take their order for drinks. "It's a beautiful night to eat on the deck. What can I get for you?" she asked, smiling broadly. "I'm Jean, and I'll be your waitress tonight."

"Water for me. A Coke for the young man," said Emily. The waitress handed them menus and said she would be right back. Before leaving, she looked down at the table and saw the flier. Squinting at Nicole's picture, she said, "I know her. That's Nicole Preston. She used to work here." So, it was true. Nicole *had* lived in Elkhart.

"I'm her mother," Emily said, surprised to hear that the waitress had known Nicole. "She's been missing for a long time, and I'm trying to find her. Do you know where she is?"

"Actually, no. I haven't seen her in quite a few years. You might want to talk to Tom Doyle. He's our manager."

Emily thanked her and asked where she could find Tom. "On the way out. He's usually at the reception desk."

They ordered steak tips and salad and after Emily paid the bill, they went to see if they could find Tom Doyle. "I think that must be him at the cash register," she whispered. Evan nodded, and they approached him. "Are you Mr. Doyle?" Emily asked.

"Yes, I am. What can I do for you?"

When Emily explained why she and Evan were looking for Nicole, Tom Doyle stood there shaking his head. "She was one of my best waitresses," he said. "Regulars asked for the tables in her area all the time. They liked her that much. Then one day she didn't come to work. I was worried about her when she didn't show up for two or three days. I knew she lived out at Maddie Hathaway's place and went out there to see if something had happened to her. That's when I found out why she left." He looked at Emily and wondered if he should continue.

"Go on," she said.

Gail Lowe

"Well, I'm not sure you want to hear the rest of the story."

"I do. What happened?"

"Well, to begin with, Maddie Hathaway owned an RV park with her husband before they closed up shop and moved back to Alabama. Nicole rented one of their RVs. To hear Maddie tell it, Nicole took up with a married man who also lived in the park, and when his wife found out about it there was a big stink. Nicole didn't stick around after that. One day she just didn't come to work and that was that. Except . . . "

"Except . . .?"

"Well, I did get a call from someone in Chicago not long after Nicole left. It was a woman, and she was looking for a reference. I'm sorry, but I don't remember the name of the company. I don't know if Nicole ever got the job."

"It's okay. At least we know we're on the right track." The story he had told about Nicole troubled Emily, and she wondered what her daughter had been thinking when she took up with a married man. She had raised her daughter to be an honest person, not someone who would break up a family. She hoped Nicole had learned her lesson.

Tom Doyle called Jean over and asked her about Nicole. "She was a good person. Fun. Lighthearted. And a hard worker," she said. "That's really all I knew about Nicole. She never talked much about herself, and we never really became friends outside of work."

Emily and Nicole looked at each other, thanked Tom Doyle and Jean, and went on their way.

CHAPTER FIVE

The next morning they were on the road again, this time bound for Willowdale.

They arrived around noontime and set up the RV in a campground a half-mile from the downtown. Before settling in, they'd taken a drive around and found that Willowdale was a small, well-planned community. Emily was happy about that. Surely in a compact town like this one everyone knew everyone else, and that would make their search much easier. If they failed to find Nicole here, they'd have to give up hope of ever finding her. The Internet people search site had stopped at Willowdale, and there were simply no other options left.

Back at the campground, Emily and Evan ate an early supper and watched another Tom Hanks' movie, this time *Saving Private Ryan*. Emily cried at the end. After the credits they called it a night.

At twenty minutes past midnight, the sound of an explosion woke them out of a sound sleep. A moment later, the first of three thundering booms sounded.

Evan jumped to the floor from his bed above the cab, ran to the window, and pulled up the shade. Gazing out into the dark night, he saw the black sky lit up in flames. Emily rushed to his side and stood behind him, clutching his shoulders in fear. "What is it?" she said. "A bomb?"

"I don't know. Something horrible. I've never seen anything like it."

"God help us," she whispered.

Gail Lowe

They stood transfixed while watching the giant blaze rise higher and higher in the sky. Another explosion followed, then another. So entranced were they by what they were witnessing that they didn't notice the interior lights going on in their neighbors' RVs. A few minutes later, a cluster of people stood in a wide circle on the campground whispering in the dark.

"Could have been a chemical explosion of some kind out on the highway," said one man wearing only his pajama bottoms.

"Or natural gas," said another.

One man went back inside his RV to grab an emergency radio. His wife was on his heels to get her bathrobe. He came back outside, police radio in hand, and fumbled with the dial. High-pitched squeals sliced through the dark until he found a local station.

" . . . emergency . . . Main Street . . . first responders," they heard the dispatcher say between radio static. "Firefighters . . . multiple victims . . . transported to hospitals . . ." Emily and Evan continued to listen. " . . . Red Cross . . . triage support . . ."

The signal was cut then, and the dispatcher's voice was replaced with even more static and high-pitched squeals.

"Hundreds of people could be dead," said Emily, her hand over her mouth. "How awful."

Another explosion sent the conflagration skyward again, and this time they could feel the ground rumble underneath them. Emily heard someone standing nearby whisper, "A terrorist attack."

She turned to Evan. "Could it be?"

"I hope not, but anything's possible."

"What should we do?"

"What do you mean? There's nothing we *can* do."

"We have to do something, Evan," said Emily, recalling the years she'd spent in the emergency room at Portsmouth Regional. She knew that the hospital staff would need every volunteer they could get.

She recalled, too, the countless nights she'd worked alongside Martin Jackson when they were treating trauma victims—

Former Things

people who had suffered burns in fires and were thrown from cars after an accident, the overweight men who suffered heart attacks, the pregnant women who'd had no time to get to the maternity ward. They'd never had to treat people who were injured as a result of a disaster, but many times they were called to work in the wee hours of the morning to save the lives of victims who'd been involved in other kinds of traumatic events. She'd never forgotten the sense of urgency during an emergency. The teamwork and cooperation among the medical staff were almost beyond human comprehension. Everyone had known what their roles were, and they all worked as fast as they could. Time, they had known, was the most crucial factor in any life or death situation.

"I need to help out," Emily whispered, more to herself than Evan.

Evan wasn't sure he heard her right. "You what . . .?"

"I need to help the injured. I'm not licensed to practice nursing in Illinois, but I think they'll welcome me anyway. There's the Good Samaritan law . . ."

"There's nothing you can do . . ."

"Yes, there is. I've never forgotten my nurse's training. I need to go, Evan. We have to find the hospital where they've taken people."

"Emily, please be reasonable. They probably don't even know what they need at this point. For all we know, there might not be any survivors."

"But there might be. And if there are, like I said, they'll need all the help they can get. I was a nurse long enough to know how these things work. Every disaster story is different in its own way, but the casualties are always the same. Evan, you've got to drive me there. I'll be needed."

Evan stared at the woman he had come to love like a grandmother. Leave it to her, he thought. Never once did she worry about her own safety. She was thinking about the well being of others. He admired her even more at that moment. "We need to find out what happened first," he said. "What if it *was* a terrorist

Gail Lowe

attack? The disaster site might be off limits to everyone. Police might not want vehicles in the vicinity, especially an RV. They'll need a lot of room for ambulances and fire engines. Let's see if a local station is broadcasting something about it. Come on." He pulled her toward the RV and left the other campers standing there, none of them knowing what to do next.

Inside the RV, Evan turned on the television and used the remote control to find a local station. Seconds later a woman appeared on the screen with a microphone in her hand. She was standing at the edge of the disaster scene, telling viewers that many people had been evacuated from their homes. Emily knew the newscaster was taking a tremendous risk standing so close to the ball of fire behind her, but she had no choice but to do her job. In another time and in another place, the newscaster could just as well have been Evan.

". . . we just received word that more than one hundred and twenty people have been taken to Willowdale General Hospital as a result of a serious accident involving a tanker truck carrying nine thousand gallons of gasoline. A fire has broken out, and it has already consumed a major portion of the downtown area," she said. "There's not enough medical personnel to treat all the victims, so about half are being transported to the high school gymnasium and surrounding towns are providing mutual aid. We'll have an update as soon as we can locate Chief of Police Burt Iverson. Stay tuned for more news . . . Maria Johnson, live from the scene."

"I need to go, Evan. You don't understand. Nursing—it's in my blood. I'm programmed to respond to emergencies." Her eyes were pleading, insistent.

"But we don't even know where the hospital is," Evan protested.

"We can find out. I need to help out any way I can, even if it's nothing more than holding the hand of someone who's been injured . . . or, God forbid, dying."

"Let's at least wait until morning. We'll have more news by then."

Former Things

She went to the window and looked at the people gathered outside. One by one they returned to their RVs to turn on their own television sets and radios for the latest updates. Evan clicked through station after station until he came to the local broadcast. This time a newscaster dressed in a yellow HazMat suit appeared on the screen.

"What we have here, folks, is the worst disaster to have ever struck this area," he said, repeating the same story. "For those of you who have just tuned in, a car filled with five teenagers collided with a tanker truck. The impact forced the truck onto its side, and the fuel has flooded the entire downtown area of Willowdale. That entire section went up in flames and has been flattened. Other nearby neighborhoods have been affected, as well. We don't know how many people have been killed at this time, but the number so far is well over one hundred. Victims are still being transported to Willowdale General. Most of the victims have severe injuries, but many are being pronounced dead on arrival. Eliot Manson, reporting live from the scene. We'll have more for you as word comes in."

Emily covered her face with her hands, and Evan put his arm around her shoulders to comfort her. "In the morning I'm going there. I have to do what I can to help."

"Then I'll go with you," Evan said, finally relenting.

"We'll both go."

They spent the remainder of the night in the living room of the RV, Evan sprawled on the couch, Emily stretched out in a chair. After a while, Emily heard Evan snoring softly, and she tried to sleep herself, but it would only come in fits and starts. All she could think about were the victims, the poor helpless people who desperately needed her. Around five in the morning, she finally fell into a restless slumber.

Around six o'clock, the sun was pouring through the window, waking Emily first, then Evan. She went to the window to see if anything had changed, and at first she wondered if perhaps

Gail Lowe

the previous night's events had been a horrible dream, but when Evan joined her they both saw flaky black soot floating in the air above the campground.

"What should we do?"

"Probably shower first, then hit the road. We can grab a cup of coffee and something to eat later."

"Then let's get going."

CHAPTER SIX

The emergency room at Willowdale General was a frenzied and chaotic scene with victims lying on gurneys, doctors and nurses running in all directions, and phone lines jammed with calls from people asking if their relatives and friends had been injured in the explosion or, worse, killed. Triage units from the Red Cross had been called in, and emergency medical personnel had converged on the town in the middle of the night to set up a clinic inside the high school's gymnasium. Cots, medical supplies, mobile communications units, and doctors, nurses and volunteers were on hand to do what they could to help the victims.

Screams, groans, and shouted orders came from every corner of the gymnasium. One man wheeled in on a gurney had had his eyes impaled with six-inch shards of glass. Another man was bleeding profusely after half his arm had been torn away from his body. A woman in her sixth month of pregnancy sobbed when she was told that the baby she had been planning to give birth to in October had no heartbeat. Homes had burned to the ground, and the entire south end of the town was ablaze. No one understood how any of the victims had managed to survive the disaster. In all the local newspapers the following day, photos and stories about the accident and resulting inferno dominated the front page.

Just before nine o'clock, Evan pulled the RV over to the side of the road when he spotted a police car near the hospital. He ran over to speak to an officer who was directing traffic at the clogged intersection.

"Excuse me, sir. I have a nurse with me who wants to volunteer her services. Where should she go? And where can I park this RV?"

"Back there, in that lot," he said, waving his hand in the direction of the hospital parking lot. "The guard there will show you where to park. As for the nurse, tell her to see Dr. Prince. He's head of the emergency room."

Evan went back inside and told Emily he'd meet her inside the hospital. She got out of the RV and went to the police officer who told her where she should go. While Evan was parking the RV, she went to the main desk inside the hospital and told the receptionist she was a registered nurse and wanted to see Dr. Prince.

The receptionist told Emily she would let Dr. Prince know she was on her way. "Go down that corridor, turn right, and take the elevator to the lower level. When you get off, take a left and you'll find the emergency room beyond a set of double doors," she said.

Evan caught up with her minutes later. "You can't stay here," a doctor told him. "Not unless you have medical training."

He thought quickly. "I'm a reporter," he said. "Working on a story." In his mind, what he had just said wasn't far from the truth. He *was* working on a story.

"I'm sorry, we're not allowing the press in here."

"Where can I wait then?"

"The cafeteria. Or somewhere outside. But not in here."

Evan went back to the RV. At least he'd have a television to watch as news of the disaster unfolded. He'd keep notes, maybe even start writing his story. He told Emily his plan, and they agreed to meet at twelve sharp for a lunch break in the hospital cafeteria.

Dr. Prince studied Emily's license. "I know I'm not licensed to practice in Illinois, but I had a feeling I'd be needed," she said. "There's the Good Samaritan law, and I thought . . ."

All around them were the pitiful cries of the victims, some barely clinging to life. Compassion for the wounded and dying filled her heart and mind, and she said a silent prayer for them all.

Former Things

"You're right. We desperately need your help, but you do realize the potential legal problems that could result."

"Yes, I'm well aware of the risks."

Dr. Prince knew that he was racing against the clock. For this one time, he decided to overlook the law and medical ethics. Lives were at stake.

"Patients in Suite B need their vitals taken. You can start there. Note your findings on their charts." He handed her a stethoscope and showed her where to find thermometers, blood pressure cuffs, and other medical supplies. "I won't be far away. If you need me, just holler. If I'm not around, ask someone to page me."

After listening to his instructions, Dr. Prince showed her where to find Suite B and she went to her first patient, a man of about forty. According to the notes in his chart, he'd lived in one of the homes that had been flattened and it was miraculous that he was even alive. Emily took his blood pressure and listened to his heart, all the while encouraging him to hold on to life. On the other side of the curtain separating his bed from the one next to it, she could hear a woman sobbing and crying out for someone named Mike. Odd, she thought, how people in despair all seemed to sound alike when they were in the depths of misery.

Satisfied that her patient was doing as well as could be expected, she moved to the next bed. What she saw lying before her nearly took her breath away. The explosion and fire had reduced the woman's face to what looked like melted wax. Mercifully, according to the woman's chart, she'd been given a heavy dose of morphine to ease the pain of her massive burns. She took the woman's vital signs, noted them in her chart and moved on to the next victim, also a woman.

The patient's face was turned away from Emily, and she was apparently having episodes of periodic breathing characteristic of impending death, according to Dr. Prince's notes. She willed the woman to live, taking her hand into her own, feeling her pulse at the wrist. She was someone's wife, mother, sister, and daughter, maybe all four. The flesh of the woman's hands was soft and yielding, the fingernails cut in perfect ovals

Gail Lowe

and polished in pale pink. There were no rings on her fingers, Emily noticed, perhaps having been removed by medical personnel and placed in the hospital's vault for safekeeping. She moved to the other side of the bed, careful not to disturb the IV drip line that was helping to keep the woman alive. She checked the heart monitor and found the rhythm satisfactory and stable before moving toward the woman's head to adjust the oxygen prongs in her nose. When Emily looked down, something inside her responded to the woman's face. A flicker of recognition. A knowing. She stood fixed to the spot when she realized that she was looking directly into the face of someone she had seen before, someone she knew. At first, she told herself that it couldn't be, that she was tired and her mind was playing tricks on her. Yet, on a second, much closer look she knew she was not mistaken. She picked up the woman's left hand and turned it over so the palm was exposed. In an instant she had her answer. There was the scar at the base of her thumb, the scar left on Nicole's hand after she had fallen from her toboggan and split it open so many years ago. Emily had stood the toboggan against a tree and left it there while she and Nicole ran across the snow-covered field, Nicole's blood dripping on the ground as they hurried along. Martin Jackson had been supervising the emergency room that day and stitched up her hand after numbing it with a local anesthetic. Nicole screamed while Martin patiently stitched her up and after the bandage was in place, he'd reached inside his pocket and pulled out a twenty-dollar bill. She remembered his words. *"You're a brave girl, Nicole. Much braver than I would have been. Ask your mother to take you to the store and buy yourself a reward."* After leaving the hospital, Emily and Nicole had gone to downtown Portsmouth where Nicole bought a magic kit. All winter she entertained herself and her friends with tricks she learned from the booklet inside the kit. Yes, these were Nicole's hands. She knew it to be true the way she knew Tuesday followed Monday. They were the hands Emily had held so many years ago when she and Nicole crossed a busy street together, the way mothers and their children do.

They were the hands that had played *Clare de Lune* on the old Steinway, the hands that had pulled the fake rabbit out of the hat, the hands that had broken her mother's crystal bowl and slammed the back door the day she stormed out of Emily's kitchen twenty years ago.

Dropping Nicole's hand, she gripped the side rail of the bed to keep from falling. She felt as if her head were spinning and thought she might faint. Shaking her head, she tried to clear her thoughts. For a long moment, she couldn't think what to do next. All the medical training in the world could not have prepared her for this. Never in her wildest dreams had she ever thought that her reunion with Nicole would be in the emergency room of a hospital. For the first time, she noticed the strands of silver in Nicole's dark hair, the web of lines radiating from corners of her eyes, the frown lines etched into her forehead. Nicole's face was fuller now and more mature, but it was her face without question. Twenty years had passed and Emily had not been able to watch her daughter progress from one decade to the next. So much time had been wasted, time she could never get back. The tears came now as she moved closer to Nicole.

"My poor Nicole . . ." she whispered, a sob catching in her throat. "Don't leave me now. Please . . . live." In an instant, the twenty years Emily and Nicole had been apart melted away like an April snowfall.

Numb, she moved away quickly from Suite B to find Dr. Prince. Maybe he could make arrangements to move Nicole to the intensive care unit. Or to another hospital. Anything to help Nicole survive. She had no idea about the depth of Nicole's injuries, only that Dr. Prince had noted in her chart: *Intracranial bleeding. Drug-induced coma.* A head injury. Emily knew all about them. She'd seen enough head trauma victims over the course of her career. The prognosis could go either way, depending on how long a victim remained comatose.

When she found her way back to the central area of the emergency room, a gray-haired, overweight nurse looked up

Gail Lowe

when Emily approached. "I need Dr. Prince," she said. "Can you page him?"

The nurse, disheveled and exhausted after hours on the job without a break, spoke in a sharper tone than she intended. "What's the problem?" she snapped.

"It's about one of the victims." Emily refrained from saying too much. She had no intention of telling her story to a complete stranger. "I need Dr. Prince to check on an intubation."

"Can't you do it yourself?"

"No. Dr. Prince told me to have him paged if I need him. And I need him right away. Please page him."

"Okay," the nurse said, sighing resignedly.

As soon as he heard his name paged over the public address system, Dr. Prince appeared almost instantly from around the corner. "What's going on?" he asked the charge nurse.

"She asked me to page you." The nurse pointed to Emily.

"Dr. Prince, I can explain if you'll follow me."

Together, they walked back to the suite where Nicole lay in her bed. "Unbelievable as it sounds, one of the patients you assigned me is my daughter. I can't take time to explain this, but I'm desperate to get her into the ICU or a hospital that's equipped to handle her injuries."

"Where is she?"

"Third bed down."

Emily took Dr. Prince to Nicole and he checked her chart. "Yes, she was one of the first victims to arrive. You say she's your daughter?"

"Yes. Nicole Preston. It's a very long story, and some day maybe I'll tell you about it, but right now she needs the best medical care available."

"She has a head injury. There's bleeding inside her skull," he said. "I'll see what I can do about getting her airlifted to Stroger in Chicago. They have an excellent trauma center."

"Thank you, Dr. Prince. You have no idea what this means to me. I'll do what I can to help the other patients until she's transferred."

Former Things

"Just give me a few minutes. I need to write the orders and see that calls are made."

He left then and went to the nurses' station and asked the supervisor to arrange for Nicole's MedFlight. Less than an hour later, she was on her way to Chicago in a helicopter with Emily at her side. She'd had to call Evan to tell him what had happened, and when he heard the news, he could hardly believe his ears. "Nicole was among the victims? You can't be serious."

"I've never been more serious in my life, Evan. I've got to do what I can to keep her alive. Meet me at Stroger Hospital. It's somewhere in Chicago. You'll have to find out the street address."

CHAPTER SEVEN

The helicopter landed on the rooftop of the John H. Stroger Jr. Hospital fifteen minutes later, and they were met by a team of doctors who whisked Nicole away to the intensive care unit. Minutes later, Emily stood next to her bed, holding her hand. "Nicole," she whispered again and again.

Nicole's eyelids fluttered and she opened her eyes only once before closing them again. Emily stayed with her until Evan arrived, and he urged her to go with him to the hospital cafeteria. He wanted to hear the details of how Emily had found Nicole and to learn about her prognosis.

Over a cup of coffee Emily told Evan how she'd taken the vital signs of two patients before coming upon Nicole. "She was lying with her face away from me, so I didn't know at first who she was. When I got to the other side of her bed and looked down, it began to dawn on me that I was looking into the face of my own daughter. And when I turned her left hand over and saw a scar near the base of her thumb . . . well, I knew it was Nicole for certain. Mothers never forget details about their children—I knew then it was Nicole even after all these years. I remember everything that happened the day she got that scar."

Evan sat across from Emily, dumbstruck. They'd been on the road for seven weeks and it had taken a disaster to bring Emily face to face with her daughter—in a hospital emergency room, no less. When he first suggested they take the trip, Evan had no idea what the outcome would be, nor did he know the high drama that would be awaiting them. The story he wanted to write was beginning to take shape in his mind, and he couldn't wait to begin.

"What are you going to do now?" he asked.

Former Things

"Go back to Nicole. Spend the night in her room if I have to. I want to be there in case she wakes up. Where did your park the RV?"

"I explained what happened to the security guard downstairs. He's letting me stay in the back lot temporarily, but I have to move before seven tomorrow morning when the hospital shift changes."

"Well, then, go ahead. We can keep in touch by cell phone. You don't mind, do you?"

"No, of course not. I'm going to find a place to settle for the night and think about how I want to write my paper."

They walked back to the intensive care unit then and Evan left Emily where he'd found her. A nurse was adjusting Nicole's IV drip, and she was mumbling in her sleep and thrashing about in the bed. A mesh tent surrounded the bed to keep her from falling out. In an instant, Emily was at her side again.

"Are you a relative?" the nurse asked.

"Her mother."

"She's scheduled for an MRI."

"When?"

"As soon as we can get her transported."

"Can I go with her?"

"I don't see why not."

The nurse eyed Emily and wondered if she knew how serious her daughter's injuries were. According to the chart, the pressure inside her skull had increased since she'd arrived, a definite indication that she'd entered even more dangerous territory. The nurse wasn't about to say anything, though. That was the doctor's job.

CHAPTER EIGHT

Dr. Richard Meisner, a short man with gray hair and blue eyes and considered the leading neurosurgeon in the Chicago area, approached Emily to talk about Nicole and the treatment necessary to keep her alive.

"I can't make any promises, Mrs. Preston. Nicole has a subdural hematoma, as you know. That puts her at great risk, but if we don't get her into surgery, we'll most assuredly lose her."

She considered what he had just told her, then turned and looked directly into his eyes. "Do you know Dr. Martin Jackson?"

"Yes. He's semi-retired. Why do you ask? Do you know him?"

"I worked with him a long time ago in New Hampshire. I heard through the grapevine that he might have moved to the Chicago area. I wondered if you knew him."

"I've worked with him on dozens of cases."

"Then let's call him in for a consultation."

"I'm not sure if he's in the area right now. He has a home in Florida and spends a lot of his time there."

That came as a surprise to Emily. She wondered if he was still married to Melinda. "We can try, can't we?"

The doctor could see that Emily was dead serious about her intent. "All right," he said, "I'll give him a call."

Emily left the room and sat in a chair near the nurses' station. Then she lowered her head and prayed. While she was sitting there, she didn't notice the young woman who had come through the double doors of the intensive care unit. About twenty years old, she had long brown hair parted in the middle and was wearing a pair of jeans and a dark green sweatshirt that

226

Former Things

said Columbia College across the front. Emily also didn't notice the young woman approach the nurses' station just a few feet away from where she sat.

"I'm Rebecca Preston. I think my mother might be here," she said to a nurse.

Rebecca Preston? The name cut into Emily's consciousness like an ice pick. She glanced in the direction of the nurses' station and saw the young woman standing there.

"What's your mother's name?" the nurse asked.

"Nicole Preston. She was injured in the Willowdale fire. I was told she was brought to this hospital."

Emily waited and listened, a million thoughts racing through her mind, each one colliding with the other. Her emotions were as confused as a jumble of jigsaw puzzle pieces scattered across a table. She watched the young woman, studied her from top to bottom. Nicole's daughter. Her granddaughter.

Emily stood up and took a few tentative steps toward Rebecca. "Excuse me," she said. "Did I hear you say you were Nicole Preston's daughter?"

The young woman faced Emily, and for a moment Emily thought she was speaking to Nicole, the resemblance between mother and daughter was so great. "Yes, I'm her daughter. Do you know her?"

"Yes, I do." Emily couldn't just spring it on the girl that she was Nicole's mother and her grandmother so she suggested finding a quiet place to talk.

"What for? Do you know my mother? She's all right, isn't she? She's not . . ."

"The doctors don't know yet. She has a serious head injury and needs surgery. Come with me so I can tell you about it."

"But . . ."

"Please . . . come with me."

Rebecca stood there wondering who the stranger was and why she was so insistent about talking to her in private. She knew all of her mother's friends, or at least she thought she did, and her mother had no living relatives, at least that she knew about. She detected a New England accent in the woman's voice

Gail Lowe

and found herself letting Emily take the lead. When she took her arm and guided her out of the intensive care unit, Rebecca did not resist. And when they were seated in the softly lit, vacant waiting room, Rebecca spoke first.

"Who are you? A friend of my mother's?"

"You might say that."

"Well, then, what's your name?"

Emily bit her lip and took a deep breath before answering. "Emily Preston."

"Preston? You have the same last name as us."

"That's right, Rebecca. I am your grandmother. Your mother's mother."

In an instant Rebecca was on her feet. "My grandmother? That's impossible! My grandmother is dead."

"Dead? I don't think so. As you can see, I'm very much alive."

"But my mother told me her mother had died. I don't understand. I don't believe you. Why are you lying to me at a time like this?" Her eyes filled with tears and Emily thought she might start crying, too.

"Rebecca, I'm not lying to you. Your mother and I . . . we . . . please bear with me . . . this is not going to be easy for either of us. The truth is, your mother and I haven't seen each other for twenty years."

Rebecca swallowed hard and shook her head, not knowing what to say. Her mother was in need of surgery, and this stranger was sitting there telling her lies.

"Why haven't you seen each other for twenty years? And why did my mother tell me you were dead? There must be some mistake," she said, trying to grasp what Emily was telling her.

"Like I said, this is not easy. Your mother and I had a falling out—she thought I was being unfair to her, you see—I never meant to harm her or cause her pain, and when I tried to make things right between us, she had already left town. She just packed up her apartment one day, took what she could, and left the rest behind. I tried to find her, but she was good at covering her tracks. Twenty years went by with no word from her. I tried

Former Things

everything I could to find her. I asked for help from the police and hired a private investigator, but I couldn't find your mother. Then I met a young man a few months ago—a college student—who offered to help me find her."

Emily then told Rebecca about learning that Willowdale was one of the places where Nicole had lived and that she and Evan had taken a gamble that she might still be there. "Before we had a chance to ask people if they knew your mother, the accident and fire happened. I'm a registered nurse and wanted to help. When I went to the hospital in Willowdale, I was taken to the emergency room so I could help some of the victims, and miraculously one of them happened to be your mother."

Rebecca stared at Emily, wanting to believe her but finding her story too preposterous to be true. "Prove to me you're my grandmother."

"How do you want me to prove it? I can show you my driver's license. My name is on it."

Rebecca leaned over in her chair, and held her head in the cup of her hands. She thought for a long moment before responding. "My mother told me one time that she had a sister who died. If you're my grandmother, you'll know her name." So, Nicole had known about Becky after all. Emily recalled the dream she'd had so many years ago when Nicole confronted her about Becky. Maybe it had been a premonition of what was to come.

Emily hesitated before answering. She looked at Rebecca and wondered what else Nicole had told her. Then she got up from her chair and looked directly into Rebecca's eyes. "Her name was Rebecca, just like yours. I called her Becky."

Rebecca was on her feet in an instant. "How can this be?" she cried. "Then you are my grandmother. Why didn't my mother tell me? Why did she say you were dead?" Rebecca was crying now, and a lump had formed in Emily's throat, so sorry was she for Rebecca, for Nicole, for all three of them.

"I'm sure she did what she thought was best at the time. I have no other answer than that. Come with me now and let's go see how your mother is doing."

Gail Lowe

Rebecca wiped her eyes, and they returned to the intensive care unit where they saw a group of doctors huddled around Nicole's bed. They appeared to be in serious discussion, and one of them was nodding in response to what another doctor was saying. The man looked familiar to Emily. She recognized the broad shoulders and hair that had turned from sandy blond to silver. Martin Jackson. He had come after all.

Emily felt her heart do a somersault as she approached Nicole's bed. Martin turned to her and held her gaze. "You came," she said.

He went to her then and pulled her aside. "Emily, I can't believe it—it's so good to see you, but certainly not under these circumstances. I'm so sorry. Nicole needs surgery and she needs it now," he said. "It can't wait."

Rebecca, hearing this, spoke up. "Do whatever is necessary to keep my mother alive."

Martin looked from Emily to Rebecca, then back to Emily again. "Your granddaughter?"

"Yes, I'll explain later. Will you be part of the surgical team?"

"If you want me to be, yes."

"Of course. It's why I asked Dr. Meisner to call you in."

"There are papers to sign. Does Nicole have a health care proxy?"

They looked at Rebecca for an answer. "No. I mean I don't know."

"As her daughter, you can sign for her."

"Whatever I have to do . . ."

CHAPTER NINE

While Rebecca was signing permission forms, Emily and Martin talked. "I only ask one thing, Martin."

"What's that?"

"Nicole must not know that you were part of the surgical team."

"Why not?"

"Because I haven't seen Nicole in twenty years. She'll probably remember you from the time she had to have stitches for the cut on her hand. I need to take things slow with her as we re-establish our relationship."

"What do you mean you haven't seen Nicole for twenty years? Why on earth not?"

"I can't go into details right now, but I promise to tell you later. Right now, it's not important. What is important is Nicole's recovery."

"I understand. I promise that once the surgery is over, I'll relinquish all her medical care to Dr. Meisner."

"Thank you, Martin. You have no idea how I appreciate your help, how much this means to me."

They joined Rebecca at the nurses' station, and once her signature was on the last form Nicole was moved from the intensive care unit to a surgical suite two floors above while Martin went into surgery to scrub. Emily and Rebecca returned to the waiting room and sat down, each of them lost in their own thoughts. The minutes crawled by, but they felt more like hours.

"Do you live in Willowdale?" Emily asked after a long silence.

Gail Lowe

"My mother lives there. I only come home for semester breaks and the summer months. Otherwise, I live in a dorm at Columbia College."

"Where were you when the accident and fire happened?"

"At school. When I heard about it on the news, I went home and found our house had gone up in flames. The police told me the victims had been taken to Willowdale General. Only when I got there, I found out that my mother had been transferred here."

"I see."

"What about you? Where do you live?"

"In New Hampshire. But I arrived here in an RV," Emily explained. "The young man I told you about . . . he's traveling with me. Why don't you come with me? We can rest in the RV while your mother is in surgery, maybe have something to eat. You can meet Evan."

Rebecca hadn't noticed she was hungry until Emily mentioned it. "Come on. It's not far . . . right here in the parking lot. There's plenty of room in the RV."

An RV? That should be a trip down memory lane, Rebecca thought, recalling the RV she'd lived in when she and her mother were in Elkhart.

On the way to the parking lot, Emily asked Rebecca about her school and what she was studying. She wanted to ask about Rebecca's father, too, but that would have to wait. She knew enough not to overwhelm her with a lot of questions. Rebecca would need to adjust to the idea that she had a grandmother, and she, too, would have to adjust to the idea that she had a granddaughter. Emily wondered what other lies Nicole had told Rebecca. And why had she told the girl that she was dead in the first place. How could she have kept Rebecca from her all these years? She'd cheated her daughter out of a grandmother who could have offered her love and support. Emily had never been able to understand Nicole, and even less so now.

When Nicole awoke from her surgery, she hoped to have some answers to her questions. Most of all she hoped Nicole would recognize Rebecca. Head injuries, Emily knew, could severely damage memory, depending on the area of the brain affected and the extent of the injury. She contemplated how she would approach Nicole and what she would say to her when she did wake up.

When Emily and Rebecca got to the parking lot, Emily saw that Evan had parked the RV in the back. "Over there," Emily said, pointing to the rear corner of the lot.

She gave a quick knock to let Evan know that she was back. After unlocking the door and stepping inside, she saw that he was sprawled across the couch, sound asleep. Standing over him, she reached out and gently shook his shoulder. He opened his eyes and glanced up at Emily, not knowing she had someone with her. "How's Nicole?" he asked, awake now.

"On her way to surgery. Evan, I have someone with me."

He asked Emily what she was talking about. "Who do you have with you?"

Emily moved aside and Rebecca stepped forward. "I'd like you to meet Rebecca. My granddaughter."

Evan looked from Emily to Rebecca, not knowing what to think or say. "Wow . . . your granddaughter? Nice to meet you, Rebecca." Something inside Evan stirred at the sight of Emily's granddaughter. She had pretty dark hair that hung to her shoulders, and he could see that under her sweatshirt and jeans she was in possession of a petite, shapely figure. He had a vague feeling that he had seen her somewhere before, then realized she was a much younger version of her mother and grandmother. Emily explained that she'd heard Rebecca ask about Nicole at the nurses' station and had put two and two together, finally concluding that Rebecca was Nicole's daughter.

"I had no idea I even had a grandmother," said Rebecca.

Emily and Rebecca sat near Evan. No one spoke for a while, each of them mulling over the circumstances that had brought them all together. Emily was both elated and angry over the fact that she had a granddaughter she'd known nothing about. Rebecca, too, was angry and disappointed that her mother had lied to her. Evan could only shake his head in wonder over the measures people took to hide the past and their secrets.

Gail Lowe

"I worked with one of the doctors who'll be operating on Nicole," said Emily finally.

"Who's that?" Evan asked.

"Martin Jackson."

"The one who taught you how to play chess?"

"Yes. I'd heard that he'd relocated to the Chicago area. Dr. Meisner took a gamble that he was in town and called him in for a consultation. He's with Nicole right now. I would trust him with my life."

They were quiet again for a time before anyone spoke. "How long do you think it'll be?" Rebecca asked.

"Any kind of neurosurgery is a delicate procedure under the best of circumstances," said Emily. "We won't be hearing anything until late afternoon. That's my guess. Are you hungry?"

"I hadn't thought about it, but yes," said Rebecca.

"Why don't we find some place to have lunch then."

CHAPTER TEN

The day was warm with a soft wind blowing off Lake Michigan, and Emily needed some fresh air. "Let's take a walk and see what we can find," she suggested. While they walked along the street in front of the hospital, she heard Evan asking Rebecca about her college and what she planned to do after graduation.

As they walked past apartment buildings and construction sites on West Harrington Street, Emily's mind was a jumble of confusion. Three months ago when Evan suggested renting an RV and going on the road to find Nicole she'd never once imagined that it would end like this. Yet, in the span of twenty-four hours she'd not only found Nicole but Rebecca, too. She thought about the events of the past twenty years. Somewhere along the way, Nicole had met a man and had given birth to his child. And Emily had known nothing about it. She now realized that she had missed out on so much and so had Nicole and Rebecca. There were so many questions she wanted to ask her granddaughter, but this was not the time or place. There would be plenty of time for them to get to know one another later—if Rebecca was willing. For her entire life she'd lived without having a grandmother, at least on Nicole's side of the family. What if she had no interest in pursuing a relationship with her? Anything was possible.

At the end of the block they turned onto West Taylor Street and stopped to read a menu taped to the window of Hawkeye's Bar & Grill. The place was nearly empty when they went inside, and they chose a table near the window. It occurred to Emily suddenly that the last time Nicole had been in a medical setting the reason had been very different. She shuddered at the memory of the abortion clinic now and pushed all thoughts of it aside. Some things were better left in the attic of one's memory, and that experience was one of them.

After placing an order for sandwiches, Emily listened while Rebecca and Evan continued their discussion about college and other subjects of mutual interest. While they talked, Emily learned that Rebecca was twenty-one years old and would graduate from Columbia the following May. Like Evan, she'd worked her way through school and hoped one day to own a business. Just like her grandfather, Emily thought. Already she had a job waiting for her at a marketing company in Chicago where she had interned during her junior year. While working, she said she planned to get her master's degree from Northwestern University. Soon it was well after two o'clock, and after paying the bill, Emily asked Evan to check his cell phone to make sure the power was turned on. She didn't want to miss any calls that might come in from the hospital.

Under different circumstances, Emily would have suggested going to a museum or getting tickets to a play, but she could think of nothing but Nicole's surgery. They walked back to the RV in silence and checked at the hospital's main desk to see if there was any word about her condition. Still in the operating room, they were told. Emily looked at her watch. Three-fifteen. Nicole had been in surgery for five hours already, and they probably wouldn't hear anything more until five o'clock or later. Emily decided to get some rest and suggested that Rebecca and Evan explore Chicago. After reassuring them she would be fine by herself, they set out on a walk that took them through the theater district where colorful blinking marquees advertised the latest Broadway musicals.

Rebecca and Evan stopped at a bookstore and while they were browsing the shelves, Rebecca used the rest room. When she returned, Evan was standing in line waiting to pay for the day's edition of the *Chicago Tribune*. "There's a story on page

Former Things

one about the Willowdale disaster," he said. "I figured you'd want to read it. Emily, too."

"What does it say?"

"I didn't read the whole story yet, but I do know that more than two hundred people were killed. And twice that many injured." Rebecca looked over Evan's shoulder and read:

WILLOWDALE, Ill. – More than 200 people are confirmed dead and twice as many were injured after a tanker truck carrying 9,000 gallons of gasoline collided with a sports car operated by an 18-year-old youth while he was allegedly speeding at the intersection of Main and Cedar streets, said police. The impact of the two vehicles resulted in a fuel spill that minutes later exploded into an inferno.

According to an early report from Fire Chief Michael Harrison, the impact tore into the side of the truck and seconds later a river of gasoline rushed into downtown streets and basements of homes in the vicinity of Main Street, igniting a hot water heater in one and a stove in another. Both homes were reduced to rubble while flames shot into the sky more than one hundred feet in some areas. Several other explosions flattened an entire neighborhood close to the downtown. Firefighters from surrounding towns have been on the scene since the explosion occurred shortly after midnight Monday . . .

"Oh, no . . . people I probably know were killed. I hope Sara is all right."

"Sara?"

"Someone I used to be friends with."

"Unfortunately, you could be right about knowing people who've died. We have to hope for the best. Did your mother live with anyone?"

"No, she lived alone. She didn't even have a pet."

"Well, that's one good thing. I just hope she makes it through surgery all right."

Gail Lowe

Rebecca turned to face Evan, her expression curious. "How do you know my grandmother?"

"I work at the place where your grandmother lives. Emerald House. It's in New Hampshire. A beautiful place on Great Bay. She taught me how to play chess and we became friends. When I found out she hadn't seen your mother in twenty years, I suggested we rent an RV and go on the road to find her. I figured it would be an interesting subject to write about for my term paper. Emily had an idea that she might have a granddaughter, but she wasn't sure. When we found your mother's name on one of the people search websites, she wondered who Rebecca Preston was. Your name was listed under your mother's, so she figured she might have a granddaughter and she was right."

"My mother must have had a good reason for not telling me about my grandmother."

"I suppose. People have their reasons." He stopped short of asking what Rebecca thought about her mother lying to her. She had enough to deal with right now. Soon enough, she'd have to come to terms with what her mother had done.

As if to read his mind, Rebecca said, "My mother lied to me, though. Why couldn't she have told me the truth?"

"I think that's something you'll have to ask her. It's four-thirty. Do you think we should go back now?" he asked, changing the subject.

"Probably. My grandmother—it feels so weird calling her that—she's probably wondering where we are."

They walked in silence, neither of them knowing what to say next. When they got to the RV, they saw Emily in the window watching for them. She gave them a wave and smiled.

Evan's cell phone rang just as he stepped through the door, and he grabbed it from the clip on his belt. The caller ID showed that the call was from the hospital. Hitting the receive button, he answered and heard a man's voice ask for Emily. Crossing his fingers, he handed her the phone.

"Yes, this is Emily Preston," she said, then listened. "I see. We'll be there in a few minutes."

After she hung up, she turned to Evan and Rebecca. "Nicole is out of surgery and in the recovery room. We can see her tomorrow morning, but the doctors want to talk to Rebecca and me now."

"Is she going to be okay?" asked Rebecca.

"I don't know. They didn't say. Only that they wanted to talk to us."

"Would you like me to come with you?" Evan asked.

"It's not necessary. It's probably best that you wait here."

Emily and Rebecca walked across the parking lot and past the security guard at the gatehouse. He waved them on after having been told that they were family members of a patient who had been injured in the Willowdale disaster. They went inside the building and headed toward the elevators to the third floor where they found Martin Jackson and the other doctors waiting. Martin took Emily by the hand and led her and the others into a conference room down the hall.

"I will not sugar coat our findings, Emily. Nicole is gravely ill, but the good news is that she opened her eyes in the recovery room and spoke for the first time since she was brought here. That's nothing short of miraculous," Martin said.

He then drew a diagram on a piece of paper showing the extent of her injuries and what was done while Nicole was in surgery. "We had to relieve pressure that was building in her brain," he said. "We got to her just in the nick of time."

Emily and Rebecca breathed a sigh of relief. "Martin, Rebecca is my granddaughter. I never knew about her until Nicole was brought here from Willowdale," she said.

"I figured that. The resemblance between you and your mother is remarkable," he told Rebecca.

Emily then told Martin a short version of how Nicole had left twenty years before without going into detail. Telling him the entire story could wait until later when they were alone. She was hoping now for reconciliation with Nicole but that remained

Gail Lowe

to be seen. At this point, she decided she'd settle for some kind of relationship with Rebecca, but even that might turn out to be wishful thinking.

"What did you want to talk to us about?" Rebecca asked.

"Right now Nicole's chances for a complete recovery are fifty-fifty," Martin said, "but we could run into problems, too. She's not out of the woods yet. What we need to talk about is a delicate but practical matter. Someone has to decide whether to order DNR if her current condition slips. Let me rephrase that. One of *you* needs to decide what to do."

Rebecca spoke up first. "I know my mother wouldn't want to be on life support," she said. "One time we were talking about Christopher Reeve, and the subject came up. She felt so bad for him, and she said she would never in a million years want to live as a vegetable. She said she'd rather die."

"Emily? Would you agree?"

"I haven't seen Nicole to talk to in many years, but my guess is that she wouldn't want to be on life support. I have to agree with Rebecca."

"We need one of you to be her health care proxy. Which one of you will take the responsibility?"

Emily looked at Rebecca. "I will," said Rebecca.

"And now we come to the matter of finances. It's our understanding that Nicole lacks health insurance. Is that correct?"

"She doesn't have health insurance," said Rebecca. "She just started a new job and her health insurance wasn't going to start for another two months."

Martin looked from Emily to Rebecca. "The hospital has a medical emergency fund we can tap, but it won't cover all the expenses."

Emily was silent for a moment. Rebecca certainly couldn't be expected to pick up the costs, and as far as Emily knew Nicole had no husband. "I'll do what I can to help with expenses," said Emily.

"You would do that? After my mother rejected you all those years ago?" Nicole looked at Emily in surprise and shock.

"Yes, I would do that. Nicole is my daughter, after all."

Former Things

The room was quiet as a chapel, and Rebecca started to cry softly. "I can't believe you would help her after the way she's treated you," she said through her tears. "After what my mother did . . . you're still willing to pay for her medical treatment? I'm so sorry. So very, very sorry." Rebecca was sobbing now, and Emily put her hand on Rebecca's to let her know it was all right. "I'm here for you, too, Rebecca. No matter what happens, I'm here for you. You're my flesh and blood."

"I need to see my mother . . . to make sure she's all right." She looked at Martin, pleading with him. "I need to see her."

"I'll take you there, but you have to promise not to try to wake or upset her. And Emily, I would advise you not to come with us. Nicole needs to hear the news that you're here in a way that won't impede her progress and recovery. We need to keep her as calm as possible. Let's not take any chances. Just in case she's conscious. Please understand."

"Of course. There'll be time enough for me to see her."

Martin left with Rebecca then and they went to the recovery room where Nicole was sleeping. When they arrived at her bedside, Rebecca touched her mother's hand and found it as cold as an ice cube. She saw the tubes and needles inserted into her body at every angle and flinched. "Mom? Can you hear me? It's Rebecca."

The heart monitor beat out a steady rhythm, and Nicole's eyelids fluttered slightly but she did not open her eyes. She moved her lips as if she wanted to say something, but the words would not come out.

"She can hear you, Rebecca. She knows you're here. Why not tell her you love her?"

Rebecca lowered her head, confused and angry. The fact that her mother had lied to her all these years had unleashed something inside that frightened her. She wasn't sure how she felt at that moment. "I can't," she said. "Not now. I want to wait until she can talk to me. She has some explaining to do."

CHAPTER ELEVEN

After Nicole's surgery, three days passed before she opened her eyes. When it happened, Rebecca was sitting beside her bed reading a book. Out of the corner of her eye, she saw her mother's hand move. Rebecca looked up.

"Mom? Are you awake?"

Nicole nodded and turned toward Rebecca. "Where am I?" she murmured.

"There was an accident. A fire, then an explosion."

"What explosion? Why is my head pounding?"

Rebecca told her mother about the gasoline spill and the fire, but she did not tell her about the extent of the damage in the south end of town. She also told her about her surgery and how close she had come to losing her life, but she didn't mention Emily. "You were flown to Chicago, Mom. That's where we are now. You had surgery for a brain injury three days ago."

"I don't remember . . ."

"That's probably a good thing."

"No . . . I want to remember. I was walking home from work . . . and just turned the corner . . . there was a blast, then flames. I fell . . . and I can't remember what happened after that."

"There was an accident. A car and a tanker truck. They hit head on, and downtown went up in flames. Someone found you and called an ambulance. They got you to the hospital, but your injuries couldn't be treated there. They flew you here. You're in Chicago. You're one of the lucky ones. A lot of people were killed and injured."

"I'm so tired . . . and the pain . . ."

"I know. You need to rest now. Get some sleep. I'll come back tomorrow."

Former Things

"What am I going to do? I have no medical insurance."
"Don't worry about that. The bills will get paid somehow."

Back at the RV, Evan and Emily waited for Rebecca to return. When she came through the door, they were both relieved to hear that Nicole had finally awakened. After hearing the details of what had happened, Emily made some sandwiches and told them she needed to rest, she was so exhausted.

"Another headache?" Evan asked.

"It's tension. All this worry about Nicole is getting to me. I'll be all right."

Evan asked Rebecca if she knew how to play chess and was surprised to learn that she did. While Emily slept, they played two games before calling it a night, even though neither of them felt like it. Around midnight, they shut off the lights and went to sleep.

CHAPTER TWELVE

The following week when Rebecca visited her mother she found her much more alert, and a month later Nicole was able to sit in a chair next to the window. Her head had been shaved on one side and was heavily bandaged, but the pain had subsided.

"When can I go home?" she asked.

"Not for a while yet. Have any of the doctors been in to see you?"

"One this morning. Dr. Meisner."

Rebecca studied her mother's face and decided enough time had passed and her mother had healed enough to bring up the subject of her grandmother.

"I was thinking . . . family is so important at a time like this . . . it's a shame that your mother didn't live. She'd probably be here if she were still alive."

Nicole turned to the window and gazed out at the city below. "I suppose if your grandmother were alive she would be here. At least I would hope so."

"What happened to her? You've never told me."

"She got sick and died. I was a little older than you, but not much."

"Sick? How do you mean?"

"I don't know. Cancer, I suppose. Or maybe it was her heart."

"You don't know how your own mother died?"

"Why the questions, Rebecca? My mother died, and that's the long and short of it. It happened a long time ago."

"But there must have been some reason . . ."

"I don't know. I really don't, and if it's all the same to you I'd like to drop the subject. I'm not feeling well."

Rebecca returned to the RV an hour later, downhearted. For the first time in her life, she was viewing her mother through a different lens. It was as if a black curtain had darkened her view, so disappointed was she to learn that her mother had lied to her so many years ago and continued to lie to her even now.

She apologized to Evan and Emily for her dour mood and went straight to bed without eating, leaving them to wonder what had happened during her visit. "Better to leave her alone, Evan," Emily said. "She has a lot to sort out in her mind. It's all been so hard on her—her mother's surgery, finding out about me—and it's going to be even worse when she confronts her mother."

Evan knew Emily was right. "How about a chess game?"

"Anything to get my mind off what's happened in the last few weeks," she said.

The following morning after breakfast while Evan went to buy a newspaper, Emily took Rebecca aside and told her it might be best to let sleeping dogs lie.

"Maybe it's better that you don't tell your mother about me at all. I know she's going to be all right now, and I'm so happy to have met you. It's not that I wouldn't want to be reconciled with your mother, Rebecca. I would love that, just as I would love having you as my granddaughter. I just don't know if it would be in your best interest, or your mother's, for me to come back into the picture after all these years." Emily tried to explain to Rebecca the best she could what it had been like to lose her only daughter, to face each meaningless day, to wonder every day of her life what had become of her daughter.

Gail Lowe

"I know this is hard for you to understand, but eventually I grew accustomed to living without your mother, though I continued to grieve her loss every day. I worried about her and wondered if she was eating well and getting enough sleep. Someday when you're a mother, you'll understand. But I'm an old woman now, and I've already lived my life. In some ways, I think it was foolish of me to try to find her. Your mother has a right to live her life as she sees fit. Maybe what I'm trying to say is that I feel satisfied knowing that your mother is alive and well. Maybe that's all I could ever hope for."

Rebecca listened while Emily talked, all the while remembering her own past. Her earliest memories were of a woman she called Auntie Rayelle who helped take care of her while her mother worked at some casino in Connecticut. The year she turned six, they moved to New York City where they lived with a man her mother had met in Central Park. She had long forgotten what Danny looked like but would never forget the smell of liquor on his breath and the times he invited her to sit on his lap and kiss her when her mother was working. When she told her mother about it, they packed their luggage before Danny got home from work and were on road, this time to Indiana where her mother got a job working as a waitress.

They had lived in an RV park, and when her mother quit her job they moved to Willowdale a few months before Rebecca's thirteenth birthday. Her childhood had not been a happy one, she now realized in hindsight, because of all the moving around, but she'd never once faulted her mother. Not after what she'd told Rebecca about being orphaned as a child and how she'd had to make her own way as a single mother after Rebecca's father died from some kind of freak accident while he was stationed at a U.S. Marine boot camp in South Carolina. Rebecca had felt sorry for her mother, a young widow having to move from pillar to post, and Rebecca had done what she could to help out, mostly by being an obedient child who got good grades, one who had never given her mother an ounce of trouble.

Now, she was left to wonder about her mother's charade. All the instability of her childhood might never have happened if

246

Former Things

her mother hadn't left New Hampshire. Emily Preston seemed like a good woman, someone Rebecca would have enjoyed knowing as a grandmother. Her mother, she knew, could be difficult. Very difficult, if the truth were known. As a child, Rebecca had been left alone night after night while her mother was out on a date with a new man or with a girlfriend. Just as often, she got her own meals because her mother was too tired to cook. She remembered, too, the day she went to school with a scratch along the side of her face and when her teacher asked what had happened she lied and said she'd been playing with her cat and that it had scratched her. How could she tell her teacher the truth—that her mother had raised her hand to her, red-polished fingernails like tiny arrows aimed straight for her face and raking her skin, leaving a bloody trail along her cheek. She justified her mother's actions by telling herself that it had been her own fault for not doing her homework when she got home from school. She remembered all these things now while her grandmother sat next to her.

"*No.*"

The word was blunt, and the sudden thrust of it took Emily off guard.

"No? What do you mean 'no'?"

"No, you will not leave here without seeing my mother. Regardless of her medical condition, she needs to face her past—and the truth. More important, she needs to be held accountable for the huge lie she told me. And I will see to it that she is."

"Rebecca . . . no. This isn't the time."

"You know, I've given this a lot of thought and the bottom line is that the timing will never be right. My mind is made up. Tomorrow when I visit her we're going to have a little talk. While we're doing that, you can wait somewhere in the hospital. The cafeteria would be a good place. When I'm ready, I'll come and get you."

CHAPTER THIRTEEN

Emily didn't sleep the entire night. She had opened a Pandora's box by coming to Illinois. She knew that now. She should never have agreed to the trip. She wanted to go back to Emerald House where she belonged and the sooner the better. Maybe she was meant to live her life alone. The past was the past. Why drag it into the present? For the first time, she recognized that what she'd said to Rebecca was true—that Nicole had a right to live her life as she saw fit. If she chose not to include Emily, that was her daughter's business. Still, Rebecca had been lied to and she deserved to know the truth from her mother, didn't she? She failed to understand how Nicole could have lied to her own daughter about something so important, something so crucial. What if Rebecca had never found out about her? Emily had a certain amount of wealth to leave when she died, but without an heir who would it go to? Her attorney would have had a terrible time tracking down Nicole. Now that she thought of it, did she really want to leave everything she'd worked so hard for to a daughter who'd gone to so much trouble pretending she was dead? The answers were not clear in Emily's mind, and her thinking was as muddy as a spring puddle. There was so much to think about and so little time to sort it all out. She felt the pangs of another headache coming on and got out of bed to take an aspirin. Tomorrow she'd ask Evan to give Rebecca and her some privacy so they could talk about her granddaughter's childhood. She wanted to know about her father, where she'd lived, and how she had ended up in Illinois.

In the morning, Emily took Evan aside and asked him if he'd mind taking a walk to get the newspaper. He knew that Emily was asking for some privacy, and he left without another word.

248

Former Things

As soon as he was out the door, Emily asked Rebecca if she would like a cup of freshly brewed coffee.

Seated at the table, Emily told Rebecca that she was curious about her early childhood and wondered how she had ended up in Illinois. Rebecca told Emily that she and her mother had moved from state to state and that her childhood had been unstable and often frightening when her mother wasn't home. She also told Emily about her father, a man she had never met. He'd been a U.S. Marine who had died while on military maneuvers in South Carolina, she told Emily. When Rebecca spoke about her father, Emily wondered if what Nicole had told her about him was also a lie.

Later in the afternoon, Emily and Rebecca went to the hospital to see Nicole and while Rebecca talked to her, Emily waited in the cafeteria for Rebecca to come get her.

The door was half closed when Rebecca got to her mother's room. She opened it slowly and poked her head inside. Dressed in a pink robe, Nicole was seated in a chair near the window reading a book, her back to Rebecca. The bandages had been removed that morning and Rebecca could see stubble growing near the incision at the back of her mother's head.

"Mom? How're you feeling today?"

"Come on in," Nicole said, closing the book and putting it on the bedside table. "I'm much better. The incision is starting to itch. A good sign it's healing, the doctor said. I can't wait to go home."

Rebecca entered the room and sat on the corner of the bed. They were silent for a while, then Rebecca spoke. "I don't know if you *can* go home. The neighborhood is still blocked off because of the fire. They're putting some people up in hotels. Speaking of home, I'd like to talk more about the home you grew up in. I mean, do you ever wonder if your life would have turned out differently if your mother hadn't died?"

Nicole shifted in her chair and clutched the front of her robe. She thought the subject of her mother had been dropped yesterday.

Gail Lowe

"Differently? How do you mean?"

"You know . . . maybe you would have stayed in New Hampshire. I might not have been born. You might not be in the hospital right now if your mother hadn't died."

Nicole glanced toward Rebecca but did not meet her eyes. "I've never thought about it, to be honest."

"How come you've never told me stories about my grandmother? What was she like?"

"Well . . . I suppose she was a simple woman with simple needs. She was content to be a housewife and mother."

"Did you get along with her? Was she nice?"

Pin dots of perspiration popped out on Nicole's upper lip. Why, all of a sudden, was Rebecca asking so many questions about her mother? She hadn't given her much thought in years, and now all of a sudden she was taking up way too much space in her mind. For all she knew, her mother *could* be dead.

"Your grandmother and I were not close, Rebecca. We didn't get along. I don't think she ever wanted children. I think I was probably a mistake."

"Why do you think you were a mistake?"

"Rebecca, what's with all the questions? You've never asked anything about her before," she said sharply.

"I don't know. Just curious, I guess. Why do you think you were a mistake?"

Nicole wracked her brain trying to think of what she could say. "Trust me, Rebecca. I can't put my finger on anything in particular right now. You'll just have to take my word for it. "

"But I want to know what it was like for you. Didn't she love you?"

"I don't want to answer any more questions. I'm tired and I don't feel well. My head is starting to throb again."

The room went silent. While Rebecca sat on the bed looking down at her hands, Nicole stared straight ahead out the window. It had begun to rain hard, and the drops pelted against the glass. A bird flew by, a hawk maybe, or a gull. She didn't know what kind. It seemed directionless and lonely as it swooped up and

Former Things

down in flight. "I know what it feels like to be that bird," Nicole said quietly, a sudden sadness rising up inside of her.

"What?"

"Nothing. It wasn't important."

Rebecca continued, determined to get the answers she wanted. "Tell me about the time you hurt your hand. When you were eight."

Nicole started and turned toward Rebecca. Her heart began to beat faster.

"My hand? What do you mean? I never hurt my hand."

"Yes, you did . . . the day you fell off the toboggan. The day you nearly sliced your hand to the bone. Tell me about it. I want to know how you got that scar on your hand."

A slow heat crept up the back of Nicole's neck and her face flamed. She turned her left hand over and stared at the jagged line at the base of her thumb left there by a row of hastily stitched sutures. She remembered the accident as if it had happened yesterday. She was eight years old when she had fallen off her toboggan and cut her hand when she went into a tree. Her mother had been frantic while driving her to the emergency room where Dr. Jackson had rushed her into a surgical suite and quickly stitched her hand. She even remembered his words. "She's likely to have a nasty scar, but at least she gets to keep her thumb."

"How do you know about that?" Nicole looked at Rebecca, locking onto her eyes. When Rebecca didn't answer, Nicole pressed further. "Rebecca, I asked you a question. How do you know about that accident?"

Inside, Rebecca was shaking with rage. She clamped her jaw shut to keep from screaming at her mother and balled her hands into fists.

"Answer me! How do you know about that accident?"

The room was thick with tension, the way the atmosphere is tense when black storm clouds gather before a torrential downpour.

"Emily Preston."

Gail Lowe

At the sound of her mother's name, Nicole gave a small gasp. She felt queasy and thought she might faint. She reached for a tissue to wipe the drops of perspiration on her upper lip and forehead. "I think I'm going to be sick," she said. "Hand me that plastic wash basin."

Rebecca handed her the basin and watched while her mother retched, then vomited. Nicole wanted to pretend that she had not heard Rebecca say her mother's name, but when Rebecca repeated it, there was no mistaking what she had said.

"Tell me about Emily Preston."

"What about Emily Preston? She's been dead for years."

"Are you sure of that?"

"What kind of game are you playing, Rebecca? You know that your grandmother is dead."

"How come we've never visited her grave? Where is she buried?"

"In New Hampshire, of course. We've never visited because we've never been to New Hampshire. I feel bad that she died, but she was very ill . . . and I . . ." Nicole knew her words had a false ring to them, and she knew also that somehow Rebecca had learned the truth. How she had learned it was a mystery.

"I need to make a phone call. I'll be right back," Rebecca said.

"Wait . . . I . . ." But Rebecca was already gone. Nicole only hoped that when she got back the subject of her mother would not come up again.

Rebecca left Nicole's room and went to the cafeteria where she found Emily staring off into space. They took the elevator to the third floor and on the way Emily continued to protest, but Rebecca refused to listen. She was determined that her mother and grandmother face each other and for her mother to explain to both of them why she had lied.

They came to the door of Nicole's room and when Rebecca peeked in, she saw that her mother had gone back to bed. Nicole was lying on her side, her body turned toward the window where rain continued to tap against the glass. How appropriate, thought Rebecca, tears raining down from the sky for a mother-daughter

252

Former Things

relationship that might have been, if only her mother had not been so selfish. Twenty-one years of living hand to mouth. That's what she'd had to endure because of her mother's poor choices. Her life had been as barren as an empty flower box in the deepest part of winter. She kept her fury under tight control when she spoke.

"Mom?"

At first, Nicole said nothing and continued to lie on her side and stare out the window. Then she said almost in a whisper, "How did you know about my toboggan accident?"

"Because I told her," said Emily, moving toward Nicole's bed.

At the sound of her mother's voice, Nicole turned and saw Emily standing there. It couldn't be true. Her mind was playing tricks on her. She looked from Rebecca to Emily and back again to Rebecca.

"You lied to me all these years. You let me believe that my grandmother was dead," Rebecca said evenly, her face like steel and gray as granite.

"Rebecca . . . please, don't," Emily interrupted. She did not want her reunion with Nicole to be melodramatic in any way. Rather, she wanted Nicole to explain the truth in a manner she was comfortable with. Rebecca backed away and looked at Emily.

"Then you ask her why she lied. Ask her why she made me suffer all through my childhood. Ask her why she raised me without having you around for all those years."

"Nicole, what would you like to tell Rebecca?" Emily asked softly.

"What would I like to tell Rebecca? Okay . . . I'll give it to her plain and simple. And you, too. Yes, I lied. But you're the one who taught me to do it. You lied to me all the while I was growing up. About my sister."

"Nicole . . . I don't know . . ."

"Don't you dare tell me you don't know what I'm talking about. I know that you had a baby before I was born. And I know her name was Rebecca."

Gail Lowe

"Please . . . don't . . ."

"Don't what? Don't tell the truth?"

"Your father and I . . . we thought it would be best that you didn't know . . ."

"Know what? That I had a sister you loved more than me? Do you have any idea how much I suffered when I was a kid because of her?"

"Your father and I didn't lie to you."

"Don't you tell me you didn't lie. You're smart enough to know there are two kinds of lies. Those that are spoken and those that are not. You withheld information from me, and that's lying, at least in my book."

The room was quiet, then Nicole spoke again. "How did you find me? And why did you bother coming?"

Emily paused before answering. "The world is small these days. The Internet is a powerful source of information. That's how I found you. Why did I bother? Because not a day has gone by in the last twenty years that I haven't thought of you every single day and missed you every single minute. As a mother yourself, surely you understand that I needed to know you were okay, that you . . ."

"You shouldn't have come."

"But why? When you left me standing in the kitchen that horrible day twenty years ago I had no idea you'd leave for good. It's true about your sister, but your father and I wanted to close that chapter of our life. We did that by starting fresh when you were born. As for your anger over your father's will, surely it must have subsided over the years. Can you honestly say that you never thought of coming home even once to straighten things out between us?"

Nicole *had* thought of it. In fact, she'd thought of it many times. When she had no place to go, she considered calling her mother, but her pride wouldn't allow her to. When she needed advice about raising Rebecca, she could have asked her mother but her stubbornness had always stood in the way. How could she ever tell her mother she had made such serious mistakes?

Former Things

She looked at Rebecca now. "Yes, I lied to you. My mother didn't die. Our relationship did. And that was the same thing to me."

"But all those times we had to move," Rebecca said. "When there wasn't enough food to eat. Your mother—my grandmother—would have helped us. I've come to know her and she's a good and generous woman. She's someone I would have loved knowing. You took that away from me. You robbed me of having a grandmother to love."

"I took nothing away from you, Rebecca. I gave you a good home. A good childhood."

"You took my grandmother away from me! And you did not give me a good home. You weren't there half the time. How could you be so selfish? How could you do that to me? To your own mother?" She was crying now, and she turned to Emily for comfort.

"I did the best I could. Mothers always do the best they can . . ." She glanced at Emily then and was forced to acknowledge for the first time that her own mother had done the best she could, too. "I'm not perfect. No mother is perfect. Please, Rebecca . . ."

Emily released Rebecca and moved to the side of Nicole's bed. She reached for her daughter's hand.

"Don't you touch me!" Nicole cried. "Rebecca, get over here."

"When hell freezes over. You can go to hell for all I care!"

Rebecca ran from the room, sobbing, and nearly knocked over a nurse who was walking by. Puzzled by the commotion, the startled nurse watched as Rebecca fled to the stairway with Emily on her heels.

"Leave me alone," she said, facing Emily. "I'll get in touch with you later. As for her, I meant what I said. She can go to hell! I hope she dies!"

Rebecca was gone before Emily could say another word. She walked back to Nicole's room and went inside. "Now look what you've done!" Nicole yelled. "Why couldn't you just stay

Gail Lowe

away! Everything was fine until now. It's why I left in the first place. You were always trying to do me in. And I'm the one who's selfish? Get out of here and leave me alone!"

"Nicole . . ."

"I said get out! Now! Before I have you thrown out!"

Emily picked up her purse and left the room in a haze of tears and misery. She never should have come to Chicago. Nicole had made that very clear. She should have left well enough alone.

CHAPTER FOURTEEN

Later that night, Emily called Martin to tell him what had happened and how sorry she was to have interfered with her daughter's life.

"So the reunion didn't go the way you'd hoped."

"Not at all. I never should have come here."

"I don't agree."

"And why is that?"

"Because not only did you find Nicole, you found me. Or maybe I found you. In fact, I'd like to take you to dinner tonight. We can talk about what's happened and catch up on what's kept us busy over the years." Emily accepted his invitation, thinking that after her abysmal encounter with Nicole she needed a friend to talk to. Evan was a friend of one kind. Martin was another.

"My hotel is an RV. It's parked in the back lot at the hospital."

"An RV?"

"It's a long story."

"Okay, I won't ask any questions now. Are you parked in the visitor's back lot?"

"Yes."

"I should be able to find you. How about six o'clock?"

"I'll be waiting for you."

Martin took her to Cloud Nine, a restaurant on the shores of Lake Michigan, and while they dined on prime rib they talked about their days at Portsmouth Regional, their travels over the years, and Emily's discovery of Rebecca. Their conversation finally circled around to Nicole.

"Somewhere along the line I failed her, Martin. I probably just never got over Becky's death. Maybe John and I should have told Nicole the truth about her sister. I tried hard to give Nicole

257

Gail Lowe

what she needed. I really did. But when John died and Nicole made her demands for money, well . . . that was the proverbial straw that broke the camel's back, I'm afraid. Maybe I should have just given it to her. That would have settled the whole matter."

"No, Emily. It would not have settled the matter, and you didn't fail Nicole. You were a good mother. Remember, I was there. I saw how caring you were. You know, it's funny, but just last week I read an article in a magazine about how young people are distancing themselves from their families, so maybe your situation isn't all that rare."

"That could be, but I still have nothing to show for all the years I was her mother."

"Yes, you do."

"And what's that?"

"One word. Experience. You had the experience of *being* a mother. A good one, too. Emily, don't ever sell yourself short. Were you perfect? Probably not. No parent I've ever known is perfect. Look, how about if I stop in to see Nicole tomorrow? Maybe she'll listen to me," he offered. "I know you don't want her to know I was part of the surgical team, but what have you got to lose?"

Emily thought for a long moment before responding. "Maybe she will listen to you," she said. "I'd be so grateful, Martin. It's certainly worth a try."

"Emily, there's something I haven't told you. Something that happened after I left New Hampshire. Melinda . . . my wife . . . she had a drinking problem but stopped when she found out she was pregnant. We had a son. Jonathan. A wonderful boy, smart. He had a promising future." Martin paused and took a sip of wine before continuing. "The summer he graduated from high school he was killed in a car accident. Jonathan was seventeen years old and getting ready to start his freshman year at Georgetown University. He loved Washington and history and politics. He'd been on the debating team in high school and wanted to be a lawyer." He stopped then to gain control of his emotions. "After his death, Melinda started to drink again. We divorced

Former Things

almost ten years ago. So, you see . . . I know what it's like to lose a spouse as well as a child."

Emily placed her hand on top of his. "I'm so sorry, Martin. I feel terrible, burdening you with my problems when you've had sorrows of your own. I had no idea."

"It's okay, Emily. Time does heal. I'll always miss my son, but at least we had seventeen good years together, and I know where he is."

"Still . . ."

"I know . . . but life is what it is. I have to accept it."

After Martin took Emily back to the RV, he let his car engine run for a minute before saying goodnight.

"Any chance we can do this again?" he said, hoping she'd say yes. Though they were much older, he found her just as appealing now as he had forty years ago.

"I'd love that. I really would," she said, leaning over to kiss his cheek.

Martin drove home, his spirit much lighter than it had been in months. After all these years, he and Emily had come together again. What was it they said about full circle? This time they were both free. This time nothing stood in their way. In the span of a few weeks, his life had taken a turn for the better. There was no telling what the future would hold for either of them. For the first time in years, he felt hopeful.

When Martin knocked on Nicole's hospital room door the following morning and looked in, he found her sitting in a chair by the window.

"What's out there that's so interesting?" he asked.

Startled, she turned and saw him standing there. "Who are you?" she asked warily.

"One of the doctors who saved your life." He moved into the room and sat at the edge of her bed.

"You should have let me die."

Gail Lowe

"Why do you say that?"

"My life isn't exactly a joy."

"It could be."

"Yeah? How?"

"By getting rid of that huge chip on your shoulder. Unfortunately, that's one thing that can't be surgically removed so you'll have to work on it yourself."

She laughed bitterly at his accusation. "I don't have a chip on my shoulder."

"Yes, you do."

"How would you know? You don't even know me."

"I'll bet I do."

"Five bucks."

"Give me your left hand."

Nicole raised an eyebrow but did as he said. "Oh, yes . . . right here. I remember how hysterical you were the day you had that toboggan accident."

She looked at him with apprehension. "What is this? Some kind of conspiracy? How do you know about that accident?"

"Because I'm the doctor who put the stitches in your hand. You don't remember me, but I remember you. I'm Martin Jackson."

CHAPTER FIFTEEN

While she contemplated Martin's visit with Nicole that would take place later in the morning, Emily sat at the little kitchen table in the RV reading the newspaper. She took a sip of coffee and struggled to concentrate on an editorial that talked about the rapid increase in murders happening in the South Side of Chicago, but she found herself reading the same paragraph over and over because her mind was on what was happening at the hospital. She had no idea if Martin could make a difference, but she was hoping Nicole would listen to him. All he could do was try, and all she could do was hope. She was in a state of mental and physical exhaustion and wanted nothing more than a few extra hours of sleep. When Evan came out of the bathroom, she got up and rummaged through her clothes to look for something clean to wear. In all the hubbub surrounding Nicole, she hadn't found a minute to do her laundry. She found her last clean pair of Dockers and a pink polo shirt and placed them at the foot of her bed. Then she showered and after drying off and putting on her robe, she told Evan she was going back to bed for a while.

He thought about what he could do while Emily rested. Maybe he'd visit the same bookstore he and Rebecca had found earlier in the week. He'd seen a book by Charles Kuralt and wanted to buy it, but there'd been a long line and they didn't want to wait. "I've got a few errands to do," he said. "Maybe I'll hop one of the tour buses, too, and see a little more of the city. I should be back around noontime. By the way, I've been trying to reach Rebecca, but she's not picking up her calls."

The news that Rebecca was not taking her calls was distressing to Emily, but she was too overwhelmed and tired to worry

Gail Lowe

about where her granddaughter was right now. Rebecca was a big girl, one who was accustomed to fending for herself. When she was ready, she would surface.

Emily heard the click of the lock and Evan's footsteps on the pavement as he walked away from the RV. Yesterday's rain had stopped, and the weather was perfect for sightseeing. She hoped he'd have some fun. She was so worn down from what had happened in the last month—the fire in Willowdale, finding Nicole in the hospital, and learning that she had a granddaughter—that in the past few days she knew she hadn't been very good company. Before going back to bed, she noticed that sticking out of her purse was a slip of paper where she had written down the phone number of a flower shop they'd passed the day before. She picked up Evan's cell phone and placed the call.

Yellow and white roses symbolized peace and harmony, the florist told her in a cheerful voice when Emily asked. "Six of each, then. In the most striking and beautiful vase on your shelf." Peace and harmony between her and Nicole. That's what she wanted most of all. Maybe a dozen roses would soften Nicole's heart.

Once the flowers were ordered, she got into bed, reviewing in her mind the past few days and recalling the events that led to her reunion with Nicole. Maybe there was wisdom, after all, in the old saying to let sleeping dogs lie. She'd done her level best to reconcile with Nicole, but at the moment Nicole wanted no part of her. Emily was ready to go home now, having reached her goal of seeing her daughter again. Nicole had made it clear that she didn't want Emily in her life. At least not now. Emily had hoped for a different outcome, but for now it was good enough that she'd found her daughter alive. She knew that Nicole had been through the mill physically and emotionally, too, and that once she thought things through she might change her mind and get in touch with her. Nicole was a strong woman, a survivor. In the past few weeks, Emily had come to think of her estrangement from Nicole in a more philosophical way. Maybe some children had to be free of their mothers in order to move ahead in life and become the person they were

Former Things

meant to be. Maybe Nicole was one of them. And maybe it was a mother's job to allow their children the freedom to follow a path apart from them, painful though it might be. In the years she had been separated from Nicole, Emily had learned to live life on life's terms. She had learned to let things be and to allow other people to live their lives as they saw fit. Most of all, she had learned not to judge herself or others.

She recalled what Reverend Lord had said so many years ago about Nicole being her consolation in the desolation. Nicole *had* been her consolation; except she'd been too filled with grief at the time to realize it. She recalled, too, what he had said about forgiveness. Yes, she forgave Nicole for leaving as she did, and she hoped that one day Nicole would find it in her heart to forgive her. Her thoughts turned to Martin then, and she wondered if they might be on the way to reclaiming their old feelings for each other. Maybe he would consider coming back to New Hampshire for a visit. The future might be brighter than either of them could possibly know. Anything could happen. A few minutes later, her thoughts began to quiet and she was about to drift off to sleep when she thought she heard Nicole calling her name.

Evan returned to the RV around noontime after a morning spent at the bookstore. He'd bought the Kuralt book and couldn't wait to start reading it. He opened the door gently, just in case Emily was still asleep. The shades were still drawn, a clear sign that she was still in bed or in the shower. When he didn't hear water running, he went to the back of the RV where Emily was sleeping.

He saw that she was still in bed sound asleep. He reached down and touched her shoulder gently, and when she didn't stir he was surprised at the depth of her slumber. He shook her shoulder a little more firmly. "Emily . . . it's twelve-thirty. Do you want me to make us some lunch?" When his words were met with silence, he was puzzled. He shook her again, this time more firmly. "Emily," he said, leaning in closer. "I'm back. Time to get up." He expected that she would open her eyes and turn to him, but she didn't move a muscle. She continued to lie there,

263

still as a model in a Rembrandt painting. He tried again, calling her name. *"Emily . . . Emily . . ."*

When he pulled back the covers and touched her upper arm, he found that it had a bluish cast and was ice cold. He went to his knees and whispered her name over and over, begging her to wake up but when she didn't, he knew in his heart that no matter how much he begged, no matter how hard he tried to wake her, it wasn't going to happen and there was nothing he could do about it.

Through a vapor of tears and with shaking hands, he pressed 911 on his cell phone. "I have an emergency here . . ." he heard himself say. Next, he called Rebecca and when she didn't answer he tried Martin Jackson.

Martin was in the middle of paying a month's worth of bills when the phone rang. He'd been thinking about calling Emily to ask if she would meet him for lunch and intended to do just that as soon as he finished stamping the envelopes. He answered on the second ring and heard Evan's voice on the other end of the line, but couldn't understand a word he was saying. His words were so garbled he could barely make out "Emily," "sleep," and "ambulance." He had no idea what had happened, but whatever it was, it did not sound good.

"Evan, listen to me. Just tell me where you are."

"The RV . . ." Evan broke down then, unable to say another word, and Martin told him he'd be there as soon as he could.

"Stay right where you are. I'm leaving now," he said before hanging up.

The drive to the hospital took Martin less than ten minutes. When he pulled into the parking lot and saw an ambulance parked next to the RV with its emergency lights flashing, he knew the situation was even more serious than he'd originally thought. Evan was standing outside the RV talking to a police officer, and when he spotted Martin he ran to the driver's side window. Martin lowered it and asked what was going on.

Former Things

"It's Emily . . . she's gone. She died in her sleep, Dr. Jackson," he said, crying. "It's my fault. It's my fault . . ."

Martin's mind went numb. It was hardly possible that his old friend had died. Only last night he'd been with her and she'd seemed fine. A bit tired maybe, but otherwise fine. Then he thought about the emotional strain Emily had been under and recalled, too, their conversation so long ago about whether a broken heart could lead to an early death. The reunion with Nicole had not been what Emily had hoped for, but had it gone so badly that the shock of it all had brought Emily's life to an end?

"Listen to me, Evan. It is not your fault. You did nothing to cause Emily's death."

"It was my idea to come here. She'd be alive if we didn't come on this trip. I never should have talked her into it."

"You did the right thing."

"How can you say that? Emily's dead!"

"You did the right thing because you brought Emily and her daughter together again. That's what she wanted most of all—to see her daughter. And you made that happen."

"But Nicole . . . "

"No one can help Nicole. No one but herself. And so far, she has chosen not to help herself. And there's something else, Evan. Something you don't know."

"What?"

"Years ago, I was in love with Emily, but the timing was all wrong. We were both married, and it wouldn't have been right to break up two households. Emily Preston was the most wonderful woman I've ever known, Evan. A real lady. To me, she was beautiful. But it was much more than that. It was her honesty, her way of looking at the world, her willingness to face her failures and correct them. Most of all, I loved her willingness to give *and* forgive. A lot of people walk through life bearing grudges, but not Emily." He paused before continuing and held back his tears. "And because of you I got a chance to be with her again, if only for a short time. Our brief encounter was a precious gift to both of us. I have you to thank for that, and I'm sure

Emily would say the same thing. But now on to more practical matters. Have you tried calling Rebecca again?"

"No," Evan said, calmer now. "I'll try again." Martin Jackson may have been right, thinking what he did, but Evan still felt guilty for talking Emily into taking the trip. Not once had he given a single thought that it might end like this and had assumed wrongly that Emily's reunion with Nicole would have a storybook ending. He was learning quickly that life could be cruel and that not everyone was as kind and gracious as the woman who had taught him how to play chess and how to live life.

He pressed the numbers for Rebecca on his cell phone, but she still wasn't answering. He left a message saying that it was urgent for her to get in touch with him as soon as she heard the message. Even then, she didn't return his call.

Martin wondered who should tell Nicole about her mother while they followed Emily's body into the hospital. Rebecca was nowhere to be found, and it didn't seem fair to shift the burden to Evan. He was her traveling companion, but he was not obliged to deliver such heartbreaking and tragic news to Emily's daughter. He asked Evan for his opinion. "Do you want me to tell Nicole?" he asked.

"If you would, yes. The less I have to do with her the better."

Martin knew what Evan was thinking without asking. He was holding Nicole responsible for her mother's death and maybe, in a manner of speaking, she was.

When he and Evan went through the revolving door at the hospital, they found the lobby filled with family members pushing their aged relatives in wheel chairs, doctors coming and going, and patients on gurneys being transported through a revolving door to waiting ambulances outside. "Where will I meet you?" Martin asked, stepping aside to let a middle-aged woman with her elderly mother pass by.

"The waiting room on Nicole's floor."

They took the elevator to the third floor, and when the door opened Martin headed for Nicole's room and Evan went to the

Former Things

waiting room. When Martin knocked and opened the door to Nicole's room, he found her coming out of the bathroom.

"It's you again," she said, her voice flat.

"Yes, me again."

"If you're here to talk to me about reconciling with my mother, you're wasting your time. I'm not interested."

"I'm not here for that reason." For the first time, Martin felt sorry for Nicole. He recalled the conversations he and Emily had had while Nicole was growing up. Emily's daughter wasn't a bad person. She was just misguided and perhaps deeply disturbed over having grown up in the shadow of an older sister who had died as an infant.

Martin noticed the vase of white and yellow roses sitting on the night stand in a shiny blue iridescent vase. "The roses are beautiful. Who are they from?" he asked, picking up a card next to the vase. He should have known. *Nicole, please find it in your heart to forgive me,* the card read. *I know I made many mistakes in the past, and I'm here to make it up to you. I love you. Mom*

She ignored his question and wished he would just go away and leave her alone. "Look, why are you here?" she asked dryly.

"I'm here because I have something to tell you. Something about your mother."

"My mother is dead. At least to me."

"For once you're right, Nicole. She is dead."

She looked at Martin, suddenly curious. "What do you mean?"

He looked at Nicole for a long moment before answering. "I'm sorry to be the bearer of bad news, but she passed away early this morning. Evan found her."

"Evan? Who's Evan?"

"The young man she's been traveling with. They were close friends. Your mother cared about him as if he were her own grandson."

"My mother is dead," she said scornfully, then laughed. "Then there is justice after all. How about that?"

Martin stared at Nicole in disbelief. "How can you be so heartless? Your mother has just died. Is that all you have to say?"

Gail Lowe

"What else am I supposed to say? Do you want me to say I'm sorry? How about if I break down and cry? Is that what you want? A little dramatic scene? Is that what you were hoping for?" Nicole brightened suddenly. "If she's dead, then she left a will, right? And she probably willed everything to me. Or at least that's what she told me she was going to do twenty years ago."

"Why would she do that? You hadn't seen each other for years before you landed in the hospital."

"Twenty years ago my mother promised I would inherit everything she owned. She told me that the day she refused to share what my father left after he died."

"From what your mother told me, she didn't refuse to share with you, Nicole. She told me she would have given you whatever you needed. But maybe when you didn't come back she changed her mind about your inheritance. Did you ever think about that?" Martin wanted to shake some sense into her. He was having a difficult time understanding how Nicole could talk about money after just learning that her mother had died, but he supposed it was part of her makeup.

"I need to call Rebecca. You'll have to excuse me now."

"Your mother and I were trying to reach her, but she isn't taking her calls."

"That's Rebecca. She can be a real pain in the ass."

"Should we try her dorm? She should know about her grandmother. Maybe the residence hall director knows where she is."

"Go right ahead. Be my guest."

Nicole recited the number while Martin placed the call. A woman answered on the first ring. "Kipling Center. Nancy Richardson speaking."

Martin introduced himself, then asked for Rebecca. "Have you seen her?"

"Yes . . . actually I have." The woman then told Martin that Rebecca had left the dorm the day before with her luggage and two big boxes. "I asked her where she was going, but she didn't answer. I have no idea where she went, but I do know that she's missed two days of classes already."

Former Things

After hearing this, Martin wondered if history might be repeating itself. Was life giving back to Nicole what she'd done to her mother? "Well, if you see her, please ask her to get in touch with me. It's urgent. There's been a death in the family," he said, giving the woman his name and phone number before hanging up.

"We'll just have to wait for her to call," he said, turning back to Nicole. When he did, he was astonished to see her holding a mirror in front of her face while she plucked her eyebrows.

Martin left without saying another word, and when Nicole noticed he was gone she looked at the rose-filled vase across the room. Tears blurred her vision and she was surprised at her sudden sorrow, but then she wiped her eyes, brushed away her feelings, and stiffened her resolve. The roses had arrived too late, as far as she was concerned, and so had her mother.

CHAPTER SIXTEEN

Disgusted, Martin walked down the hospital corridor and found Evan in the waiting room leaning against a wall. He looked up when Martin came in. "Let's go," he said. "There's no use talking to her. Nicole Preston has a heart of stone."

They walked back to the car and once inside, Evan tried calling Rebecca again. This time there was a recorded message. *The number you have reached is no longer in service.* Evan told Martin about the message and said they would have to wait to hear from her. There was nothing else they could do.

"I gave her my cell phone number the other day," said Evan. "I know she'll get in touch with me eventually. She promised to meet with me to talk about the paper I'm going to write before we go back to New Hampshire. I don't think she's the type of person who would break a promise."

The following morning, arrangements were made for transportation of Emily's body back to New Hampshire. Martin drove with Evan in the RV and once they got home, Evan called Donald Magnuson to tell him the news. "She died unexpectedly," Evan explained. "It happened while she was sleeping. The doctors think it might have been an aneurysm. She probably never knew what hit her."

"I'm sorry, Evan. I know you and Emily were close friends." Over the summer he'd had to fire Nina, but decided this wasn't the time or place to tell Evan about it. In hindsight, maybe he shouldn't have listened to the girl's complaints about Emily.

❦

Funeral services were held on Friday, and all of Emily's friends were there for the service at the Church of the Good

Shepherd. Reverend Lord, now in his eighties, came out of retirement to officiate and give the eulogy. Evan, Martin, Alice, Rita, Tess, Mikayla, Marie and residents from Emerald House sat in the front pews. Dr. Talbot and Emily's former co-workers from the hospital sat behind them, and Mary Ellen and Richard and Elizabeth Sterling sat in the pew opposite them. Even Donald Magnuson and Professor Grieg made an appearance. And Cora, the woman who had taken care of Nicole when she was a little girl, had come down from Maine and Althea Marcotte drove over from Portsmouth. The only people absent were Nicole and Rebecca.

After Emily's casket was carried out of the church and placed in a waiting hearse, the funeral procession continued on to Wedgewood Cemetery where Emily had arranged to be buried alongside John and Becky before leaving on her trip with Evan. A sugar maple grew near the plot of land, and she and John had chosen the spot when Becky died for the maple's leaves, which changed from green to the most vibrant shade of scarlet, Emily's favorite autumn color.

When Emily's attorney called Evan into his office in Portsmouth for the reading of her will a week later, Martin went with him.

"First, Evan, I want you to know that Emily left her chess set to you," Gerald Bramhall said, pausing before he continued. "Emily Preston must have thought very highly of you. In fact, I know she did. The day she came in to see me—actually it was the week before the two of you left on your trip—she told me she wished she had had a grandson just like you."

"Believe me, the feeling was mutual," Evan said, tears welling in his eyes. "Emily Preston was a special woman, and I'm going to miss her a lot. She was like family to me."

"Well, she will live on in you because not only did she leave you her chess set, she left instructions that your college loans be paid in full and she also left you her cottage on Prince Edward Island. She specified that the remainder of her assets be split

Gail Lowe

evenly between you and any biological grandchildren she might not have known about. To her daughter, she left an assortment of gifts she bought over the years, mostly jewelry. She also left Nicole a bank account with a balance of about $62,000."

Evan got up from his chair and went to the window. "I'm shocked that she would do that for me," he said, shaking his head before suddenly remembering what Emily had once told him, *"If I have something, Evan, I want to share it. That's my joy in life. Sharing what I have."*

"Now, while you were in Chicago Emily called to tell me she had learned about a granddaughter named Rebecca. Do either of you have any idea where this girl is?"

Evan and Martin took turns explaining what had happened in Chicago. "We've tried to get in touch with Rebecca repeatedly, but she changed the number on her cell phone and moved out of her dorm at Columbia College a few weeks ago. No one knows where she is, and she hasn't been in touch with her mother, either," Martin said.

"I thought I'd hear from her by now, but I guess she's still hurting over what her mother did," Evan said.

"Well, that does create a problem, doesn't it?" Emily's attorney knew what this would mean. Hundreds, maybe thousands of dollars consumed by legal notices placed in newspapers published in the Chicago area, and probably beyond, to begin the search for a granddaughter Emily never got to know. "It's really a shame," he said. "You'd be surprised to know how many of my clients suffer estrangements in their families. But when it's time for the will to be read . . . well, that's when they come out of the woodwork. Money. It's always been the great motivator and always will be."

Arrangements were made for Evan to meet with the attorney again the following week to sign papers, and they shook hands before saying goodbye. "By the way, Evan, did Emily ever show you pictures of the cottage on PEI?"

"Yes, many times," he said.

"Before or after the renovations?"

"I'm not sure. She never mentioned anything about doing the place over."

The attorney studied Evan for a long moment, then said, "I understand that you're going to make writing your career. All I can tell you is that the cottage is a writer's paradise. I used the place a few summers ago when I was in the middle of a complicated trial and needed to think in peace and quiet. Emily gave me the keys to her cottage and told me to use it. I took her up on her offer and was overwhelmed by the beautiful flower garden she planted and the million dollar views of the Gulf of St. Lawrence. The cottage itself is a masterpiece—it's made of stone and is like something you'd see in the English countryside. I hope you'll think about taking a ride up there before the end of summer."

"I never gave it a thought but now that you mention it, maybe I will."

After their meeting with Gerald Bramhall, Martin and Evan stepped outside into a beautiful warm August day. "How about some lunch?" Martin asked, squinting from the glare of the hot sun.

"Sure."

"Where would you like to go?"

"Do you know how to play chess?"

"As a matter of fact, I do. I taught Emily how to play years ago. As a matter of fact, the chess set Emily left you might be the one I gave her years ago."

"Oh, yes, she told me about that. There's this place in Newmarket. The King's Rook. I think we should go there. That's where Emily and I used to play. I think she'd like that."

"The King's Rook? Never heard of it. But if you think Emily would second the motion, then let's go."

On the drive to Newmarket along the winding country road, Martin recalled the life of the woman he had loved and lost. He was glad, at least, that they had found each other again, if

Gail Lowe

only for a little while. Evan, seated beside him, was also lost in thoughts of his own. He knew his next two goals would be to find Rebecca and start writing his paper. Maybe he'd write it while visiting Emily's cottage—*his* cottage. As they drove along, he turned his thoughts to his opening words and jotted down a few ideas in a small notebook he carried in his pocket. He hoped Professor Grieg would approve.

> *The Internet is a powerful Twenty-First Century tool for reuniting people, including family members who, for various reasons, have not been in touch for many years. Family members like Emily Preston and her daughter, Nicole. For twenty years they had not spoken . . .*

LaVergne, TN USA
'09 August 2010
192700LV00001B/11/P